MW00427589

Patricia stared at Anshar with a look that could chill
one's soul to the bone. Her breath came in deep
gasps and she could not bring herself to speak.
She didn't understand her reaction to the stranger.
Every fiber of her being wanted to run from the
room and disappear into the forest outside. She
forced herself to stand quietly and greet the angel.

"I am pleased to meet you, Anshar." Patricia
extended her cold hand in greeting and forced
herself to smile.
Anshar stared at the beautiful woman who offered
her hand to him. He looked at the glow of her aura
and forced himself to peer deeply into her eyes.
Within moments, he knew. Blinding torrents of raw
emotion flooded his heart and mind. Part of him
wanted to rush forward and embrace the woman.
Another part of him wanted to strip the flesh from
her bones with a sharp knife. Strangely, he felt
that he would find pleasure in both actions.

"You don't remember me, do you?" Anshar
questioned.

"You know this woman?" Mitchell queried.

Anshar did not look at Mitchell. He did not remove
his gaze from Patricia.

"Should I know you?" Patricia's heart began to
beat faster. She forced herself to remain calm. She
did not know how long she could keep up the
charade.

Books by Mitchell Earl Gibson

Your Immortal Body of Light

The Living Soul

Signs of Mental Illness

Signs of Spiritual and Psychic Ability

Ancient Teaching Stories

The Human Body of Light

The First Darkness

Symbols of Light

Coming Soon:

The Pot that Was Cracked

The Human Body of Light: 2012

The Spiritual Power of Prosperity

Copyright @ 2012 by Mitchell Earl Gibson MD

All Rights Reserved

Cover Art by

Balud422 of 99Designs.com

First Printing, April 2012

Tybro Publications
110 Oak Street
High Point NC 27260

www.tybro.com

www.ganden.socialgo.com

https://www.facebook.com/Djanthi

http://www.youtube.com/user/mitchellgibsonmd80
00?feature=mhee

www.thenineinsights.com

Fascinating story...filled with suspense waxes with an effortless and beckoning pace; but yet quite arresting...love it. The first spiritual thriller I have read thus far... The scene is set; the tone, color and ambience are all seamlessly woven together for what promises to be a great book.

More power to you Dr. G! J. Thompson, Minnesota

These chapters are extremely thought provoking. The whole concept of there being 'Stealers of souls", the whole maze of this world, so many illusions that stick like superglue to our being, and the path to freedom and compassion after all our lessons have been learnt. What a journey this is, magnificent and awesome and only just begun! ...Thank you for writing this book! D. Anderson, Baltimore MD

Keep it coming, Dr. Gibson. Having written some fiction myself, I especially admire your skillful and rich descriptions of the setting (which obviously come from life-experiences). Looking forward to more... Well done. M.P. USA

Dr. Gibson, as someone mentioned, "a spiritual thriller" is very unique! This book is very exciting. I am hooked, so please keep them coming! Thank you for allowing us to peak into the world that is your soul....J. Davis, London

Thank you for sharing another, magnificent book Dr. G.....More power to the light...please keep it coming! Also, with each chapter my vocabulary is put to the test; not to mention taking to task my spiritual intelligence...P. Lindsay, San Bernadino CA

Even though this book is written as a work of fiction many things in it are true. I have been witness to and partook in the Chorus and it is something you never forget. It is not something you only experience with your mind but with your whole being. It links you to the light of the Creator and is a gift from him/her. Your whole being is moved to an energy that is, all at once, one of peace, deep joy and a feeling of returning home to where you belong.

This home is not a physical place but is a state of consciousness and a vibration of the totality of who you are. I came upon the Chorus in a journey to the vast emptiness. An emptiness that was/is alive. There were beings of light in this place they were singing in praise, gratitude and love for the Creator. They sang with every fiber and photon of their being. And I found I was with them and began to "sing" too. It was the most natural thing to do I would not have chosen to do anything else. And I felt the presence of the Creator as a being of vast, golden light who knew who all of us were/are and heard/hears everyone's song. Some part of me is with them still, singing.....Thank you for writing this book Dr. Gibson......B. Henderson, London

Dr. G, this is truly a work of magnificence. It is a soothing balm for my overly-taxed soul. Thank you also for the reminder of the wonderful gift we have been vouchsafed. I look forward to adding the published work to my collection, and sharing it as a gift with friends and family. L. Jansen, Delhi India

To my wife Kathy,

You are the light of my life and
the joy in my soul.

The First Darkness

Prologue

Melvina struggled to cover herself with the tattered remnants of a shawl that she had stolen from one of the slaves in the lower dungeons. She knew that her situation was hopeless. Melvina and her sister, Salva, were surrounded, desperately attempting to flee from a growing mob of young gladiators that had been set upon them. Salva was barely 10 years old. Melvina had hoped to see her eighteenth birthday in a few days. That was before the centurions burned their home, slaughtered her parents, and took the two of them captive. Now their lives had been reduced to sport.

Salva had been wounded by the first band of men that had rushed toward them. They had been thrown into the arena naked, hungry, and covered in honey. The shawl provided little more than a scant semblance of dignity. Fortunately, Melvina had been able to pick up a broadsword that had fallen onto the ground during the struggle. She had nothing to lose by at least trying to use it.

Melvina's brother, Taras, had taught her some rudimentary broadsword fighting moves, but in her dazed and weary state, she had little hope of holding the men off for any significant length of time. Salva was frozen with fear and Melvina circled her sister's body warily. Three men lunged at her and she gored one cleanly in the liver with a clumsy but effective strike. The remaining two looked at their fallen comrade for a moment, kicked him aside, and renewed their awkward attack.

The crowd grew quiet as they approached. The other slaves scampered away and cleared a path to the two girls. Melvina looked at her sister, smiled, and began swinging the sword in wide circles. Her hand grew sweaty with perspiration as she nervously gripped the handle. The crowd remained deathly quiet. The two men laughed as Melvina quickly tired herself, swirling the heavy broadsword above her head. After a few moments, she could barely lift the sword. Faster than her eyes could follow, one of the men grabbed her throat and yanked her off the ground. Her tiny feet dangled above the dusty coliseum floor. She dropped the broadsword as she gasped for air. The crowd began a muffled cheer.

The young gladiators in training were expected to rape and murder the newly captured slave girls thrown into the arena. The act was considered to be a sort of reward for their hard work. The biggest of the two men grabbed the shawl and threw it to the ground. He pinned Melvina's arms back as his companion ceremoniously removed his tunic. Melvina glanced to her side and saw that Salva was already being ravaged by three new gladiators who had rushed into the fray.

White-hot rage began to build within Melvina as she saw her sister screaming in agony as the men seized her body. The three of them grabbed her and attempted to hold her still. In a desperate lunge, Melvina tore her arm away from her attacker and grabbed a small bloody knife that she spied lying half hidden in the dirt. She thrust the blade into the chest of one of her attackers and then, just as swiftly, cut Salva's throat. Bright spurts of red blood stained Salva's face as she closed her eyes in anguished relief.

The crowd roared its disapproval at the sudden turn of events. The larger gladiator tore the knife from Melvina's hand and thrust the blade deep into her stomach. Melvina spit into his face and fell flat onto the dust of the coliseum floor. The weight of her attacker's body fell onto her chest. The crowd cackled and cheered as the remaining gladiators flung their dead companion's body aside and took brutal advantage of the fleeting moments of warmth that gradually left the dying girls' frail bodies.

Melvina's fragile spirit slowly separated itself from its now lifeless body and floated silently into the cold night air above the arena. She tried to strangle one of the gladiators, but she could not grasp his throat with her spirit hands. She saw her sister's weak spirit energy hovering several feet above her blood-soaked corpse. She willed herself to her sister and grasped her form. Unseen by the cheering crowd, the two spirit forms walked away from the coliseum floor and disappeared into the silent darkness of the neighboring forest.

Chapter One

The Trouble with Beetles

Mitchell sat quietly with his legs crossed in the lotus position on the silk cushion pillow. Kathy, his wife of seven years, was out shopping for groceries, and his children, Tiffany and Michael, had not yet come home from school. He had planned all day for this moment. For the next two hours, with any luck, he would be able to meditate in complete peace and quiet, which was a truly rare commodity in the Gibson household.

Mitchell had begun meditating when he was a small boy. At first, meditation was the only way that he could get away from the stress of growing up hungry, cold, and poor in the backwoods country house that he called home. Soon, however, he realized that if he went deep enough, he could escape his body altogether and explore the neighboring cities and towns that his family rarely visited. Sometimes, on his nightly out-of-body sojourns, he would peek in on his brothers, Dennis and Chris, as they slept, and contemplate scaring the living daylights out of them with a ghostly nudge. He also wondered what it would be like to make himself appear to an adult, someone he didn't know, and scare them just for the heck of it.

After making the costly mistake of telling his pastor about his meditative exploits, Mitchell's mother beat him with a peach tree switch. He learned to keep his out-of-body travels, and his more mischievous thoughts, to himself. Meditation was to become his very secret getaway from the life that he desperately wanted to escape.

His breaths came slowly as he willed himself down into a well-rehearsed trance. His heartbeat slowed evenly and his thoughts stilled to a calm and placid whisper. He felt his energy begin to center in his chest. The sensation grew to the intensity of a large, white-hot flame that slowly enveloped his entire upper body. Mitchell willed the energy away from his chest and up into his brain. The energy resisted briefly, but gradually submitted as he redoubled his efforts. After a few furtive moments, the flaming energy mass coalesced and obediently rose to his forehead.

Sometimes the energy was more cooperative than others. Over the years, Mitchell had learned to master the art of moving the energy mass to whatever part of his body that he chose. He learned early on that allowing the mass to remain in any part of his body other than the brain was a recipe for trouble. If the energy did not enter the brain, he could not get out of his body. There was no point to meditating if he could not get out of his body.

As the flaming energy mass bathed his brain, Mitchell willed his spirit to rise through the ceiling of his home. His spirit rose with practiced ease and floated over the roof. As he floated, he surveyed the forest behind his home. He had grown to love the countryside residence that he and Kathy called home. They had moved to North Carolina from Arizona five years previously. Phoenix was beautiful, but the congestion, smog, and crime had gotten to be a bit too much. Raising two small children was now their priority, and Summerfield, North Carolina, population 7,018, was perfect in many ways.

Mitchell hovered over the thick grove of pines that draped the two-acre plot upon which he had built his home. The April spring air was warm and sweet and it filled his being with peace. There was nothing quite like floating out of one's body. Using his astral vision, he looked back into the meditation room and saw his physical body slumbering peacefully. He wished that he could do this every day. Time, however, did not permit that luxury.

Suddenly, he heard a loud explosion. At first, he thought he was hearing the peal of an approaching spring thunderstorm. They were common in North Carolina during this time of the year. He looked up at the sky and saw the fleeting wisps of cloud that

dotted the tree line. He dismissed any
thoughts of a coming deluge. Then, he heard it
again.

The thunderous sound turned into a long wail. The
noise rippled through his astral form like an
explosion. He strained his senses to find the source
of the commotion. Amidst the din, he could make
out a few words.

"Help me, I'm trapped!...Help me! Help me!"

Meditation was supposed to be peaceful. The
children were not due to return home for at least
another two hours, and Kathy had left for the
market only minutes before. Her car was not in the
driveway. That ruled out family trouble as the
source. Mitchell followed the sound and quickly
found himself hovering over the rose garden near
his front step.

He spied a large black beetle lying flat on its back,
screaming as loudly as it could. Its legs churned
the air furiously. The little creature's lungs were
strained to capacity as it shouted and yelled for all
to hear. Most humans would never hear the sound.
The only reason Mitchell heard the creature's cry
for help related to a certain Word of Power that he
had memorized years before. Unfortunately, in his
astral form, all of his senses were heightened and
the beetle's yell took on monstrous proportions.

Mitchell lowered himself down to the beetle. He
willed his hand to become solid enough to touch
the creature, and he set it upon its legs. The beetle
looked at Mitchell, breathed a heavy sigh of relief,
and grinned widely at the human who had become
his rescuer.

"I thought I was a goner. This yard is crawling with
frogs, birds, and cats. You outta do something
about it, Mitchell."

Mitchell could not believe that the beetle knew his
name.

"How do you know my name?" Mitchell asked.

"I've been living in your yard for two years. Don't you think I woulda heard your name a few times by now? By the way, thanks for flipping me over."

"Don't mention it, friend. By the way, what is your name?"

"You couldn't pronounce it...humans have a hard time with the beetle language. I speak your words a little better than most of my people only because I am brave enough to go into your house on a regular basis. You got the best cookies in your pantry...oops, guess I said too much, huh?"

"As unsettling as the thought of you eating the cookies in my home might be, the thought of having a conversation with a bug strikes me as a bit more curious...something tells me that you wanted to get my attention. What's on your mind?"

"Ray..."

"What do you mean 'Ray'?"

"You can call me Ray."

Ray the Beetle crawled up onto the lower step and began munching on a pink rose petal that had fallen from a nearby blossom.

"Okay...now, tell me what's bothering you, Ray. You took a big chance flipping yourself over like that."

"It's the ants. They're driving everybody in the yard crazy. You know what I'm talking about...Those big, black, hairy suckers that eat everything in sight...and I mean everything."

"We have been dealing with them in the house as well. They don't listen to reason very well."

"You telling me! They're building these mounds all over the forest out here and nothing is safe. You gotta do something."

Ray the Beetle was right. For the last two weeks, Kathy and Mitchell had tried unsuccessfully to deal with the horde of invaders that had begun to call their kitchen home.

When people talk about getting rid of black ants, they are generally referring to one of two different species. The first is the carpenter ant. The second is the black soldier ant. Black soldier ants (Monomorium minimum) are excruciatingly annoying and fertile pests. A single colony can consist of more than 2,000 ants that are active both day and night. Ants are one of the most single-minded and obsessive creatures on the planet.

Mitchell had not been able to find a good Word of Power that would allow him to negotiate with them without harming the queen or their young. In their opinion, the land, the trees, and the house that Mitchell and his family lived in belonged to them. After all, by their count, they had been there for 26,000 years. According to all their citizens—and Mitchell had spoken to a number of them—they had rights. The Gibson family was lucky that the ants didn't decide to attack en masse and take the yard by force.

"I don't know what to do about them, Ray. We are looking at some options."

"Well don't wait too long. I'm planning to reproduce in a few weeks, Mitch...if you know what I mean. I don't want my kids to be ant food. How would you like it if your kids were eaten by a horde of ants?"

"Ray, for a beetle, you have some unsettlingly human elements to your personality. I see your point, however. I will do what I can."

"Okay, doc. Sorry for the commotion...I had to get your attention. Somebody had to do something."

Ray finished the rose petal that lay on the lower step and began to crawl stealthily toward the larger bush of roses. He glanced at Mitchell and grinned sheepishly.

"I love these things. Do you mind?"

"Kathy minds, Ray. Take one petal and leave the rest. I will see what I can do."

Mitchell heard the phone begin to ring inside the house. He felt the familiar heavy magnetic tug of his body beginning to weigh his astral form down. He knew that he couldn't stay outside of his physical form much longer.

"We will talk about this in a few days, Ray. And by the way, if my roses are gone, I will know who did it."

"Quit your worries, I'll spread the word. You scratch my back, I'll scratch yours."

Ray the Beetle quickly plucked a large, juicy rose petal from the plant and happily trudged off toward an opening under the stairs.

Mitchell quickly rose above the steps and flew high into the springtime sky. He surveyed the backyard for a few moments and soon saw the source of Ray's concern. With his astral sight, he was able to see both below and above ground at the same time.

Ants—tens of thousands—were massing in the yard. Ray was right; there were a lot of them. Mitchell would need to do something soon.

The phone rang again.

In a flash, Mitchell rejoined his body, drew in a deep breath, and walked out of his meditation

room to the downstairs counter. He looked at
the number flashing on the caller ID. This call
needed to be answered.

"Hello, this is Dr. Gibson."

"Mitch, thank God...I was about to hang up. This is
Gerald."

Detective Sergeant Gerald Holmes was an old
friend of Mitchell's. They were best friends from
Mitchell's UNC Chapel Hill days. Gerald was
responsible for more than a few raucous parties in
their dorm. He had straightened his life out over
the past few years and was now the lead detective
in the homicide division of Greensboro North
Carolina.

"Hello Gerald, I was out in the yard trimming the
roses...what's up?"

"We have had another case you might be
interested in. I think you might want to come see
this for yourself."

"Alright, give me the address and I will meet you
there in thirty minutes."

Mitchell placed the phone back in the cradle. He
paused for a moment, smiled, and picked it up
again. He dialed Kathy's cell phone number. After a
familiar series of tones, he heard her pick the
phone up.

"Hi sweetheart. Is everything okay?"

"I got a call from Gerald. There's been another
case. He wants me to come take a look. I might
not be back in time for supper. Go ahead and eat
and I will get something when I get in. What are
we having by the way?"

"Your favorite...fried catfish with wild rice."

"You know I love your catfish...you know how to
hurt a guy, don't you, my love?"

"I'll see if I can manage to save you a plate,"
Kathy quipped.

Kathy was an excellent cook. They had met during
Mitchell's residency at Albert Einstein in
Philadelphia. Kathy was tall at five feet nine inches,
and she had won a full track scholarship to the
University of Southern California. As a matter of
fact, she was the captain of the women's track
team as well as a starting guard for the basketball
team. She was strikingly beautiful and had a laugh
that won Mitchell's heart.

"I'll try to be back before too long."

"Okay, sweetheart...I'll be home soon."

Mitchell hung the phone up and headed back
toward his meditation room. He walked toward the
far wall and paused for a moment. He removed a
large bronze medallion that hung on a thick, black
leather cord. The medallion was covered in a series
of raised arcane letters that seemed to pulse with
power. He held the medallion in his hands briefly
and whispered a Word of Power over it as he
gently rubbed the letters. The medallion began to
sparkle with a shimmering blue light. The glow
quickly subsided and Mitchell placed the medallion
cord around his neck and hid the object under his
shirt. He walked out of the meditation room,
grabbed his jacket, quickly scribbled the address
that Gerald had given him on a scrap of paper, and
headed toward the garage.

Chapter Two

Thomas

Thomas Morton was a wealthy man by any standard. Tax law was a lucrative business and in his profession, he was considered the best. His wife, Patricia, was a former beauty queen who had been a finalist in the Miss Argentina pageant. His two sons were both star athletes and honor students. They lived in a 65,000-square-foot mansion overlooking a 200-acre estate in the outer regions of Guilford County. Thomas was one of the founding partners of his law firm and if he had to imagine his life being any better, he probably couldn't do it. He couldn't understand why he had just shot his two sons to death with the model 1908 Mannlicher Schoenauer Carbine sniper rifle that his grandfather had given him two years before.

The boys never knew what hit them. Both boys had died instantly—one shot each, right through the temple. Thomas was ranked Marksman First Class at the local shooting clubs. He had taught the boys how to handle firearms as well. He watched the boys playing in the yard for more than an hour before the thought hit him. He wasn't angry. He hadn't been drinking. The thought of killing them had come spontaneously and it was just that—a plain, simple, ordinary thought.

He knew that Patricia wouldn't understand. He knew that she was probably aware of his dalliances with his new junior associate. She was a smart woman. She allowed him the luxury of an occasional affair in exchange for the life that he had given her. At least, that was the way that he saw it. Not that the affair had anything to do with what he had just done.

Thomas walked over to the bodies and calmly
fired two rounds into the chest cavity of each boy.
He then reached down and tenderly kissed each of
his sons on the forehead. Their skin was still warm
and the ruddy color had not yet left their cheeks.

Thomas placed the Mannlicher onto the ground
next to the boys. He then pulled a Ruger GP100
.38-caliber revolver from his coat pocket. He
checked the chamber and placed three rounds into
the gun. He placed the pistol against his temple,
pulled the trigger, and slumped to the ground.

High overhead, a gray misty form glowed red for a
moment, descended over the forms of the three
dead humans, and gradually disappeared into the
corpses. After a few moments, it reemerged. Its
color had now become a bright crimson red. The
crimson entity rapidly ascended into the afternoon
sky and vanished over the horizon.

Chapter Three

The Journey

Melvina didn't remember a forest beyond the coliseum. She hadn't been given much opportunity to see her surroundings from the floor of the cart on which she and her sister had ridden in. She could clearly remember the cries of the youngest children. They would be useless on the open market and even the most brazen magistrates saw no sport in placing them in the arena. Most of them were probably sold into harems. The unlucky ones went to the southern Carib tribes. She remembered her parents telling stories about the elaborate feast the Carib people prepared that featured heaping mounds of cured human flesh, vegetables, and fruit. They preferred the flesh of young children, so she heard.

She now had much larger problems to occupy her mind. She was very sure that she was dead. She had personally slit Salva's throat and had been splattered with bright spurts of her blood in the process. She was certain that her blow to Salva's throat had been fatal; but some unsettling questions remained unanswered. She felt very much alive. Salva hadn't stopped whimpering for more than an hour. Melvina reasoned, can a dead girl whimper? Why would she? What would be the point?

Salva looked down at her feet as they walked on a pebble-strewn trail through the forest. She didn't mind the walk so much as she did the hunger that raged through her body. She didn't care if she was dead. She was still hungry and, for the most part, that was the most important thought in her mind. Salva's eyes had turned red from hours of crying. She looked at her sister and shouted, "I'm hungry!"

"What do you want me to do about it? I'm hungry too!" Melvina replied.

"Where are we going? I'm tired. Can we stop for a while?" Salva complained.

"I don't know where we're going. I just want to get as far away from that place as possible."

Salva stopped abruptly and sat cross-legged on the ground. She threw her head back and let out a loud shriek.

"If we're dead, why do my feet hurt so much? Why am I so hungry? None of this makes any sense!"

"I don't have any answers for you, sister. I just know that crying and complaining aren't going to help. We're dead. I killed you. Those bastards killed me back at that horrible place. I don't understand why we're here now. I thought we were supposed to be with the gods."

Melvina's questions were not meant so much to answer Salva's concerns as to help her sort out their situation.

"Where are our parents?" Salva asked.

"You assume that they have died," Melvina replied.

"What else would the soldiers have done to them?" asked Salva.

"We have rested long enough. Let's find somewhere to sleep and then we can find someone to help us," Melvina said sharply.

Shaking her head as if trying to make Salva's questions go away, Melvina struggled to sound as reassuring as she possibly could. She had no idea if anyone else existed within a day's walk of where they were.

Salva grudgingly rose to her feet and walked toward her sister. After giving each other a halfhearted hug, they both began to walk back toward the pebble-strewn trail.

They walked for what seemed like hours without saying much of anything. Salva complained about the cold. Melvina reminded her that dead girls don't feel cold. Salva showed her the goosebumps on her arms.

Melvina spotted a fire in a clearing just a short distance down the road. Salva saw it too. They both looked at each other with a sigh of relief.

"What do you think, sister?" Salva asked.

"What do we have to lose?" Melvina replied.

The two girls quickened their pace and soon reached the source of the fire. In a small clearing set a small distance from the path they saw a simple thatch hut. The hut was surrounded by six large dogs. The animals appeared to be asleep and did not stir as the girls approached.

The animals had shiny black manes spotted with bits of blood and tissue from some unnamed prey. Their glistening fangs hung from their mouths, rising and falling with the rhythm of their slumber. Their sleepy growls seemed to add an ominous tone to the air.

Just in front of the hut, the two girls spotted an old man. He sat quietly and did not stir as they approached. He wore a simple green robe that covered his body completely. He was bald and was perhaps the oldest person they had ever seen. His eyes were sunken and dark. Large wrinkles lined his face and deep circles rimmed his eyes. His skin was the color of pale moonlight before a storm. His hands were wizened and the skin hung from his arms like the leaves of an ancient willow. The only ornamentation on his body was a large, brilliant red stone that he wore on a pendant that hung from his neck.

The two girls stopped to warm themselves by the fire. The dogs did not move, neither did the old man. The girls looked at each other, glanced at the dogs, and decided to sit down as they continued to warm themselves. As far as they could tell, death gave certain freedoms not normally available to young girls traveling alone in the wilderness.

The old man still did not move. He did not look at them. His eyes remained steadfast upon the fire. The girls glanced at him from time to time but said nothing.

After a while, the man closed his eyes and began to sing softly to himself. The girls could not make out the words to the song, but the sound was beautiful.

One by one, the dogs began to awaken. They quickly encircled the fire and, before they could move, the girls were surrounded. The old man continued his song. As he sang, the dogs glared fiercely at the two girls. The dogs did not approach them, but they did not need to. Their message was clear.

Abruptly, the old man interrupted his song. He rose without speaking, glanced at the two girls, smiled a wide, toothless grin, and motioned for them to follow. As he moved, the dogs parted silently in response to his gesture. The girls followed him into the house. The dogs followed the three of them to the door.

After the old man, Salva, and Melvina had entered the hut, the dogs stationed themselves in front of the door. The old man closed the door behind them. The dogs quickly fell asleep.

Chapter Four

The Case

Thomas Morton's home was magnificent by any standard. Built in 1849, the mansion had 297 rooms, 112 fireplaces, 32 kitchens, 26 baths, 17 staircases and over an acre of roof. The design of the home was strikingly similar to Chatsworth, the 17th-century Derbyshire residence of the Duke and Duchess of Devonshire. Greensboro, North Carolina was a long way from Devonshire, England. Thomas Morton's intention in building the largest house in Guilford County was to remind all who entered that he was descended from royalty.

The mansion sat on the edge of a wide oak forest. Morton found battling the elements in the country far more amusing than battling traffic in the city. The children had never wanted for anything in their lives. Each space in the home was designed to recreate the grand design of an English Tudor summer residence. The few neighbors that the Mortons had never suspected that the family would be the subject of the evening news—at least, not for this reason.

Mitchell drove past the large oak fence that draped the front lawn of the estate. The police had set up a perimeter around the entrance and he flashed his police consultant badge for the young officer on duty. The officer checked the badge studiously, nodded, and motioned to the senior officer in charge of the grounds to allow the alpine green convertible Jaguar to pass.

Mitchell paused for a moment to lower the roof of the vehicle and parked a few yards beyond the outer edge of the perimeter. He never had much chance to enjoy riding in the Jaguar with the top down. The ride out to the scene seemed like the perfect opportunity. He knew, however, that any minute now, Gerald would spot his car and demand the remainder of his attention. Mitchell removed the large medallion from his shirt, placed it over his chest, and closed his eyes. His breathing became deep and slow. After a few moments, a large ball of blue light emerged from his forehead and floated through the ceiling of the Jaguar. Mitchell took care to utter a quick word of obscuration over the ball as it left his mind.

The blue sphere floated high into the sky over the mansion. Even though Mitchell remained safely in the car, the sphere greatly extended his sensory perceptions. He could see the entirety of the estate from the vantage point of the sphere as easily as he could with a satellite orbiting from space. The sphere offered immediate access to information related to smell, taste, hearing, sight, touch, and a host of other extrasensory perceptive data streams.

Almost immediately, he picked up an unusual scent. The odor was oddly metallic, somewhat foul, not unlike meat that has been sitting too long on a kitchen counter. There was also something more—a sweet, sickening, flowery odor that cloaked the stronger foul odor. Extending his senses slightly, he saw the faint outline of a gray-red cloud. Mitchell knew that he was dealing with a murder scene. The perimeter tape, the number of cars, and the media blackout were standard procedure for crimes of this nature, especially in this neighborhood.

Curiously, he had not seen any evidence of the victims' soul forms wandering around the grounds. Shortly after a violent death, the vast majority of souls wander around for days before fully comprehending what has happened to them. Before he could investigate further, he spotted Gerald walking briskly toward the Jaguar.

Mitchell was immediately jolted out of his meditative state. He muttered a word of dissolution and the ball instantly vanished. He

looked toward the car window and saw
Gerald's smiling face. He knew that he would need
to be more careful with his practices around his
inquisitive friend.

"When are you going to let me take this baby for a
spin?" Gerald had always admired a good racing
vehicle.

"You have a standing invitation my
friend...anytime you wish."

"One day, when I get some time, I will take you up
on that," Gerald replied.

Detective Sergeant Gerald Holmes was a tall man.
He stood just slightly over six feet six inches tall.
Gerald had played basketball for the University of
North Carolina at Chapel Hill for three years during
his college days. He never started for the team but
was a valuable sixth man at the left forward
position. He loved playing the game, even after his
knee decided to give up the sport and shatter in
two places during an off-campus pickup game.
Following two surgeries, rehab, and extensive
training, he was never able to regain his playing
form. He enlisted in the Navy after college and
specialized in military intelligence. After 24 years
of duty, six tours in special ops, and three
decorations for service during highly classified field
operations, he met the woman of his dreams and
retired from the Navy. His parents both lived in the
Greensboro area and he decided to move back
home to raise his young family. His children,
Tammy and Nicholas, both attended high school at
Grimsley.

Gerald had an easy smile and a calm, good-
natured manner. People liked him and that made
doing his job that much easier. His men respected
his judgment, though some of them wondered why
he frequently recruited a retired psychiatrist as a
consultant on certain murder cases. The two men
had been good friends for more than 25 years.

"So what happened here, Gerald?"

"This is another strange one, Mitch. Walk with me while I fill you in."

Gerald led Mitchell down the long, winding garden pathway that encircled the Morton estate. The grounds were tended by a small retinue of full-time gardeners who had formerly been employed by a now deposed South American military leader. During this time of year, the gardens were alive with lavender rose bushes, pink and white dogwood blossoms, and blazing yellow tulips. Mitchell stopped briefly to admire the sculptures that lined the garden perimeter. He recognized the large replica of the Marcus Aurelius statue that faced the main entry to the home. Twenty yards away, he was certain that he spotted a replica of the Farnese Bull. The three graceful figures grappling with the majestic bull atop the beige and gray marble piece seemed to come alive as they passed.

"We have here the home of Mr. Thomas Morton. He was a very wealthy businessman, attorney, age 54, married 21 years, two children, both boys. From what we have been able to piece together, Mr. Morton was a collector of antique weapons. So far, we have found over 300 different artifacts, all catalogued on his hard drive and labeled according to age, date of acquisition, and country of origin. He used a model 1908 Mannlicher Schoenauer Carbine sniper rifle to kill the two boys. He used a .38 on himself. The security tapes show him killing the two boys and then himself."

Gerald pointed to the three body bags lying in the grass some 50 yards away. Two heavily armed SWAT team members stood near to the bodies, while one crime scene investigator hovered over the grassy area near the bodies.

"The really strange thing is, he had no history of violence...no domestic calls of any kind came up on the board...no history of drinking or drugs...as far as we can tell, this was a model family. That's why I called you."

"Did Mr. Morton have any history of psychiatric illness?" Mitchell asked.

"Not that we could find. You know these people, so secretive, but nothing on that end either."

"Has anyone questioned his wife?"

"We were kinda hoping you would do the honors, doc," Gerald said, grinning.

He slapped Mitchell gently on the back and led him through the entrance of the home.
A coffered ceiling with golden rosettes crowned the entrance to the great hall of the home. A number of 19th-century French pieces, including a boulle marquetry table, lined the hallway that led into the main room. A Louis XVI-style console stood majestically against the wall adjacent to the main stairwell. Six framed antique Ottoman manuscripts lined the walls above the console.

Mrs. Morton sat in the corner of the reception room just left of the main stairwell. She sat on a 19th-century gilt armchair that had originally been crafted for the Egyptian Khedivial family. On the writing table just in front of her sat a Seljuk terracotta bull.

Mrs. Morton rose to meet the two men as they approached. She was a stunning woman. Standing at almost six feet tall, her hair was long, thick, and dark, with curly locks draping the ends that hung by her shoulders. Her skin was dark and tanned. She wore a simple Missoni wedge maroon tunic top with a white mid-length skirt.

Patricia Morton had twice been a finalist in the Miss Argentina pageant. In her last competition, she had been first-runner up. Thomas Morton had met her during a business trip to Argentina. He had taken her to see Iguazu Falls on their first date. Even though she had grown up in Argentina, she had never once seen the Iguazu Falls.

Mrs. Morton's face was distraught. Her dark brown eyes rimmed with tears even as she attempted to remain the cordial hostess. While she'd been away shopping in Winston Salem with friends, she'd lost her husband and two children. Her world had been instantly shattered forever for no apparent reason.

Mitchell opened his vision slightly so that he could examine Mrs. Morton more closely. Her aura was large, perhaps 10 to 12 feet across. The main color was green, though the interior and middle regions were filled with bright yellow and gold inclusions. Deep red and gray clouds lined the perimeter of the aura.

The green color meant that she loved people, was very social, and would likely be quite a good teacher. The yellow color defined a soul that was a highly intelligent woman who was full of life and optimistic. The gold color pointed to some latent psychic and spiritual gifts that lay dormant within her subconscious. With the advent of the recent traumas, Mrs. Morton had little hope of fully realizing those gifts during this lifetime.

The deep red and gray clouds on the aura's perimeter most likely represented the emotional trauma and shock that accompanied the news that she had just received. As far as Mitchell could determine, Mrs. Morton was a beautiful and gifted soul who was genuinely in shock.

"Mrs. Morton, my name is Detective Sergeant Gerald Holmes. I will be in charge of the investigation. This is my colleague, Dr. Mitchell Gibson. He is a psychiatric police consultant that I have called in to help me on the case."

Gerald and Mitchell in turn extended their hands to Mrs. Morton. She shook them lightly and returned to her chair. As she sat, an attendant entered the room and placed a Bradford tea service down on the writing table. The attendant then quietly placed three rose porcelain tea cups on the table. As quickly as she entered, she left the room without making a sound.

"Thank you for coming, detective, doctor. Will you take some tea?"

Mrs. Morton was ever the perfect hostess, even under these phenomenally trying circumstances. Years of parties, state dinners, and official gatherings had honed her instincts to exquisite perfection.

"Thank you, ma'am. I think I will," Gerald answered.

"I will as well," Mitchell replied.

"Tell us, Mrs. Morton, had you noticed anything unusual about your husband's behavior over the past few weeks? Anything out of the ordinary that might help us figure out why this happened?" Mitchell asked.

Mrs. Morton sat back in her chair, closed her eyes briefly, sighed for a moment, and looked intently at Mitchell.

"We were very happy. Don't get me wrong, we argued from time to time, all couples do. But we loved each other and Thomas would never do anything like this. He was a good man. Something is wrong with all this. He loved his boys more than life itself. I just don't understand."

"We will do everything we can to get to the bottom of this, Mrs. Morton. Did your husband have any enemies? Anyone who might want to do him harm?" Gerald asked.

"I tried to keep out of my husband's business affairs. This house, our homes, our charities, our children, keep me quite busy. I just checked our main accounts, we were fine. My husband was a man of great integrity, detective. If he had enemies, they were only those who envied him. He would never intentionally hurt another person. He was a good man."

Mrs. Morton's eyes began to fill with tears as she tried to compose herself. She pulled a tissue from the silver container on the writing table in front of her and wiped her eyes quickly.

"We will try to be brief, Mrs. Morton. We appreciate your patience. Do you know if your husband had ever been treated for depression?" Mitchell asked.

Mrs. Morton smiled thinly, sighed again, and took a long sip of tea. As she spoke, the outer perimeter of her aura flashed soft tufts of brown and gray.

"A few years ago, my husband lost a big case...some company in Miami, I believe. They tried to sue my husband for negligence but they were unsuccessful. The whole thing went on for several years and I could tell it was very taxing for him. He had trouble sleeping and difficulty focusing on his work. He saw a counselor, a friend of ours, for a few sessions. The company eventually dropped the suit but I could tell that the whole thing took a toll on my husband."

"How long ago did you say that was?" Gerald asked.

"About five years ago, if I remember correctly."

"Anything else that you can recall that might have upset him more recently?...Another suit perhaps?" Mitchell asked.

"No, nothing...as a matter of fact, business has been great."

"Gerald, I think we're done here."

"I think so too," Gerald replied.

"Mrs. Morton, we will be going now. Again, thank you for your time. I want to extend my condolences to you and your family." Gerald extended his hand to Mrs. Morton. This time, however, she stepped forward to hug him. As she hugged him, she burst into a torrent of tears. The attendant walked into the room and placed her arms around Mrs. Morton's shoulders. The two women backed away from the detective and the attendant led Mrs. Morton away from the reception area.

"I hate this part of my job, Mitch," Gerald said, shaking his head sadly.

"From what I can see, my friend, this is a murder-suicide case with no easy answers," Mitchell replied.

"I just don't know why a man with everything would blow it all in one fell swoop for no reason," Gerald said.

"In many suicides, we never find out what triggered the final event. You know that."

"I know, but this one seems odd to me, you know, in a funny sort of way...I don't think this thing is as cut-and-dried as it seems," Gerald replied.

"I don't think I can do much more here, Gerald. If you don't mind, I am going to head back into town. Let me know what the medical examiner finds when he does the autopsies, and when you get a chance, send me a copy of those security tapes."

"Sure thing...Hey Mitch, when are you going to go fishing with me and the boys?"

"What about next week?" Mitchell replied.

"You got it. Lake Norman?"

"Fine. I'll tell Kathy."

Mitchell hugged his friend and briskly walked back to the Jaguar. He paused briefly to allow his vision to examine the three bodies as they were being loaded into the ambulances. He visually scoured each of the forms carefully. As closely as he could determine, none of the bodies had residual soul

material. Other than the dull, gray, misty
traces of life force that clung to the corpses, he
could see nothing. Somehow, the soul material of
these three people had been stolen. A force that
could do that was nothing to ignore. Mitchell knew
that he would need to do a much closer
investigation of this matter under more appropriate
circumstances.

Chapter Five

The Hut

Salva didn't know what to make of the old man. He
had not spoken a single word to the two girls in
days. He provided food for them. It was simple
fare by any measure—cooked meat with bread and
wild potatoes—but considering their options, he
was going far beyond any measure of civility that
they had expected. He gave them a sleeping space
and provided them with warm blankets and a large
burlap sack filled with straw to use as a pillow. In a
word, he had made them comfortable. The
unsettling question that remained was, why?

The girls did not leave the grounds surrounding the
hut for weeks. They slept, ate, and assigned
themselves simple chores around the hut to pass
the time. Salva dusted, swept, and cleaned the
floors, cupboards, and doors as often as she could.
Melvina spotted a large pile of unwashed clothing
on the floor near the back of the hut and she
busied herself with the task of sorting and washing
them by hand. She found a wooden basin and
managed to convince the old man that she needed
to fill it with water. She opened the door with the
basin in hand and walked outside. The dogs parted
silently as the old man stood closely behind her
and motioned for them to part. The two walked
silently down a long wooded path that ended in a
clearing.

Melvina could not identify the trees that lined the
path. They were tall and broad, with large, dark
trunks that bore unusual whorled patterns in their
bark. The patterns seemed to form the vague
outline of human faces, but Melvina decided that it
was an illusion—simply a trick of the light.
The old man walked silently beside her, saying
nothing. After a while, they came to the end of the
clearing. Melvina saw a small creek flowing along a

wide and crooked path that arched through the trees and disappeared beyond the field past the clearing. The water was clear and moved quickly along its path. Curiously, she did not hear the water as it moved. She stopped, looked at the old man, and saw that he had made himself comfortable on a nearby boulder. He was looking up at the sun, eyes wide open, without the least bit of discomfort. Melvina watched the old man for a moment as he sat cross-legged, entranced in a silent dance with the energy of the sun. She had never seen anyone look at the sun in that way.

As she watched him, she saw his diminutive figure begin to glow with a reddish-golden light. The energy from the sun seemed to envelop his form and, within a few moments, she could no longer distinguish the man from the glow of energy that surrounded him. Melvina could feel the energy emanating from his form. At first, she was uncomfortable with what she was seeing. The energy, however, was another matter entirely.

The reddish-golden light enveloped her as she watched the old man. She did not know how, but she felt as though she were somehow being recharged with energy by the act. Broad rivulets of energy began to course through her system. The energy began its path through her body by entering her toes. The sensation was not unlike that of a warm stream of water, but somehow it was stronger, much stronger. The current moved into her legs and gained momentum as it traveled through her body. When the energy reached her pelvis, she gasped aloud. The sensation was indescribably wonderful. She had never felt such pleasure before. In her brief time on earth, she had not had the pleasure of being with a man in the proper way. She had seen her parents' bulls mating with the cows and once she had spotted a soldier with a young girl in the fields just beyond their home. For a moment, she recalled the incident in the arena that had led to her death. Somehow, the power of the energy that emanated from the old man seemed to wash the stain of that painful time away.

Melvina dropped the basin and fell to the ground as the power began to rise to new crescendos of intensity. She closed her eyes and allowed the energy to take her. The power coursed through her pelvis and gathered strength as it roared toward her chest and stomach area. She now no longer felt the need to move or breathe. The force of the energy seemed to take over her will. Her chest expanded and filled to accommodate the force of the power being shoveled into her being. She tried to look over at the old man's form, but she could only see the reddish glow that filled the space where he once sat.

She closed her eyes once again and tried to make sense of the power that coursed through every fiber of her being. After a few moments, the energy made its way to her head. Blinding flashes of blissful pain entered her skull as the energy was now moving with a speed that she did not think possible. It seemed to be attempting to communicate with her. In her mind, she saw dozens of images move past her vision in rapid succession. She could not make out any of the visions individually, but she could sense that somehow they were imparting some knowledge to her that she would come to understand. Each image lasted only fractions of a second, but one image purposefully tore itself away from the stream and leaped from her mind.

She saw a ball of light floating in front of her. Within the ball, she saw the image of the old man, floating, smiling, and pointing to a flat moving image that glowed within the ball. Melvina focused intently upon the image. She saw a succession of people involved in what could only be described as mating. She saw people, young men and women mostly, of many races and cultures. Some of the women seemed to be in ecstasy, others were barely conscious of their surroundings. Each of them, in turn, looked at her, smiled, and pointed toward her with a single finger. The image lasted for perhaps a few minutes, flickered brightly, and slowly faded in the glow of the ball.

Suddenly, the intense force of the energy that erupted from the old man faded. Melvina felt paralyzed by the experience. She slowly opened her eyes and attempted to move her body. She wiggled her fingers and toes and attempted to stand. Her breath came in short gasps and her heart was racing. She managed to get to her feet after several furtive attempts. She looked around and saw the old man sitting on the boulder. His eyes were now closed and his form was no longer emblazoned with the reddish glow that she had seen earlier. The old man said nothing as he looked at her very intensely.

He slowly rose from his meditative position, walked toward Melvina, picked up the basin, and placed it in her hands. He then motioned for her to go to the stream.

Melvina quickly walked to the stream, filled the basin with water, and rose to return to the boulder. As she turned with the basin, she saw that the old man had already begun to walk back toward the treelined path. She also saw that two of the dogs now trotted quietly alongside him as he walked.

Melvina picked up her pace in order to catch up with the old man and the dogs. In a few moments, she caught up with them. She knew that the old man was not a normal person. She had never seen or experienced anything like what she had just gone through earlier. She wanted answers.

"Who are you? What do you want from us?"

The old man did not answer. He did not slow his pace. He did not look in her direction. He made no indication at all that he had heard her question.

"Did you hear me?" Melvina demanded, raising her voice slightly.

Again, the old man said nothing; he
maintained his pace, did not look toward her, and
continued to make no indication that he had heard
her.

Melvina grew impatient and decided to get his
attention in the only way that she knew how. She
placed the basin upon the ground, cupped her
hands, and splashed a large handful of water onto
the old man's robe. The old man stopped in his
tracks.

He turned slowly toward Melvina. He looked at her
without smiling or moving his face in any way. His
eyes seemed to blaze with a reddish-golden light.
After a few long, tense moments, he began to
laugh. He reached down into the basin, cupped his
hands, and launched a large handful of water back
at Melvina. She was soaked in seconds.
Melvina froze in her tracks. She looked at him in
shock. She had not expected him to return the
favor. Without thinking, she splashed him again.
He splashed her right back. After a few splashes,
they were both soaking wet. Melvina looked at him
intently without blinking. Despite herself, she
began to laugh. Deep, rolling laughter filled her
body as she looked at her own clothing and that of
the old man. She could not remember the last time
that she laughed. She felt good, alive, in a manner
of speaking.

The old man looked at her, smiled, pointed his
finger at her soaked clothing, and began to laugh.
The sound of his laugh was sweet, yet coarse. The
vibration ripped through Melvina like a bolt of
lightning and her whole body shook involuntarily.

"What is your name?" Melvina asked, after
regaining her composure.

"My name is Anshar," the old man replied.

"What happened back there? Wh-what did you do
to me?" Melvina stammered.

"I gave you a reward," Anshar replied.

"A reward? For what?" Melvina asked.

"Services rendered, of course."

"Services? What do you mean, services?"

"You completed your mission."

"What mission? I don't know what you're talking
about."
"Salva. You were charged with bringing me her
soul. I must say, you discharged your duties
admirably. Now go and refill the basin, you have
clothes to wash."

"What are you talking about? I didn't bring you any
soul! My sister was killed by those butchers, just
like me."

"On the contrary, if you will recall, you dispatched
her before they could kill her. By our agreement,
dying by your hand gives me the right to claim her
soul."

"I didn't kill her for you! I did what I did so that
she wouldn't have to suffer."

"A most expedient solution...admirably creative,"
Anshar replied.

Anshar turned and began to walk down the path
again. He chuckled quietly to himself.

Melvina stood in silent horror. She could not
believe the words that had just fallen upon her
soul. Her mind whirled with a cacophony of
confusing thoughts and images that made her
nauseated. After a few moments, a single blinding
thought raged through her mind. She had to get to
Salva.

Melvina's heart began to race and her breaths
quickened. She began to run as fast as she could
toward the hut. She did not think of the old man or
the dogs that accompanied him. She looked back

only once. She saw the old man and the dogs walking slowly, both staring intently in her direction. They did not quicken their pace in the slightest.

She ran as fast as her legs could carry her. She moved faster than she ever thought possible. She wanted to run away from this place, wherever it was, take Salva, and never return. As she ran, the trees seemed to cast long glances upon her. Their shadows trailed long, straight patterns on the trail behind her as she gradually neared the hut. The hut appeared on the horizon.

Melvina saw the remaining dogs sleeping near the fire in front of the hut. She wondered if that fire ever went out. She looked back toward the trail again. Still, she saw no sign of the old man or the dogs that were with him. This gave her some small bit of relief. She slowed her pace as she neared the hut. She did not know what the dogs would do if she tried to rush into the hut without the old man. The more she thought about it, the more she realized that she should stop and walk as calmly as she could toward the door.

Breathing heavily, she slowed to a brisk walk and cautiously approached the dogs by the door. The dogs did not look up. Two of them seemed to be fighting over some large, flesh-covered bones. The others were satisfying themselves with some fresh meat. None of them bothered to stop her.

Melvina pushed the door open and walked into the hut, shouting for Salva.

"Salva! Salva! We have to leave here now!"

The scene that greeted her as she entered the hut left her speechless.

The old man sat cross-legged on the floor in front of a large plate of meat and vegetables. He did not move as Melvina entered. Two dogs sat beside him slowly munching on a pile of raw meat that had been placed before them on the floor.

Melvina froze in horror.

"Where is Salva?"

The old man did not speak. After a few moments, Melvina took a deep breath and began to repeat her question. Before she could speak again, Salva walked into the house from the back entrance.

"Melvina, I was worried. You were gone so long," Salva said calmly.

Melvina was speechless. She stared at the old man and looked back at Salva. The old man grinned at her and began to hum quietly as he ate.

"Melvina, come sit down and eat. Your food will get cold," Salva said.

"How did you get here so fast?" Melvina snapped.

"What do you mean? He has been here with me this whole time while you were gone getting the water," Salva replied.

Melvina felt her thoughts begin to spin and whirl inside her brain. She backed away from the entrance to the door and slowly stumbled toward the fire. The world around her seemed to tumble and fall away in a blur of motion and chaos too confusing to follow. In a moment, she fainted and fell to the ground, fast asleep.

Chapter Six

The Meeting

Driving home from the manor, Mitchell was struck by the suddenness of the tragedies that claimed the lives of the Morton family. The force that had taken the soul material of these victims was powerful. Soul material was sacred to the powers that ruled this world. After the death of a human, certain angels are assigned the task of collecting soul material and transporting it safely to the next world.

Granted, the angels did not always arrive at the most opportune times, nor did they always arrive on the day of the victim's death. For the most part, however, the system worked and soul material was kept out of the hands of demons, elementals, energy parasites, and other lower-class soul feeders. Thus far, the force that had claimed eight lives in the Guilford County area had moved in before the Angelic Protectors could salvage their souls. This act alone required a tremendous amount of spiritual knowledge and power. Guilford County, North Carolina was not likely to be home to such evil.

Prior to relocating to North Carolina, Mitchell and Kathy had lived in Phoenix, Arizona. Kathy was an executive sales person for a large telecommunications firm in Scottsdale. She was born in Madera, California. Her father was a master brickmason and pastor at a local church. He was a strong-willed man who also championed many civil rights causes. He found it necessary on more than one occasion to shutter the blinds and stand by the doorway with a shotgun throughout the night to protect his home and family. Nothing ever happened that truly endangered the family, but Kathy had been with him on many of those occasions. Her father passed the time during those nights by telling her Bible stories. From that time, she developed a deep love for the sanctity of home and the protective power that came with a strong father. Her father died 25 years ago from complications secondary to pneumonia.

Her mother was a powerhouse of strength and love for the family. She cooked, cleaned, and made the clothing for her growing family. She was an expert singer and she imparted a deep love of music and art to all her children. Her greatest gift to Kathy, as far as Mitchell was concerned, was her gift of cooking. Kathy's mother was one of the best cooks to ever grace a kitchen. Her recipes had won numerous accolades throughout the state of California. Kathy had watched and learned to cook from the best. As a result, Kathy's cooking was superb. She had taken care of her mother during the final years of her battle with pancreatic cancer. That struggle had emotionally devastated the family. Kathy had been quite close to her mother. Even now, 12 years later, the anniversary of her passing was a difficult time for the family.

Kathy attended the University of Southern California on a track scholarship. She was a champion long jumper and was an All-American basketball player. She had started for the women's USC basketball team that played in the final four. Kathy had planned to attend the Olympics and participate in the long jump, but American politics had precluded any team participation in the Olympics that year. Kathy finished college and worked briefly as a nurse in a hospital in Philadelphia. That is where she met Mitchell. Marriage and two children quickly followed.

Tiffany, the youngest, was a precocious young girl with a flair for languages and a love for all things television. She was tall and very petite, just like her mother had been at the same age. Tiffany was the noise in the house. She loved to laugh, joke, make fun, sing, and do everything she could to let everyone around her know that she loved life. Her main aspiration in life was to become a lawyer. At the moment, she was focused on convincing her parents to get her a dog, despite the fact that both Kathy and Mitchell were allergic to dogs.

Michael, their eldest, was very tall and strikingly handsome. He was very athletic and played on the school basketball team. He also played AAU basketball and was team captain. He was quieter than Tiffany but his sense of humor was extraordinary. He loved pretending to be different characters in an ongoing series of plays that he would create in his head.

Sometimes, he would adopt an Italian accent and pretend to be a street person looking for a handout. He also liked pretending to be a peculiar aristocratic character who sported a thick Russian accent and had a penchant for drinking diet cola. His favorite character was a country farmer with a deep southern accent who followed Mitchell around the house asking for dipping snuff. Michael was an honors student and he wanted to major in a science field. He hadn't decided whether he wanted to major in mathematics or physics. Mitchell always thought he should consider the theater. Michael was a great accomplice to Tiffany's case of the moment. Together, he and Tiffany had decided that the Gibson family needed a dog.
As Mitchell entered the driveway, he saw Michael and Kathy shooting hoops. Tiffany was keeping score in what seemed to be a rather heated game.

"Who's winning?" Mitchell asked.

"Score's tied, 19-19!" Kathy shouted.

Michael grinned and prepared to drive the ball toward the basket. He looked up briefly and waved to his father. In that moment, Kathy stole the ball, backed up behind the three point line, and drained a perfect jumper.

"Game time!" Kathy shouted.

"What do you mean 'game time'?" Michael asked.

"Three pointers are worth two points in 21, Michael!" Tiffany shouted.

Michael stood transfixed in shock as Kathy ran to Mitchell and kissed him on the cheek. Tiffany ran to pick the ball up and then threw in a perfect layup shot.

"Did you see that, Dad?" Tiffany asked.

"I did, sweetheart. Now let's try that with someone guarding you."

Tiffany took the ball and began to dribble toward her dad. She faked right and backed up slightly to assess her defender. Mitchell had never played organized basketball, but at six feet one inch, 215 pounds, he was a formidable defender. Tiffany grinned, bit her lip in determination, performed a perfect crossover dribble, switched the ball behind her back, and blazed toward the left-hand side of the basket. Mitchell followed and blocked her path while planting both feet firmly under the basket. Tiffany stepped back, squared off, and drained a clean ten-foot jumper.

"In your face, Dad!"

"You looked like your mother doing that shot, young lady. Good one," Mitchell replied.

"Let's go eat supper, guys. Everything should be ready in about twenty minutes," Kathy said.

Michael took the ball and ran behind the three-point line. He drained a clean shot and peered over at his mother.

"Next time, Mom...next time."

"Whenever, wherever, Michael...just bring it,"
Kathy replied.

Tiffany grabbed the basketball and raced toward
her father.

"Dad, we have got to do something about those
ants! There are billions of them all over the
kitchen!"

"Billions? You counted them, sweetheart?" Mitchell
replied.

"You know what I mean, Dad! They're everywhere!
We gotta get some kinda exterminator or
something in here to kill them."

Mitchell paused for a moment as they walked
toward the house. He looked up the hill toward a
large crepe myrtle tree that grew near the edge of
the driveway.

"Before we talk about killing all the ants, let me
show you something. Come with me, Tiffany.
Michael, you are welcome to come along if you
wish."

Both children knew the look on their father's face.
He was about to show them something. They
never quite knew what, but they knew it was going
to be different, and very, very weird.

Mitchell led the children up the hill to the crepe
myrtle tree. Kathy went into the house to finish
preparing supper. She had a good idea what the
children were about to see.

The children saw a large, conical object attached to
the north side of the crepe myrtle. The object was
about three to four feet long and about two feet
wide. It was made of a material that appeared to
be an amalgamation of paper, sawdust, and wood.
The material had been laid down in a layered spiral
pattern. As they neared the object, the children

could hear a loud buzzing emanating from its center.

"What is that, Dad?" Michael asked.

"It's a white-faced hornet's nest. I just spotted it a couple of days ago. Don't get too close. These hornets are very aggressive and there are likely to be thousands of them in that nest."

Tiffany stepped back from the nest and placed her hands over her mouth in shock. Michael stood transfixed in awe.

"How did we not see this?" Tiffany shouted.

"They must have built this some time ago. Let me show you why I brought you here. And no, Tiffany, we are not going to call the exterminator," Mitchell said.

Mitchell calmly held his hand out over the nest. He projected a cool beam of blue light into the center of the hive. The children had not developed significant vision at this point. All they could see was their father holding his hand out over a large hornet's nest.

Mitchell then recited an ancient Aramaic prayer over the nest. The prayer was over 2,800 years old and held the secret to the 42-letter Name of God. All creatures in creation knew the energy of the prayer and obeyed any command accompanying its use.

A-na B'cho-ach
gdu-lat y'min-cha ta-tir
tze-ru-ra

Ka-bel ri-nat am-cha,
sag-vei-nu, ta-ha-rei-nu no-ra

Na gi-bor,
dor-shei yi-chud-cha,
k'va-vat sham-rem

Bar-chem ta-ha-rem ra-cha-mem,
tzid-kat-cha ta-mid gam-lem

Cha-sin ka-dosh b'rov tu-cha,
na-hel a-da-te-cha
Ya-chid ge-eh
l'am-cha p'neh,
zoch-rei k'du-sha-te-cha

Shav-a-tei-nu ka-bel,
ush'ma tza-a-ka-tei-nu,
yo-de-ah ta-a-lu-mot.

As he spoke, invisible fingers of golden energy filled the
nest. A couple of sentinel hornets emerged from the nest
to investigate the disturbance, but they remained calm and
unalarmed. None of the normally aggressive hornets
approached Mitchell or the children.

Mitchell then addressed the nest in English.

"My name is Dr. Mitchell Earl Gibson. I am the
current owner of this property and I come to you
in peace."

Michael and Tiffany looked at their father in total
disbelief.

"Dad, do you think they understand you?" Michael
asked.

"Yes, Michael, they do. Now, give me a moment to
show you why we're here."

A giant sentinel hornet emerged from the nest and
gathered three equally large guards to accompany
him. The hornets crawled to the lower tip of the
cone and sat motionless. They seemed to be
listening intently to Mitchell's words.

In his mind, Mitchell could clearly hear the words
of the queen hidden deep within the nest. The
sentinels and the guards were her eyes and ears.
She alone, however, spoke as the voice of the
nest.

"I hear you, One Who Speaks the Name."

Mitchell knew instantly that he had gotten the queen's attention. He decided to continue in English and to direct his thoughts toward her.

"I come in peace, Great One. Your presence in this place will bring danger to my children and to the humans who live near this land. I ask that you move your people to another tree nearby. There are many for you to choose from."

"We have chosen this tree, One Who Speaks the Name."

"It is my desire to resolve this matter with you peacefully. I will personally guarantee your safety in transfer. I will ask that your new home be blessed with much food and many healthy young."

"You will use the Name of the One on our behalf?"

"You have my word."

"Such a blessing would bring great prosperity to my people."

"Upon your agreement to these terms, I will place this blessing upon your people."

"You have my word, One Who Speaks the Name."

Mitchell raised his hand once again and repeated the prayer three times. After the third repetition, the hive began to pulsate and shake. Mitchell pushed the children back and asked them not to move.

One by one, hundreds of hornets began to emerge from the nest. Each one was about the size of a penny. First, the largest sentinels emerged. Once they saw that the hive was safe, they circled the nest in a large swarm. The sentinels freed the nest from its moorings in the tree. Then the main body of the hive emerged. Guided by the sentinels, the hive hovered over the nest in a swarm. Within seconds, the swarm descended onto the nest, lifted it into the air, and flew away. As they ascended, the conical shape of the nest was enveloped by the mass of the hive. The nest climbed higher and higher into the sky. After a few moments, they were gone.

Michael and Tiffany stood in silence. Tiffany was the first to speak.

"Dad, how did you do that?"

"I asked them to leave."

"You don't just talk to insects and tell them to leave. That's not possible," Tiffany answered.

"It's only impossible if you don't try. By the way, Tiffany, that is what I am going to do with the ants," Mitchell replied.

"You mean you're gonna talk to them and make them leave?" Tiffany replied.

"Yes, in the same manner that you saw here."

Tiffany looked at the tree and gently touched the spot that used to anchor the nest. She approached it cautiously, as if the hornets might return at any minute. She poked it gingerly and looked back at Mitchell. Mitchell nodded, smiled, and motioned for her to continue.

Tiffany shook the branch and, within moments, the whole thing was covered in a shower of leaves and flowers. There was no movement or any sign of the hornets.

Both children looked at Mitchell, looked back at the tree branch, shook their heads, and ran down the hill toward the house. Sometimes, the attention span of a teenager could be a blessing, Mitchell thought to himself. He knew that the children would regale their mother with every detail of the event.

After supper, Mitchell and Kathy sat together quietly downstairs by the fireplace so that they could catch up on the day's events.

The Gibson home had three levels. Each floor had its own personality. The bottom floor had been designed to play host to their love of movies, meditation, and fireplaces. The previous owners had built a large wine cellar in the center of the bottom level. The room had been lined with volcanic rock and was climate controlled. Mitchell and Kathy immediately decided to turn the room into a meditation space. Directly across from the meditation room, they had installed a large movie theater and fireplace for long, cozy evenings such as this one.

"I wish that I could find the answers to these murders as easily as dealing with the nest. This string of murder-suicides has me baffled."

Mitchell slid toward the end of the black leather couch that sat in front of the fireplace.

"Eight people in such a short time. What do you think it means?" Kathy replied.

"The first four cases all involved former mental patients who had previously attempted suicide. The Brown case was the first one to involve a non-mental patient. Doris Brown had no history of mental illness," Mitchell said.

"But she did own a gun. Actually, she owned several guns," Kathy remarked.

"The papers never miss a trick. She did have that particular piece of history in common with all the victims. They all owned guns. Mr. Morton, the man I just saw, was no exception. He owned antique as well as modern weaponry. Even though suicide by handgun or rifle is not the most common method employed by most people, it is not unusual. What is unusual is that so many people in such a short time, in such a small geographic area, would

choose to kill themselves that way," Mitchell
answered.

"Did you see something clairvoyantly at the
Mortons that might help you to find some
answers?"

"Just like the other cases, there were no soul
fragments present in any of the victims. It is as
though the bodies were sucked dry before the
angels had a chance to get to them. I have never
seen that before."
"What kind of force could do that to a human...in
defiance of Angelic Providence no less?" Kathy
questioned.

"Something quite powerful...and if we don't
identify it and stop it soon, there is no telling who
or where it will strike next."

"You don't believe these people are killing
themselves voluntarily do you?"

"No, I don't. Something or someone is behind this.
I picked up a faint reddish glow at each of the
crime scenes. I saw the same thing at the Morton
place this evening. I wanted to investigate it
further, but Gerald interrupted."

"Well, you know Gerald."

"I do. He almost caught me before I had a chance
to return to my body."

"What do you think this reddish glow means?"

"Not quite sure. The intensity and charge of the
glow seem to point to a rather potent
source—someone or something that has access to
the Higher Powers."

"You mean a demon?"

"Perhaps. I will need to go back there later and
check it out properly. Care to come?"

Kathy often accompanied Mitchell on his occult investigations. She had spent the last six years honing and developing her own clairvoyant gifts. Her empathic ability combined with the ability to see entities had proven invaluable on more than one occasion.

"I would come with you, but I have so many emails to catch up on, and Tiffany wants me to go over a presentation that she has for AP World History on Friday."

"I will be very happy when she finishes that class," Mitchell replied.

Suddenly, the fireplace began to hiss and roar. The flames changed into a brilliant blue torrent and leaped out of the fireplace. The long tongues of flame formed a spherical iridescent shape that hovered above the table in front of the couch.

Mitchell leaped to his feet and formed a protective mudra. Kathy began to draw a protective rune in the air. Bluish-gold energy shapes formed in the air around them as they feverishly invoked a protective ward.

The shape grew in size and began to take the form of a large man. The figure sprouted wings and a flaming sword appeared in its left hand. Mitchell instinctively lowered his defensive mudra posture and fell to his knees. Kathy gazed upon the figure for a moment, glanced over at Mitchell, and soon fell to her knees.

The figure grew in size and soon filled the room with a bright golden light. Its wings glistened with raw golden energy that rippled throughout its form. The figure was covered in armor that seemed to be composed of a material that was at once metal and sunlight. The material seemed to pulsate with a life of its own. The figure solidified and floated in front of the fireplace. The room seemed to dissolve slightly as the figure materialized.

The entity's head was humanoid in form,
though one could not tell whether it was male or
female. The head was surrounded by a soft nimbus
of light that revealed the shimmering outlines of a
nose, eyes, and lips. Its eyes blazed with the fury
of a thousand blue-white stars and the entire room
was soon filled with their glory. A large silvery-gold
medallion added dazzling energy and power to the
figure's presence. It looked exactly like the
medallion that Mitchell had worn earlier.

"Mitchell Earl Gibson, your Creator summons you."

Mitchell and Kathy briefly raised their heads and
gazed upon the figure. The words spoken by the
entity were loud and clear, though neither Mitchell
nor Kathy could see movement around its mouth
or head. The words flowed into their minds like the
gentle breeze of a warm midnight wind flowing
over the ocean. As the entity spoke, they both
became overwhelmed with sensations of
indescribable joy, warmth, and power.

Kathy's eyes were already brimming with tears of
joy and elation.
Tears began to form in Mitchell's eyes but he
fought them back and held his composure. Long
years of meditation had helped him maintain his
focus in the presence of this being.

"I hear the words of my master, and I will obey,"
Mitchell replied without moving or rising to his
feet.

"Shall I accompany him?" Kathy asked reverently
as she composed herself.
"Know this, soon shall your services be required,
my child."

The figure flashed a brilliant incandescent white for
a moment, and just as suddenly as it had
appeared, it vanished.

Mitchell and Kathy sat transfixed in awe and
wonder for a few moments. Mitchell rose to his feet

and reached his hand out to Kathy. She slowly rose to her feet and reached out to hold her husband.

"I will return as soon as I can," Mitchell said softly.

"I know you will, my love. We need to prepare."

Kathy and Mitchell made their way to the master bedroom. They both knew that a formal summoning from the Creator must be answered quickly. Several points of preparation and decorum were, however, essential to one's proper presentation to the Most High.

Mitchell removed all of his clothing and took a quick shower. As he exited the shower, Kathy anointed his body with jasmine, cinnamon, and myrrh oil. Mitchell walked into the master closet and removed a long white and gold robe. The robe was simple in its design. The outer arms were lined with two golden roses, which were small and had been hand sewn into the garment by Kathy herself.

The children were both in their rooms busily catching up on homework and emails, though not necessarily in that order.

Mitchell and Kathy made their way down the stairs into the meditation room. Before they reached the bottom flight of stairs, Kathy stopped in the kitchen, opened the large set of doors under the sink, and retrieved a wide-mouthed tin bucket. She filled the bucket with water and carefully placed it on the floor beside the sink. She then traced two rune signs above the water. The air above the bucket seemed to crackle with power as Kathy focused on the working. Mitchell recognized the first rune as Thurisaz, the rune of blessing. The second rune was Ingwaz, the rune of power. After she completed the rune working, Kathy plunged her right hand into the water and uttered a final Word of Power for protection. She then took the pail and carried it down the stairs.

As they reached the bottom of the stairs,
Mitchell opened the door to the meditation room
and removed his robe. He quietly sat on the
meditation couch, closed his eyes, and began to
pull himself down into trance. Kathy removed a
clear container of blessed rainwater from the shelf
near the couch. She poured two drops of the water
into the bucket. The blessed rainwater mixed with
the water in the bucket, which then turned a soft
blue-gold in color. Kathy knew that they were
ready.

Mitchell was already deep in trance. She lifted his
feet and placed them into the water. She removed
the large bronze medallion from its spot on the
wall where Mitchell had placed it earlier that
evening. She held the medallion in her hands
briefly and whispered a Word of Power over it. The
medallion sparkled with a shimmering blue light.
She then placed it around Mitchell's neck. Within
minutes, the medallion began to shimmer and
pulsate with new life. Kathy seated herself
comfortably by Mitchell's feet and held the bucket
steady. She watched intently as his spiritual body
rose from his physical form. She closed her eyes
and followed her husband's journey with her
vision.

Chapter Seven

A New Charge

Mitchell felt the cool energy of the charged water surround his feet. Even while deep in trance, he could feel the power begin to surge into his spiritual form. With his spiritual eye, he looked lovingly at Kathy as she sat vigilantly by his side. She smiled at his form as he gazed at her. Soon, he felt a familiar crescendo of warmth begin to build within his spiritual form. The energy rose from the base of his spine, swirled around his pelvic region, and swiftly rose toward his third eye. The energy pulsated and crackled as it gathered intensity. It moved with a will of its own as it traveled through Mitchell's form. He gathered as much of the energy as he could with his will and focused intently.

He turned his spiritual vision inward. He saw the energy form into a large comet-like shape, pick up speed, and race off toward what appeared to be a star-like presence in the distance. Mitchell focused all his will on keeping pace with the comet.

The comet rushed past planets, stars, nebulae, and galaxies filled with life. Mitchell could still feel the power surging into him from the water that Kathy had prepared. Its flow and current added mightily to his own power as he focused on the journey at hand. The star-like presence in the distance grew larger with each passing moment. The intensity of the light surrounding its presence was blinding, even to Mitchell's spiritual vision. Mitchell adjusted his concentration and trained his will upon the center of the light. Soon, the comet form seemed to slow its pace. The stars and galaxies had disappeared. There were no nebulae present in this place. Mitchell knew that they were nearing their destination. He focused his concentration upon the comet. Up to this point, it was all that he could do to keep up with the racing comet form. Now he knew that more was required.

Mitchell willed his spiritual form to take the shape of a tiny ball of light. The tiny form picked up speed and soon overtook the comet. Mitchell then merged his tiny light form with the comet energy. The comet began to pick up speed and began to move in a convoluted and erratic motion. Mitchell knew that he must not lose contact with the form. The comet bucked and roiled as it attempted to lose him. Once, it stopped suddenly, flung itself backward, and dropped sharply at a steep 90-degree angle.

The comet then began to constrict itself around Mitchell's tiny form. Mitchell could feel powerful bands of energy struggling to squeeze and threaten his life force. He fought the constriction with all his will. The comet then stopped suddenly. The constriction eased and he sensed that he had stopped moving. Suddenly, the comet's energy dissolved into a shower of a billion rivulets of silvery-gold light. As it dissolved, Mitchell could clearly see the outline of six angelic figures standing before him. He had arrived.

Mitchell opened his spiritual vision as widely as he could. Before him he saw six impossibly tall, winged angelic beings. Each of the angels appeared to be some 50 feet in height. Their wings were burnished gold and they wore no discernible clothing. They were neither male nor female in appearance. Their skin was bronze in color and glowed with an inner light that seemed to emanate from the entire bodily structure. Each figure formed a sacred mudra with its hands. The mudras were different for each angel.

The space surrounding them was almost indescribable. The stars seemed to hover around them like pinpoints of light flickering in the forest on a dark night. The sky was illuminated with a bluish-gold glow that held the angels and the stars in place. A thick, sweet, intoxicating aroma filled the expanse; it almost took Mitchell's breath away. He focused his awareness on the bluish-gold light and steadied his energy.

A voice emanated from the bluish-gold energy. The words took form of their own accord with the benefit of a body to hold them. The angels did not move as the words filled the expanse. Mitchell instinctively kneeled as the words entered his consciousness.

"In your last lifetime, you had mastered the movement of your vessel to a much greater degree."

Mitchell held his kneeling position and answered without raising his head.

"This vessel is young, my lord. In time, I will master the work."

"Rise, my child. I would speak with you."

Mitchell slowly lifted his head and rose to his feet. He saw the angels begin to shimmer and glow. Each one gradually softened in appearance and, within moments, they disappeared. Mitchell was alone in the expanse.

A large, solitary figure formed above him. The image was vaguely human in shape, though there were no discernible features that would identify it as male or female. The voice, however, was unmistakable. Each syllable carried the sensation of love, power, and grace. The force of the words battered Mitchell's tiny form like a small ship in the grip of a storm at sea. Mitchell drew more energy

from the bluish-gold expanse that hovered
above him in order to steady his form.

The figure descended and shrank in size as it
neared Mitchell. Within moments, the figure had
assumed the mien of a young man, about 25-30
years of age. His skin glowed with the same bluish-
gold energy that filled the expanse. His eyes
sparkled like diamonds. He was the same height
and build as Mitchell, but his race was clearly
indeterminate. He could have been Asian, African,
Caucasian, Indian, Hispanic, or some admixture of
all of the above. He looked Mitchell in the eye,
smiled, and took his hand.

"Walk with me."

Instantly, they were transported to a tropical
beach lined with palm trees and a large
mountainous cliff that jutted over the bay. The
sand was warm and soft under Mitchell's feet. The
wind kissed his face with the smell of fresh sea air
and the promise of warmth.

Mitchell had been on this beach many times. Each
time, however, was just as magical as the last.

"A great storm approaches you, my child. The
force of darkness threatens your world in a way
that you have never before seen."

"Father, I have seen crimes that point to a new
darkness. Can you tell me what it is?"

"You know the answer to that question. I can tell
you that you will need the assistance of one whom
you have recently met."

"May I ask this person's name?"

"Her name is Patricia Morton."

"She has only recently lost her entire family,
Father. How can she help in this work?"

"Within her soul resides a seed that must be nurtured. You have seen this with your own eyes. Her gift is the key to understanding the power that is the center of this darkness."

Mitchell thought back to his first meeting with Patricia Morton. He recalled the gold color that adorned her aura.

"How may I be of service, Father?"

"Recruit this soul. Train her. Bring her gifts into your world."

"She has no experience or training in this lifetime, Father. And, she is in mourning. This task will require much time."

"You must perform this work quickly, my son. Her gift has been placed in your hands. Use your knowledge."

"Yes, Father. I have one question."
"Yes, my son."

"If she refuses...?"

"She will follow her destiny. You must show her the path. Return now, and remember that I walk with you always."

"Yes, Father."

The figure slowly dissolved and Mitchell felt himself being drawn back toward his physical body. In a few seconds, he stood again at the feet of the six silent angels. He looked up at each one and bowed his head in thanks. The figures did not move nor did they seem to acknowledge his presence.

One of the pinpoints of light that Mitchell assumed were stars began to grow in size. The light descended from the firmament and assumed a familiar form. The figure was covered in armor that seemed to be composed of a material that was at once metal and sunlight. The material seemed to

pulsate with a life of its own. Mitchell
recognized the being immediately.

"I will escort you back to your world, Mitchell."

The figure's voice filled Mitchell with the same joy
and elation that he recalled from their meeting
earlier that night. Once again, he could barely
control his desire to cry out in exultation.

"Master, I would be honored."

"The Father has permitted me to speak with you
on this matter. There are several facts you should
know before you approach the woman."

As the angel spoke, Mitchell felt the energy around
his tiny spiritual form grow and expand. His sense
of perspective changed and he had the feeling that
he was moving at immense speed, though he did
not see the movement reflected in the stars and
planets around him. He felt that he was at once
being escorted back to his body and filled with
some sublime form of healing energy. He had
never experienced the sensation during his many
journeys with the angel.

"You speak of Mrs. Patricia Morton?"

"The woman is in possession of a unique and rare
gift. It is known as the power of assignation. When
a being is to be born in your world, it is granted
one soul for the purpose of completing the work of
that lifetime. With her power, Patricia Morton may
gather souls from whomever she chooses and
assign them to any being she may choose. There
are powers within the darkness that would seek to
use her gift to gain entry to your world."

"If she does not know of her gift, how can she be
of use to these powers?"

"You will understand this and many other
questions in time. But know this, she must be
trained and made aware of this gift. Do not
underestimate the importance of this task."

"I will train her, master."

Mitchell began to feel the familiar tug of his physical form. His spiritual vision began to fade and his physical eyes began to flutter. The angel smiled at him and disappeared. Mitchell descended into his body, drew a deep breath, and shook his head briefly. He opened his eyes and smiled at Kathy, who sat quietly awaiting his return.

"How long was I gone?"
"About five minutes."

"I can never discern the passage of time properly while I am with him. It seemed like I was gone for hours."

Kathy smiled and helped Mitchell remove his feet from the bucket. He stood slowly, walked around the meditation room for a moment, and knelt in front of the altar. Kathy joined him and they both prayed silently.

"We have to get in touch with Mrs. Morton."

"Why?"

"I will explain later. She holds the key to many questions."

"The Creator told you something?"

"Yes, and it would appear that I have a new charge to train."

Chapter Eight

Into the World

Melvina awoke on the bed that Salva had made for her in the back of the hut. Her eyes hurt with a deep pain that penetrated to the core of her being. Her vision was fuzzy and when she tried to focus, she became nauseated. Salva held a hot cup of broth next to Melvina's lips and asked her to drink.

"What happened?" Melvina asked.

"You fainted."

Melvina drank the warm broth slowly. The taste was rich and delicious, unlike anything she had ever tasted. The more she drank, the stronger she became. Soon, she felt her old strength return and she sat up easily. She stared at Salva for several long moments, took a deep breath, and sank slowly back onto the bed.

"We have to leave this place, sister," Melvina said.

"Why? Where would we go? We died, remember?"

"I remember. But this place makes me uneasy. There is something wrong about the old man. We have to leave here."

"But if we leave, where would we go? He has been kind to us."

"Listen to me, sister. Today, I saw something...something that I can't explain right now. I want you to trust me on this. He is not as he appears...there is something—"

Before Melvina could complete her statement, the old man walked into the room. Two of the dogs from the pack stood passively by his side.

"I am happy to see you are well. I was worried. If you are up to it, please walk with me."

The old man extended his hand and motioned for Melvina to come with him.

"Shall I come as well?" Salva asked.

"If you don't mind, I would like to speak with your sister alone."

Melvina rose quietly from the bed and took the old man's hand. They walked through the back door of the hut and slowly approached the dirt trail that ran adjacent to the stream.

Salva ran to the door to watch the two of them walk away. The two dogs lagged a few feet behind, pacing silently.

The old man did not speak until they had lost sight of the hut.

"She will not believe you, and she will ignore your fears. She feels safe here with me."

"My sister is young and impressionable. I know better. You are not as you appear."

"You would do well to remember who I am. I have given you certain freedoms upon your return in exchange for the service that you have provided. Your sister will make a fine addition to my collection. Perhaps I shall even keep her as my slave."

Melvina looked at the old man and violently wrenched her hand from his.

"You do not own me. I am not your servant. My sister is not your plaything."

"Perhaps I should remind you of the true nature of things, my dear."

The old man stopped and picked up a smooth gray pebble from the path. He spit on the rock and spoke softly over the stone as he rubbed the spittle onto its surface. He then set the rock gently upon the path once again.

In a few moments, the rock began to glow and sparkle. Red and orange smoke rose from its surface and clouded the entire stone. As the smoke cleared, Melvina saw a small rabbit arise from the stone. Amazingly, the rabbit grew to full, robust, adult size in seconds.

The old man picked the rabbit up, stroked its ears gingerly, and kissed it on the nose. He looked at Melvina, smiled, and threw the rabbit to the dogs. The rabbit tried to hop away, but the dogs were upon it in seconds. They tore the animal in half almost immediately, spewing blood and tissue over a wide circle. Even torn in half, the rabbit managed to breathe an unearthly scream.

Melvina watched in horror. She was speechless.

"You see, you are one of my creations. You have a special purpose, unlike the rabbit that you saw. Would you like to know what you were before I gave you this form?"

Melvina felt the broth begin to broil within her stomach. A few seconds later, she bent over near a large boulder and threw up.

"Yes, I believe you understand now."

""Wh-whyyyy...are you...doingggggg...this to me?" Melvina stammered as she struggled to wipe her mouth.

"You gather souls for me, my dear. That is what you have always done."

"What do you mean 'gather souls'?"

"I collect the souls of humans for a very special purpose. For reasons that I cannot explain to you, I am unable to do this myself. However, you, my creation, are able to circumvent certain rules. You have been rather useful in that regard."

Melvina felt her stomach begin to boil and rumble once again. She grabbed her sides and bent over. This time, she could only manage dry heaves.

"How long have I been doing this for you?"

"Not quite long enough, I'm afraid. Which brings me to the reason for our chat. It is time for you to return to Earth."
"I'm not going anywhere without my sister!"

"I am afraid you have no choice in the matter."

"I won't do it. I'll run away, and I'll take my sister with me."

"And go where?"

"Away from you!"

"That will be rather difficult, considering that in a very short while you will be reborn."

"What do you mean?"

"The broth you drank...the vomiting...the dizziness you are about to feel...all part of my plan for your rebirth."

Melvina began to feel her mind spin and reel again. Her senses refused to focus on the path or on the

old man's grinning form. She barely managed
to force herself to speak.

"Rebirth plan?"

"That is the only way to send you back into the
world, my dear."

Melvina fell to her knees. Her insides began to boil
and churn anew. She felt a strange, squeezing
sensation grip her head, shoulders, and chest area.
Without meaning to, she closed her eyes and lay
down in a curled-up, fetal position. Slowly, her
body began to glow and sparkle.

Within moments, she felt her body begin to shrink.
She wanted to cry but her voice could only create
a feeble whimper. She tried to open her eyes, but
she could not. The intensity of the squeezing
sensation increased around her head and chest.
She wanted to scream, but her desire was once
again met with tiny, feeble whimpers. Her mind
continued to reel and spin as her senses refused to
lock onto her surroundings.

She felt her body shrink further. As the pressure
from the squeezing grew stronger, her urge to
scream became greater and greater—but she could
not.

Soon, she felt the sensation of something like
hands touching her body. Suddenly, she felt the
odd sensation of a sticky, cold fluid surrounding
her. The squeezing intensified until it was almost
unbearable. She felt as if her head were about to
burst from the pressure. Suddenly, just as she felt
that she could bear no more, the pressure
subsided.

She felt a warm liquid flowing over her body. She
heard voices. They seemed to be those of women,
but she did not recognize any of them. The
sensation of the liquid was soon replaced by the
slightly warm but rough touch of what felt like a
blanket.

Melvina mustered as much willpower as she could. She forced her eyes to open. She saw the face of an old woman whose skin was wizened by too many days in the sun. She wore a thick shawl that was covered with a strange and elaborate design. The woman smiled as she looked at Melvina.

The old woman spoke and the words crashed onto the shores of Melvina's consciousness like a ship lost in a storm.

"It is a boy, my lord."

Melvina began to scream.

"He is very healthy," the old woman said.

Melvina's cries were quickly drowned out by the cheers and songs of praise that surrounded her new parents. Lord Evans and his third wife Linda were the proud parents of a new baby boy.

Chapter Nine

Two Souls

Ten years later...

In the year 1329, Lord Williams Evans was a man of considerable means. He had made his fortune during the Siege of the English Fortress of La Réole on the Garonne. The English forces had been led by Edmund of Woodstock, Earl of Kent, but were forced to surrender after a month of bombardment by the French cannons. Their promised reinforcements never arrived. Unknown to his superiors, Lord Evans had led a small contingent of his own loyal men deep into a neighboring village. During their forays, they had plundered and sequestered a small hoard of wealth from the local merchants. After the hostilities subsided, Lord Evans reported one of his lieutenants to the earl for planning the forays.

The hapless man was quickly tried and imprisoned for treason. He tried in vain to persuade the earl that he had acted upon the orders of Lord Evans, and had even gone so far as to implicate his fellow marauders in the act. Forced to accept the word of a commoner over that of a lord, the earl personally beheaded the soldier and rewarded Lord Evans with a wide swathe of land, cattle, and properties. Lord Evans kept the hoard for himself.

As was the custom of the day, Lord Evans took certain privileges with the wives of all the men who lived and supported themselves on his land. He heartily availed himself of the delicate feminine riches of all the newest brides in the area. His newest wife, Linda, had been married to a strapping young man who had enlisted in the earl's Light Calvary. He was killed in the first hour of the charge at La Réole. Lord Evans wasted no time in consoling the beautiful young girl and soon claimed her as his own.

Melvina, now known as Gerard Evans, heir to the lands and property of Lord Evans, grew up on a sprawling 20,000-acre estate. During the first few years of his new life, Gerard clearly remembered the life he experienced as Melvina. During his screams, he tried to mouth his story to his new parents. His voice had not yet formed into anything more than the screams of a newborn. His parents and nursemaids assumed that he had a bad case of the croup, and attempted to soothe his spirit with milk, honey, and mashed vegetables. Gerard knew that he was not ill; he desperately wanted to tell his story. Over time, however, his memory began to desert him and he could scarcely hold together more than small snippets of the details of his past life.

By the time he reached two years old, he had all but forgotten his brothers, parents, and the life that had been taken away from him. But he remembered Salva and the old man clearly. He endured long, tortured nights filled with nightmares about countless deaths and rebirths. He could not make sense of them all, but knew that he must somehow hold onto the details of his previous life.

Once, while his parents were away in town, he told the story of Salva and the old man to Tracy, the nursemaid with whom he spent the most time. Tracy had been present at his birth and was a

patient and kind soul. Over the years,
however, her hearing had become a pale shadow
of what it used to be, and as Gerard shared his
story, Tracy heard only bits and pieces. She
attributed the tale to the imaginings of the fertile
mind of a young boy.

Though the nightmares continued, Gerard never
told anyone else the story of his former life. But he
did not forget the strange hut in the woods, the
dogs, Salva, or the old man.

As he grew, his muscles and intellect grew as well.
He learned that he could trust his mother, who was
a beautiful and intelligent woman, and given
different circumstances, might have educated
herself and taken a different path in life. From time
to time, she spoke of her life with her last
husband, but she always let Gerard know that she
loved his father very much and that she was happy
with her new life. He grew to love his mother and
became very protective of her happiness.

Lord Evans, on the other hand, was a different
matter altogether. He spent many hours with his
new son teaching him the ways of nobility. He
taught his son how to handle a sword, to hunt, to
fish, and how to handle himself with those over
whom he held charge. Lord Evans hired the best
tutors for the boy, and soon he learned that Gerard
had a talent for languages. He had visions of one
day guiding his son to take a seat in the
government of the new country that he had a hand
in building. He saw Gerard being very successful in
life and expanding the fame and power of the
family. Gerard did not share his father's vision.
Even though he knew that his father loved him, he
could not bring himself to trust the man.

Shortly after Gerard's birth, Lady Evans had made
him promise to stop his practice of sleeping with
the local women and to instead remain true to her.
Lord Evans agreed to the promise, but Gerard had
secretly followed him on many late nights when he
believed that everyone was asleep. The nightmares
that he endured made sleep a challenging

proposition. Walking alone on the grounds was somehow strangely calming to his nerves. At first, seeing his father leave the estate late in the night seemed out of place, but after following him a few times, he came to understand the nature of the visitations.

Countess Charlotte of Woodstock, wife of the Earl of Kent, was a stunning woman. She was the fifth of six daughters born to a wealthy merchant loyal to the king. She had been given to the earl as a gift for his many years of loyal service. The earl was an elderly man and was not given to the sexual service expected of a noble of his stature. He cared little for his wife and spent little time with her or the two children they had birthed. The earl busied himself with the affairs of war and the endless campaigns that were required to secure the borders of his estate. Lord Evans took little time to notice the unhappiness of their union.

The countess met Lord Evans in a barn some two miles from her main estate. She was always accompanied by one of her loyal maidservants who kept watch as she ducked into the building to meet Lord Evans. Gerard had on more than one occasion managed to sneak past the maidservant and see for himself what his father did with the countess. He watched for what seemed like hours as they embraced in florid and tumultuous screams of ecstasy.

He did not understand how his father could so easily break his promise to the woman he loved. As he watched, he saw brief flashes of the torture at the hands of the soldiers that he had endured as Melvina. The screams of joy and ecstasy that issued from the countess were replaced in his mind by the wails of pain and agony that Salva had endured during the final moments of her life. Frozen in horror, Gerard sat crouched behind the large wooden door of the barn. He could not force himself to look away, but he could not ignore the feeling of rage and despair that flooded his young body. He wanted to yell at his father and tell his

mother everything. He knew, however, that
the news would devastate her.

Gerard spotted a stone near the door. Without fully
understanding why, his disgust deepened further
as he looked at the stone. He picked it up, rubbed
it briefly, and threw it as hard as he could at his
father's heaving chest. The stone hit Lord Evans
hard and a large red mark grew on his body where
the stone had impacted his skin. Gerard did not
wait for his father's reaction. As fast as he could,
he ran back toward his home. He looked back from
time to time but he saw no one chasing him. After
a while, he slowed his pace and hid behind a large
oak tree that stood near the front gate of the
Evans estate.
He peered cautiously from behind the tree and
watched to see if his father had given chase.
Fifteen minutes later, he grew tired and began to
fall asleep. He shook himself a few times to chase
the sleep away from his eyes. Gerard knew a
hundred ways to sneak back into his home without
being seen. Soon, he was back in his room,
undressed, and under the covers. He lay still and
tried to calm his mind.

Less than one hour later, he heard heavy footsteps
approach his door. Sleep had escaped him and he
feared that his father would burst into the room
and beat him for what he had done. Gerard
pretended to be asleep as Lord Evans approached
his bed. Lord Evans sat quietly on the side of his
son's bed. He did not speak, he did not move, nor
did he attempt to touch Gerard in any way.
Gerard's heart pounded loudly in his chest as he
feared that at any moment, his father would rip
the covers away and demand to speak with the
boy. Just when he felt that he could not bear
another moment of agony, Gerard heard a soft
familiar voice in the background.

"Are you coming to bed, my love?" Lady Evans
asked her husband softly.

"I was just going to kiss my son. I'll be there in a
moment."

Lord Evans kissed Gerard softly on the cheek, stood up, and paused over the boy's bed for a moment. He looked around the room and spotted Gerard's mud-soaked shoes in the corner. He could see the water still dripping from the leather bindings. Lord Evans smiled to himself, kicked the shoes lightly, and walked out of the room.

When he was sure that his father had left the room, Gerard let out a loud sigh of relief. Soon, he heard screams of ecstasy issuing from his parents' bedroom. Somehow, the sounds were comforting to his ears. He knew that his father would not return to his room that night. He probably wouldn't have the strength.

The next morning, Gerard decided to tell his father everything. He didn't trust his father, but he knew that his father loved him. If his father knew everything, at least he would have the insurance of knowing that it was only his son who had discovered him. He did not want him to suffer any more than he needed to. Gerard was not afraid that his father might harm him—a beating perhaps, but nothing more.

Later that day, Lord Evans decided to take his son fishing. The streams near the main mansion were well stocked with trout, brim, and carp. The carp gave an especially good battle during their frequent fishing trips and Gerard looked forward to the outing. The water was brisk and cold that morning. As he stood knee-deep in the stream, wading out to the carp feeding area, Gerard bided his time. His father seemed unusually quiet that morning, but he attributed the silence to fatigue.

Lord Evans was a man of few words, but when he spoke, there was gravity and purpose in his voice.

"We need to talk, son."

Gerard's heart dropped. He held his breath, exhaled slowly, and tried to pretend that everything was normal.

"What is on your mind, father?"

"I know that you followed me last night."

Gerard dropped the fishing pole and the current carried it downstream. The long, thin line trailed helplessly behind the pole as it drifted.

"What do you mean, father?"

"Do not lie to me, boy. I saw you as you ran from the barn. It was you who hit me with the stone, was it not?"

Gerard was petrified with fear. His face became pale and his voice cracked with strain.

"Yes, father. I will not lie. It was me."

The burden of the strain seemed to lift as the words left his mouth. He looked at his father and waited for the blows that he knew would soon fall upon him.

Lord Evans stood silently and looked coldly at his son. After a few long, tense moments, he cleared his throat and spoke.

"You will tell no one of what you saw. You certainly will not tell your mother. Is this clear?"

"Yes, father, I will not speak of it to anyone, ever."

"Very good then. Let us never speak of it again. But you must know this, my son, I love your mother. What you saw was lust, something that happens between adults, nothing more. You will understand when you become a man."

"But you made a promise to Mother..."

"This is true. But I am Lord of the Manor...my word is law and your mother will do as she is told. I do not answer to her, nor to you, boy!"

"I understand, father."

"If you like, I can arrange for one of the servant girls to introduce you to the ways of women."

"You mean to lay with them, to make babies?"
"You are not old enough to make babies, my son, but you can know the pleasure of a woman—that is, if you wish it."

Gerard was tempted by his father's proposal. He had seen several new servant girls in the manor who had caught his eye. There was one in particular, a young Moor with light green eyes and dark brown skin, who particularly captured his fancy.

"What would mother think of this? I am only ten."

"Let us say that this will be our secret."

Lord Evans smiled, patted his son on the shoulder, and let out a laugh that echoed loudly across the stream. A nearby flock of geese took flight as the sound of his voice bellowed across the water.

"I want to give you a present, my son."

Lord Evans reached into his trousers and took out a short dagger. The ivory-laden handle of the blade was encrusted with rubies and sapphires. The blade itself was lined with gold and silver.

"This blade has been in our family for centuries. You are fast becoming a man now. It is time for you to have it."

Lord Evans motioned for the boy to follow him onto the shore. He dropped his pole and sat on the sandy bank. The sun was high in the sky and a warm breeze blew across the stream. Gerard sat on the bank beside his father.

"Why do you give this to me now? Is it because of last night?"

"I need no excuse to give my son a gift. It is yours, should you choose to take it."

Gerard took the dagger from his father's hand. He shook the water that had gathered on the hilt and examined it more closely.

"It is very beautiful. Where did it come from?"

"There is a legend, told to me by my father, that this blade was at one time used by gladiators in the Colosseum. It is quite old."

Gerard felt a white-hot stab of pain shoot through his chest. One of his oldest nightmares centered around Roman soldiers and gladiators. He was almost certain that he had seen a blade such as this somewhere, but he could not remember where.

"I will treasure it always, father. Thank you."

"Gerard, you are never to follow me again, do you understand?"

"Yes, father. May I ask who that woman is?"

"It is better that you not know. Let us go and see what the servants have made for dinner. Oh by the way, which of the girls would you like to have visit you in your chambers tonight, Master Evans?"

Gerard swallowed hard at the prospect of touching a real woman in the way that he had seen his father touch the lady in the barn. He was big for his age and very strong. More than once he had secretly longed for such a gift.

"I would like the new girl, father. I believe she is a Moor."

"An excellent choice, my son!"

Day turned swiftly into night and Gerard could not wait for the sun to set. After he talked to his father, he sat on the marble steps of the main house for hours, watching the clouds move through the sky. He hated his father for what he did to his mother, but he was awash with new emotions related to the coming events of the night. Soon, he spotted the young girl who had been promised to him.

She walked past him carrying a large pail of milk. She did not look at him and hurried on her way toward the kitchens in the back. She knew her place even now, but he could not help but wonder what she was thinking.

His mind burned like fire at the very thought of the girl. He knew little of her. She was a recent acquisition from one of the local merchants. He did not even know her name. He did not know how old she was, but she was at least five to six years older than he was. She was tall, perhaps several inches taller than he was. Her hair was long, wavy, and black. She smiled when she walked, as though she knew some secret that she was not going to tell anyone. She wore mostly rags for clothing; this was common for the new slaves. Her breasts often showed through the tatters of her loose top and had caught Gerard's attention on more than one occasion.

He removed the knife, which his father had just given him, from his trousers. He fingered the finely sculpted sheath and admired the blade. Such a fine thing would make a wonderful gift for the girl, he thought, but just as quickly as he'd formulated the idea in his mind, he remembered his father's words. When they were together later, he would show it to her, and perhaps even let her hold it. Later...

Evening fell and Gerard wolfed down his supper of roast lamb, potatoes, and cool water from the spring. His father made small talk of the day's fishing expedition and his mother recalled her time with the weavers, who had been commissioned to make new drapes for the main receiving room. Gerard said little and excused himself as he finished.

"Are you not feeling well, my dear?" Lady Evans asked.

"I am fine, Mother. I merely wish to practice my Latin."

"A fine student he is, my sweet. He will surely make a first-rate lord of the manor one day," Lord Evans remarked.

Gerard kissed both his parents and headed off toward his bedroom. His father gave him a sly wink and a quick, toothy grin as he ran off.

Sometime later, after the house was dark and the evening meal had been cleared, Gerard heard a knock at his door.

"Who is it?"

"I come to bring you water and bread, Master Gerard."
Gerard knew instantly who the visitor was.

"Enter."

The girl opened the door and entered the room, carrying a large platter of freshly baked bread, honey, a wooden cup, and a wooden pitcher filled with water. She smiled nervously as she approached the small table near the middle of the room.

She quietly placed the platter on the table, removed the pitcher from the platter, and began to pour the water into the cup.

"Would his lordship like a cup of water?"

The girl poured the water into the cup and handed it to Gerard. He drank the whole cup in one gulp and then used his nightshirt to wipe his mouth.

Gerard's heart was pounding a mile a minute as he watched the girl. When she'd entered the room, she had closed the door behind her; the two of them were truly alone for the first time. He had no idea what he would do with her, but he relished the idea of finding out.

"What is your name, girl?"

"Lea, my lord."

"Where are you from?"

"Far away, in a land my people call Sephard."

"I know this place from my studies. My people call it Spain. You speak well, Lea."
"I attended some school with the priest in my village. My lord, I have a confession to make. I did not come to you simply to serve you bread."

"I know. My father told me that he would ask you to come to me tonight."

Lea held her head down and began to cry softly.

"What is wrong? Have I said something to offend you?"

"No, my lord, you have treated me with respect and kindness, not like the others in the kitchen. I regret doing such a terrible thing."

Lea began to sob and buried her face in her hands. Gerard pulled her close and motioned for her to sit on the bed beside him.

"What terrible thing could such a pretty girl as you have done?"

Gerard found himself stroking her hair involuntarily.

"Your father, my lord, asked me to see you this night. He said that he would free me and my family if I did a special service for him."

Gerard felt his heart begin to race.

"Have you already been with my father?"

Lea laughed and tossed her head back. She looked Gerard in the eye and gritted her teeth.

"No, my lord. That is not the service he bid me to provide."

"What is it then?"

"He gave me a small pouch of powder while I was in the kitchen. He asked me to pour it into the water that I was to give you. I asked him what it was, but he would only say that it was something to help you sleep. His eyes, my lord, told me that this was not the truth. I fear that I have done a terrible thing!"

Gerard looked at the pitcher of water and knocked it over with his fist. His heart began to race and he felt a strange tightening in his chest. His vision began to blur and his skin began to feel cold and clammy.

"What have you done to me?"

As he spoke, white-hot rage seized his mind and blinded his reason. He wanted revenge and he would start with the girl, given whatever time he had left.

Gerard grabbed the girl's arm and held her tightly. She tried to pull away and run but before she could budge, he pulled his knife from under the pillow. He had planned to show his new prize to the girl, but now he felt a more pressing urge.

Lea screamed and began to struggle in an attempt to get away. Gerard raised the knife to her throat and sliced her windpipe open cleanly with one swipe. Large spurts of blood issued from the wound and the girl grabbed her throat in a vain attempt to stem the flow.

In moments, Lord Evans entered the room followed closely by Lady Evans.

"Murderer!" Gerard managed to shout as he pointed the dripping blade at his father.

"You are the murderer here! What have you done?" Lord Evans shouted.

"You promised this girl to me in order to silence me for what you did, but then you made her poison me!"

Speech was the only faculty that Gerard continued to control. His vision began to swirl and he felt his heartbeat become slow and erratic. He could no longer feel his hands and his legs became heavy and numb.

As the poison took its final effect, his spirit began to leave his body and he saw Lady Evans rush to his side.

She shook him violently, pleading with him to wake up. His mind was still racing as he felt the life drain from his muscles. His breath came in long, tortured gasps, but he was determined to say one last thing to his mother.

"I saw father...with a lady in a barn...and he has...killed me for it."

Gerard's spirit slipped away from his lifeless body as he heard his mother begin to scream.

Gerard floated free from his body and watched from the ceiling as his mother took the blade from his cold, dead hands. In fury, she attempted to slash her husband. The blade missed its mark and Lord Evans grabbed her arm. He shook her and slapped her fiercely across the face.

"You dare threaten me! I am your lord and husband, woman!"

"Look at what you have done! You have killed my son!"

"He was poisoned by the slave girl! I had nothing to do with it!"

"You are lying to me! Why would he accuse you of adultery with his dying breath?"

"I will not tolerate your accusations, wife!"

"You are a liar! Liar! Liar!"

Lady Evans backed away from her husband. Several slaves had gathered near the door, awakened by the sounds of shouting and screaming late in the night. She stared at them and glared at her husband.

She then looked down at the dead girl and the growing pool of blood staining the floor. A wave of despair and agony washed over her and she felt nauseated. She grabbed the blade firmly, brandished it briefly at her husband and, in a flash, thrust the knife deeply into her own heart.

Lord Evans rushed toward her and attempted to pull the knife from her chest. Lady Evans fell to the floor, smiling. Her body fell atop the body of her son.

Her spirit clawed its way out of her dying form and began to coalesce near the ceiling. She saw the ghostly form of the slave girl crouched in the corner of the room watching the proceedings. Gerard's ghostly phantom slowly formed next to the girl's spirit. He motioned for his mother to take his hand.

She descended from the ceiling. He smiled at her and she took his hand. Together, they began to walk toward the rear wall of the bedroom. Gerard looked back and saw Lea still crouching on the floor. He shook his head, drew a deep, ghostly breath, and motioned for Lea to follow them. Lea slowly got up and cautiously walked toward Gerard. Without looking at him, she took his hand.

Together, the three of them walked through the rear wall of the bedroom. Within minutes, they had reached a clearing in the forest. In the distance, Gerard could see the figure of an old man standing in a clearing.

"Do you know him, son?"

"Yes, Mother, I do."

They reached the old man within minutes. The old man smiled, took Gerard's hand, and kissed it tenderly.

"Two souls this time. You have done well."

The old man spoke an almost incomprehensible Word and waved his hands over Lady Evans and Lea. Their ghost forms shimmered for a moment and began to glow with an unearthly orange and red light. Seconds later, both their forms were transformed into large dogs.

The old man spoke another Word, and the animals froze in position, looked the old man in the eye, and lowered their heads submissively.
The old man glanced at Gerard and smiled.
"They will be happier as dogs I think," the old man said.

"You have earned the right to know who you are and why you are in my service. Come, let us go and see what Salva has made us for dinner."

Chapter Ten

The Hunt

Anshar loved the freedom of flight. Rodare did not seem to mind the endless hours of time that they spent going over the details of capturing the new charges. After all, human souls were not very complicated. The beings that fed upon them, however, were another matter entirely. Anshar understood the need for preparation, planning, and tactics in battling the enemy. Sometimes, he wondered if the archangels enjoyed their control of the hunt a little too much.

The sun beat down upon his wings and made the effort of flight much tougher than he could recall in recent centuries. By his side, Rodare, his long-term partner, glided effortlessly through the clouds. They had worked together for almost 10 billion years, gathering the souls of human, fairie, E'ndar, H'al'al, and other assorted races spread out over the temporal world. They seldom spoke during flight, but Anshar wondered sometimes if Rodare still enjoyed the work.

Anshar flexed the bronzed muscles of his upper back and veered downward toward a small sleeping village in the northern region of a small country that was on the verge of organizing itself into a power to be reckoned with on this planet. The charge had been king of this land during his living years, and his soul was now prize game for the denizens of the lower world who wished to use it for a number of nefarious purposes. The soul of a human king would bring a high price on the astral slave market, if the demons could get their hands on it.

Rodare followed Anshar down toward the castle edifice. The king, Kildaran of Toran, had died a peaceful death. The Actus Record, kept by Archangel Ramirael, cast Kildaran of Toran in a wonderful light in this regard. He was, by measure of the Actus Record, a good and kind man. He had married six times and fathered 18 children by three of his wives. Contrary to the custom of his country, he claimed all of his children, sheltered them, and took care of his wives in an equal standard of measure. He did not take a lead wife, second wife, or third wife. All of his women were treated as equals in his castle. He also provided equally for the welfare of all of his children. In this regard alone, he was a rare human indeed.

His thirst for war, conquest, and plunder was typical of the humans of this world, and this placed him squarely on the demon's radar. No human was perfect, and Anshar had no delusions about the saintliness of this charge. Like any other human, he had good and bad traits. Only the Creator decided which human souls were to be collected and transported directly to the Celestial World. Most were processed for re-implantation in new bodies by the lower angels. The lucky few, like Kildaran of Toran, were escorted back to the Celestial World by Gatherers, specially trained Celestial Warriors who were equipped to handle the challenges of removing a human soul from the cycle of carnage known as the physical world.

However, the demons that now pursued his soul knew this, and in their world, the soul of a truly good human was a rare and precious commodity. Anshar realized that he and Rodare would have to fight for this charge, but then, that was truly no different from any other day. Anshar loved the hunt.

As a Gatherer, both he and Rodare were issued three weapons—a light spear, devil sword, and an angelic mace. Anshar checked his light spear and carefully twirled it once in the air to test its readiness. The light spear was forged from the fires of a large Cepheus-class blue-white star. The shaft of the spear measured 10 feet in length and the pointed blade at the tip was designed by the Demiurge Michael himself. The gold-titanium-ultrium alloy was made exclusively for Gatherer-class angels and was unbreakable. From top to bottom, the light spear was over 14 feet long. The weapon sparkled in the sunlight like a bolt of lightning. Though long and powerful, the weapon itself was surprisingly light. As a backup, Anshar kept a small devil sword, which was some four feet in length and designed by the Demiurge, hidden in a sheath behind his main wing attachments. The light spear had never failed to dispatch a fallen one. Anshar loved the power it gave him.

Rodare carried only the angelic mace. In reality, that was all that he had ever needed. Standing at over 15 feet tall with a nearly 60-foot wingspan, Rodare was one of the largest and most powerful of all the Gatherers. Even though Anshar stood at nearly 13 feet, his wingspan of 50 feet was nearly dwarfed by Rodare's magnificent plumage. The angelic mace was a weapon of awesome power and energy. At nearly 20 feet in length, the flanged angelic mace was a weapon feared by all demons and fallen ones. Forged in the fires of the red giant star, Antares, it was made from a Celestial alloy of ultrium, angelic iron, and gold. The mace was designed to penetrate even the thickest armor. The four flanged blades at the end of the shaft had been sharpened to the thickness of a single atom and tipped in gold. The weapon was also surprisingly light and well balanced. Rodare had never once been defeated in combat while using the weapon. Even though most Gatherers carried at least two of their issued weapons, Rodare dared to be different, and thus far, the choice had proven to be a very good one. No one in the Celestial Kingdom, save the Demiurge Michael, had ever dared to challenge him in single combat. Anshar felt fortunate that the Creator had seen fit to pair the two of them together.

They circled the castle and surveyed the outer perimeter. Long years of battle-tested experience had shown them that rushing in to gather a charge was unwise in the extreme. According to intelligence gathered by the Anakim, the reconnaissance wing of the Celestial Guard, the soul was being pursued by the Caecodemon Guratham. Guratham was unique in his standing among demons. He was once half-human. In the 12-billion year history of the Underworld, only two humans had risen to a level of leadership and royalty. The first was a conqueror known as Anaius, a blood-thirsty human who had once killed 30,000 children in a single city because he did not want his men to be tempted to sell them on the black market. Killing them, in his opinion, was the more merciful act. After his death, 100,000 of his most loyal soldiers killed themselves and followed him into the Underworld. Under his leadership, the soldiers overthrew three Underworld district capitals and two regional provinces. Anaius changed his name to Barburatham and sired three Caecodemons with a half-fairy half-human slave whom he captured from the Upper World. Guratham was his third son. Guratham was not content to accept the riches gathered by the labors of his father, Barburatham. He wanted to make a name for himself. As a result, Guratham had gathered unto himself 25 legions of demons, humans, and halflings that he had forged into a formidable army. He used these legions to plunder the Upper World for souls that he could sell for profit on the Astral slave market. The money that he received was used to expand his territory. Barburatham did not trust his son and he knew

that, at some point, Guratham would need to
be confronted, most likely on a field of battle.

Guratham had been on the Celestial Most Wanted
List for centuries. To date, more than 50 Anakim
Warrior-class angels and hundreds of lower-class
battle angels had been dispatched to bring him in.
The Creator knew that eventually Guratham's theft
of good human souls would upset the balance of
power on Earth between the forces of light and
darkness. For this reason, the Creator chose to
dispatch his two best Gatherers. On this day,
Anshar and Rodare sought to end Guratham's reign
of terror.

Anshar cautiously descended onto the grounds of
the main castle courtyard. Rodare circled overhead
as he carefully scoured the area for the presence
of demons. They both knew that there would be a
fight. The yard was too quiet. The humans were in
mourning for their king. The women were dressed
in long, thick cotton robes, their faces covered in
thin, sheer, red gauze, a custom well known in the
region as part of the mourning ritual for royalty.
The men sat stoically around the grounds dressed
in full armor. Many of them drank heavily and
passed the time by regaling themselves with
stories of the king's battle heroics. None of them
noticed Anshar's presence. Anshar walked past the
men unseen. He hated the smell of human flesh. It
was the least pleasant part of his job. He pitied
their miserable lives—the tedium, the aging,
decay, and death. He would never understand why
the Creator loved them so much. Anshar walked
slowly through the castle courtyard. He had not yet
gotten the scent of the soul. Sometimes, after the
death of a human, the soul is slow to free itself. He
remembered instances in which the soul would
take hours to free itself. Neither he nor Rodare
could smell a soul that was bound to the form of a
physical body. He had heard that a few Anakim
scouts had developed this ability, but they had
never seen them demonstrate the gift on a
mission.

Anshar signaled to Rodare to keep watch while he went into the castle. During the briefing, they were shown where Kildaran had died. Kildaran's castle was old, even by human standards. Standing for more than 1,300 years, most of the original outer curtain wall was still present and could be seen stretching away to the right and left on either side of the heavily fortified outer gatehouse straight ahead. Arrow slits could be seen on both sides and on the left there was a crenellated parapet with a walk behind it on which defenders of the castle would have stood to shoot. There was also a walk, called an alure, behind the parapet at the top of the gatehouse and behind most of the parapets in all places on the castle.

Demonic intruders would not easily gain entry to the castle structure as it was encircled by a deep moat filled with snakes, crocodiles, and poisonous fish. The wide drawbridge had been raised early that morning as a sign of respect for the passing of their king. The bridge had chains and ropes attached to its outer end and could be pulled up when necessary. The demons would also have to face the next hazard of missiles, traditionally comprising boiling oil or molten lead, which could be thrown down the wide shoot below the outer parapet of the gatehouse. The whole castle was built of locally quarried liassic limestone and Anshar could see stalactites below the projecting supports of the parapet.

Two long lancet windows lined the outer side of the gatehouse and a large, hooded fireplace of hardened granite faced the guardroom. This fireplace gave light to the entire surrounding courtyard and, during the day, it was used as a spit upon which a variety of game meats were prepared. Anshar stood quietly next to the fire and warmed his skin. Calming his thoughts, he opened his senses to the area and scanned it for the presence of Kildaran's soul. Despite the smell, standing next to the fire helped him to focus.

Rodare did not need much time to find the soul. Human souls had very distinct smells. A highly developed soul smelled distinctly of roses—aromatic and beautiful. Lower souls smelled of coal and stone—gravelly and metallic. Average, undeveloped souls carried a variety of scents, varying from that of freshly bathed human flesh to that of clean rainwater or the oaken woody aroma of pine trees in a vast forest. The rosy smell of an evolved soul was a rare scent indeed and Rodare knew it immediately.

Following his nose, he rose into the air and dissolved his form into a rainbow shower of light. Moments later, he reformed himself in the main bedchamber. Kildaran's soul floated near the ceiling of the room, having recently freed itself from the slowly stiffening corpse on the bed. The soul was magnificent.

The human soul was composed of more than 617 separate faceted gems that bound themselves tightly together to form a cohesive unit. The healthier and more evolved the soul, the more facets it contained. Most souls were green to orange in color, though some of the more evolved variety could attain the rarified colors of white and gold. Kildaran's soul was brilliant gold with the full complement of 617 facets. Each facet shone brightly and filled the room with effulgent light and splendor. Rodare liked gathering souls of this quality.

Slowly, Rodare approached the soul. He knew that Guratham was somewhere nearby, but he had not yet detected his presence. There were no demons, no lower forms, no elementals, no cerebral parasites of any kind. Perhaps the intelligence reports that he'd received had been wrong for once. Rodare mentally signaled to Anshar that he had retrieved the soul and was preparing to leave the castle. Anshar responded mentally with his usual aplomb and continued to stand guard outside.

Rodare gathered the soul into his arms and cradled it gently. The soul pulsed gently with the divine force that once carried life into Kildaran's body. He spoke a Word of Power and the soul slowly rose into the air above his head. Rodare then allowed the soul to hover briefly above his crown as he raised himself into the air. Under the influence of the Word, the soul gradually disappeared into Rodare's form. It would now be safe for its journey to the Celestial World.

Anshar willed himself into the air and soon rejoined his partner in the sky high above the castle. He looked at Rodare and smiled.

"You have the soul?"

"Yes."

"I have seen no sign of the enemy. Perhaps we will return home in time for the Symphony after all."

"Perhaps, but let us not be too careful. Remember who the enemy is."

Rodare nodded as they flew. Neither of them dared speak of the Symphony while they were carrying a charge. They knew well the potential dangers that they still faced.

Every angel was nourished by the gentle rays of the Symphony every day of their lives. Quite simply, the Symphony functioned as the primary sustaining force of the universe. Each day, corresponding to a 28-hour cycle in Earth planetary time, the highest angels of the Celestial Horde banded together forming a large circle. One angel, a Seraphim, usually began singing one note of power. The note was based upon the principle of the Word. All functions of the universe could be traced back to the principle of the Word. Each Word controlled a primary force of creation. A note was a single syllable of a Word.

As the Seraphim intoned the note, the remaining angels in the circle joined in. All angels were given at least one Word of Power at the time of their creation. Depending on the level of responsibility assigned to the angels, they may have been given more Words as time progressed. The Words of Power were either spoken or sung, depending upon their usage. Singing a Word generally gathered and released more power than a simple verbal intonation. As the angels each intoned their Words, the Symphony was formed. Over time, hundreds of thousands of angels adopted the practice of joining the Chorus of the Symphony. It is said that the Creator himself sometimes led the Chorus.

The Symphony lasted for 20 minutes each day. The overall effect of the power and sound of the Symphony was nothing short of miraculous. The Seraphim Moriel wrote a lengthy treatise on the virtues and benefits of the Symphony; it was entitled "*Moratus Symphoniel Verautis Domineisus.*" The text was required reading for all angels. In the text, the Seraphim Moriel described his first experience with the Symphony as follows:

"Nothing could have prepared me for the beauty and majesty that befell my senses as the first strains of the Chorus graced my senses. I had heard of the Chorus and Symphony, but I had never personally experienced it for myself. My service to the Lord required me to venture into the Nether Lands, and in this place, no light may be welcomed, no prayers may be heard.

Upon my return from service, I beheld a strange light flickering in the heavens. The light shimmered gold and iridescent blue as it approached me. Each moment that passed brought the light closer and closer to my being. In time, I began to hear a voice emanating from the light.

At first, the voice was faint, childlike in its presence, but as the light approached, it grew louder. Within a few moments, the light enveloped

me. The voice that I had initially heard as one
gradually became many. The sound lifted me from
my path of flight and carried me aloft. I know not
of the force that lifted me, but as it carried me, my
being was filled with a serenity, ecstasy, and peace
that I had never before experienced. I wished to
cry out, weep, pray, and sing all at once, but I
could not. As I was swept along by the tide, the
sound grew in intensity, and I feared that I might
at once be ripped asunder. All of my wings glowed
intensely with the light created by the sound.
Every fiber of my being was enlightened and filled
with the majesty that could have only been created
by my Lord. After a brief time, during which I felt
that I might be swept away by the force of my
experience, the sound stopped and the light
dissolved.

I regained my senses, righted myself, and checked
my wings to see if they had been changed by the
experience. All 48 pairs were intact, but I noticed
that they were somehow stronger, denser, and
more powerful than before. I drew a deep breath
of the primordial air that filled the Celestial space
and I also noticed that my muscles, my lungs, and
my mind were stronger, sharper, and somehow
renewed by the force of the energy. I gave a quick
prayer of thanks to my Creator and willed myself
as quickly as I could back to my seat on the
throne.

I reported my experience to my superior, the
Seraphim Anmtiesel, and he, too, reported that he
had experienced the light and sound in the same
way that I had. Thus was my first experience with
the Symphony.

(Moriel-Seraphim of the First House-Fifth Choir-
Second Seat: Recorded this Celestial date
2031:23:654:9:.008)

Initially, all beings in creation took part in the
Symphony. Over time, however, the Creator saw
that many beings were becoming dependent upon
the rapture brought on by its power. In the human

and astral worlds, many beings simply sat around all day awaiting the arrival of the Symphony. They neglected their families, responsibilities, and service requirements to creation itself. The Creator sent the archangel Raphael to warn them of their mistake and its impending consequences, but most did not listen. The Creator, in his mercy, did not take the Symphony away from the residents of the lower worlds. Instead, he blocked the reception of its chords from the conscious mind and buried it deep within the unconscious. The Symphony was still delivered to all beings in all worlds, but in the lower worlds, only those who learned to remove the unconscious blocks could benefit from its power. As a result, the dissonance caused by fear, anxiety, and chaos in the lower worlds rendered the Symphony all but inaudible to most elementals, humans, and demons.

Clear, unblocked, and coherent reception of the Symphony was the true source of immortality. Hearing it once gave a being the power of immortality. Hearing it on a daily basis renewed this immortality and granted increased power and vitality to the Immortals.

Anshar knew that the Symphony was coming soon. As a matter of fact, he was counting on it. He touched his chest and checked to see if the Soul of Kildaran was safe within its protective pouch. He could feel the soul beating within his chest. He smiled to himself. He permitted himself to glance briefly at Rodare flying silently by his side. Rodare, too, was smiling. The Symphony was near and they both sensed it.

Suddenly, the energy within the ethers around them grew still. Rodare was the first to sense it. The path back to the Celestial Kingdom was very familiar to Anshar and Rodare. This stillness was abnormal in the extreme.

"What do you think it is?" Rodare asked.

"I am not sure. I have never sensed anything quite like this before."

"Do you see anything that might presage trouble?" Rodare queried.

Anshar stopped in mid-flight, steadied his senses, and focused intently on the area surrounding them. Other than the stillness, he could sense no danger. He allowed himself to remain still for a few moments longer to be sure. He could sense nothing.

"I sense nothing, my friend."

"Do you think it safe to continue?"

"Yes, but we should be cautious."

Slowly, the two Gatherers began to beat their wings and will themselves onward toward home. As they flew, the space around them began to turn dark. The effect was subtle, but they both knew almost immediately that something was wrong. After a few moments, they stopped in mid-flight and drew arms.

"We know you are there. Come out and fight, if you dare!" Anshar shouted.

A large mass of gray, swirling energy began to coalesce and fill an area directly in front of them. The mass was almost twice as large as Rodare and Anshar combined. Both Gatherers instinctively recoiled and backed away from the mass as it grew in size and began to take shape. The head was the first area to become immediately recognizable. Shortly thereafter, the arms, covered in thick armored scales, became visible. A huge chest shrouded in shimmering, dark, gilded armor and chain-linked mail coverings manifested in the middle of the figure. A few moments later, the hips and legs grew under the form. Anshar immediately recognized the figure as that of Gurantham.

"You will remove yourself from our path and surrender to the servants of the one true God!" shouted Rodare.

"Well, Rodare, it would appear that we have quite the predicament. You seek to make demands of one who is not subject to hearing them. You should know that I do not serve your God."

Rodare slowly raised his angelic mace and placed it squarely on his chest. He began to mouth his Word.

"Rodare, stop. We need not fight this human. He is beneath our notice," Anshar said.

"Perhaps you are right. Perhaps I am quite beneath the notice of Heaven's greatest Gatherers. Yes, I know who you both are. But you might notice that I brought along a few friends, in case you might want to change your minds."

In the distance surrounding the now fully materialized Gurantham, a terrifying spectacle began to form. As far as the eye could see, legion after legion of soldiers began to teleport into the area. Heavily armed, drooling, and dark with arcane power that seethed through every fiber of their being, the soldiers slowly encircled the space surrounding Anshar and Rodare. The two Gatherers looked at the growing horde and smiled. They had faced armies such as this in the past and walked away without a scratch.

"Oh by the way, you might want to know that the Symphony won't be playing for either of you today. So don't count on using it to get you out of this."

"What say you, monster?" Anshar shouted.

"I have taken the trouble to invoke a small pocket of the Netherworld around us. You can't hear the Symphony here. No one can."

"That is not possible. It is an abomination to even suggest such a thing!" Rodare replied.

"I knew you would not appreciate the expertise required to lure two experienced Gatherers such as yourselves into a trap. You wouldn't believe how much it costs to find sorcerers capable of that kind of magic these days. Those humans are clever beings."

"The Creator will not stand for this. You cannot bend the laws of creation to suit your own ends, Gurantham!" Anshar shouted.

"And what is he going to do, punish me by sending me to the Underworld? Remember, I was born there...it's where I do my summers. You will give me the soul and, in return, I will allow you both to live and serve me. Refuse, and my friends here will enjoy tearing you to pieces. Without your precious Symphony, there will be no renewal, no extra strength to draw from the Chorus. You will truly be on your own. You will die."

Anshar looked at Rodare, who glanced back at him. They both knew that if Gurantham was right, they might well die trying to defend the soul of their new charge. They both strained to sense the chords of the Symphony that they knew must be present by this time. They could hear nothing. Neither of them spoke for a few moments. Surrounded, cut off from the Chorus deep within a pocket of the Netherworld, they had but one choice.

Anshar faced Rodare and smiled. Rodare looked at his partner, acknowledged the plan that he sensed growing in the space of their minds, and began to sing. Both Gatherers had learned many Words over the course of their long lives, and with each passing millennium, they mastered more and more sacred notes of power. However, one grouping of Words was more powerful than the rest.

"Esat, esot, esin...Esat, esot, esin...Esat, esot, esin..."

The Gatherers smiled as they sang. Gurantham stared at them blankly and tried desperately to discern what they were attempting. After a few futile moments, he ordered his men to attack.

The horde of demons descended mercilessly upon the Gatherers. The angels did not interrupt their chant. As the horde grew nearer, the angels began to glow. At first, the glow was dim, not unlike the bright moonlight on a summer's eve; but within seconds, the glow transformed into something quite spectacular.

"Esat, esot, esin...Esat, esot, esin...Esat, esot, esin..."

Slowly, impossibly, their angelic forms began to multiply. Each copy had exactly the same size, shape, and appearance of the Gatherer from whom it emerged. Eventually, both Rodare and Anshar were flanked by hundreds of copies of their bodies. Each copy carried the same weapon as its originator.

After a few moments, the Gatherers stopped chanting and turned toward the growing horde. Anshar's men raised their light spears and flew into the fray. Rodare's men hoisted their angelic maces high overhead and descended upon the demons, screaming as they flew.

Gurantham flew high overhead and watched.

The power and ferocity of the demon's attack was terrible to behold. The Gatherers, however, struck back with equal ferocity and might. Each Gatherer had created 1,000 copies of himself. They faced over 25,000 entities within the demonic horde. As far as they were concerned, even without the Symphony, the odds were equal.

The light spear burst into action and cleaved the armor of the attackers with ease. The brilliant luminescent ray of Celestial force that spewed from the point spread out in all directions. Each copy carried an identical weapon, full of power, charged with equal brilliance. Gradually, the demons began to fall.

Rodare's men flew into the midst of the horde and consumed hundreds of demons with their might. Each indomitable swing of the angelic mace carried the souls of dozens of demons back into the Underworld. However, for each one sent back into its domain, others quickly replaced them. Both Gatherers knew that the battle would not be quick.

Hours passed and the horde stood firm. Despite killing thousands, thousands remained. Anshar felt his breathing becoming more and more labored as he pressed on. His arms grew weary from the killing, but he knew that he had no choice. Rodare breathed more easily, but he, too, sensed the weariness beginning to creep into his bones. He missed the relief of the Symphony. The raw power that renewed them each day was more than their salvation; it was the source of their immortality. He had never been cut off from it before. He did not realize that he had become so accustomed to its strength.

Each angel gathered his strength and continued the battle. If they felt that their prayers would have been answered, they would have prayed. But in this pocket of the Netherworld, they knew that their prayers would be intercepted and consumed by the horde before the words ever reached the gates of the Celestial World. They were truly on their own. They continued their chant.

"Esat, esot, esin...Esat, esot, esin...Esat, esot, esin..."

Their reinforcements entered the fray with a vengeance. Hours passed as the sky grew dark with blood, ichor, and a mixture of expended life forces that defied simple explanation. Anshar knew that the use of the Word was potentially costly in the end. Each time they used a Word, they expended a portion of the Immortal Essence that bathed the fabric of their cells. The Symphony refilled this Essence on a daily basis, but since they were cut off, the Essence had no respite and they both slowly began to feel drained. They pressed on.

Hours slowly turned into days. Anshar and Rodare had endured many such battles in the past. Even without the Symphony, they could endure days of continuous battle without reprieve. They knew that they would prevail, but Anshar was not sure why he felt so tired. Even the effort of holding his wings aloft was almost more than he could bear. The combination of fighting and flying was normally done without so much as a thought. Now, however, he was literally fighting for his life. Rodare seemed to sense that something was wrong with his partner.

"Anshar, what is wrong?"

"I do not know."

"We should end this. I do not know how many days have passed, but without the Symphony, we risk injury of a most serious kind if we continue."

"What do you recommend?"

Rodare surveyed the remaining horde. He calculated that they had wiped out approximately two-thirds of the horde. By his estimation, less than 10,000 demons remained. Suddenly, he conceived a plan.

"Follow my lead!" Rodare said.

Rodare focused his will upon his men. He flew
straight up, high into the Netherworld firmament,
and summoned his men to follow. The demons
followed closely behind. Anshar bid his men to do
the same. As Rodare flew, he dipped his wings and
began to fly in a tight circle. As he flew, he
released his Light. The Light is the energy created
in an angel's body by the presence of the Essence.
Anshar followed suit with his men. The demons
immediately followed.

Within moments, the horde of gathering angels
began to create a spinning vortex of Light. They
flew faster and faster. As they flew, the intensity of
the Light increased. After a few seconds, the
vortex began to pulsate and shimmer with an
unearthly force. Gurantham knew what had
happened.

"Withdraw! Withdraw! Withdraw!"

Gurantham watched in horror as his horde of
demons was gradually sucked into the center of
the vortex. Anshar and Rodare had created a
pocket of Celestial Space within the Nether World.
Seconds later, they shouted a prayer. In a blinding
flash of Celestial Light, thousands of gathering
angels emerged from the center of the vortex and
quickly consumed the remaining demons of the
horde.

Two of the gathering angels grasped Gurantham
and pulled him into the vortex. He screamed as his
form was forced into the blinding light of the
Celestial World. Within seconds, the primordial air
grew still and peaceful.

Anshar sighed deeply as he watched the horde
disappear. He struggled to hold himself aloft as he
felt his strength begin to leave him. Rodare raced
toward his partner and clutched him close.

"I will take you to see the healer Raphael at
once. He will know what is wrong. I will not let you
fall."

"Thank you, my friend. It was a good plan."

Chapter Eleven

Darkness Falls

Rodare wasted no time in taking his fallen friend to
the healing archangel Raphael. Anshar grew
weaker by the moment and Rodare had never
before seen such a sickness befall one as mighty
as a Gatherer. The Healing Temple was a place
that Gatherers did not frequent.

The temple was large, even by Celestial standards.
When he was young, Rodare was taught that the
Celestial world was spoken into being by the
Creator's prayers. After the Celestial Throne, the
Healing Temple was the first building to spring into
being. The domed building was more than 50 miles
in circumference and glistened like the sun.
Standing more than one mile high, the dome was
supported by massive columns fashioned from a
Celestial alloy of gold, titanium, and iron. Each
column was guarded by a single massive throne

angel. Each throne angel was more than 2,000 feet tall and carried a light spear in one hand. The spears glistened like jewels in the light as Rodare swooped down from the sky into the portal entry.

Rodare had never personally entered the Healing Temple. He had no idea how he would find the healer. As he descended, he spotted a sentry near the opening. The sentry lifted himself majestically from his post and approached Rodare and Anshar.

"I will help you with your burden, brother."

"He is no burden to me. I will carry him. Thank you for your kindness, brother. We need to see the healer."

"Certainly."

The sentry uttered a single word of passage and Rodare instantly received an outline of the floor plan of the temple, as well as the exact location of the healer.

Anshar remained still and quiet in his arms as he flew. His breathing was still and shallow and Rodare wasted no time moving through the maze of the temple. Each section of the Healing Temple was designed to address a specific variety of conditions that befell the Celestial population. Immortality did not protect Celestials from illness and injury. Their unique body structures protected them from the permanent damage inflicted by death, but certain diseases and injuries were still capable of causing much suffering. Battling with the forces that threatened the Celestial World was a constant effort.

Rodare flew down closer to the temple floor. He had never imagined that he would see this place from so close a proximity. He knew that at some point, all things must end—even Gatherers; but he never allowed himself to think about it too much. Anshar stirred briefly in his arms, looked up at his

partner, and tried to speak. He could not
mouth the words that he wished to convey;
instead, he felt himself begin to cry. His tears
stained the darkening skin of his cheek. Rodare
looked at his partner's face and felt his own heart
begin to beat faster. He was deeply saddened to
see tears on the face of such a great warrior. He
knew that he must act. He quickened his pace as
he navigated the corridors of the temple.

He did not permit himself to think that Anshar
might die. He was not sure that he could bear such
a loss. Gatherers did not marry, create children, or
give themselves to family as did some angels. A
Gatherer's partner was all that he had. Their
relationship, their bond, had endured for billions of
years. What would he do without Anshar? He could
not bear the thought. Surely, the healer would
know what to do. He was their greatest hope.
Rodare knew that the healer could be found in the
center of the temple. His heart quickened even
more as he flew nearer to his destination.

The healer seldom left the temple. Even though he
administered to the needs of billions of Celestials,
humans, elementals, gods, and the occasional
demon, he usually summoned multiples of himself
to handle the work. Raphael was one of the oldest
of the archangels. He was created to embody the
Healing Essence of the Creator Himself. In his
purest form, Raphael stood more than 200 miles
tall. He was covered by an effulgent greenish-
golden glow that was almost too bright to look
upon. He wore only a simple golden mesh tunic
and seldom allowed himself to light upon the floor
of the temple. While administering to those in need
within the temple, Raphael shrank himself down to
a reasonable working height of 12 feet. Raphael
never slept, he never ate, and when he did have
free time, he spent it in prayer. It is said that he
was one of the most devout of all the archangels in
the Celestial World. His existence was one of total
service and commitment to healing.

Raphael had received word from the sentry and he knew that Anshar and Rodare were approaching. He prepared a fresh examination area for Anshar. He seldom treated Gatherers, but when he did have the honor to tend to their needs, he often found that they were among the sickest of his charges. Raphael prayed for strength as he felt Rodare rush into the room.

Anshar had fallen into unconsciousness and Rodare quickly placed him on the large bed space that had been prepared for him. Raphael smiled briefly at Rodare and quickly began to examine Anshar.

"It is good to see you, Brother Rodare. What has happened to our fallen comrade?"

"He became weak during a battle. He lost the ability to fly and to speak. I brought him here as soon as I could."

"I will do what I can for him, brother."

Raphael stood quietly as he examined Anshar. He did not speak, he did not move as he allowed himself to descend into a healing trance. He surrounded Anshar's body with an extension of his golden light. Within seconds, hundreds of tiny golden balls of light formed within the space between Anshar and Raphael. Each ball danced and moved under its own energy, and seemed to have a purpose known only to itself. Raphael extended his right hand over Anshar's head. A large green pearlescent sphere emerged from his hand, entered Anshar's skull, and disappeared. Without moving his hand, Raphael turned briefly to Rodare.

"This will take some time, brother. I do not know how long we might be here."

"I have nowhere to go. I will stay with him."

"So be it."

Raphael refocused his efforts and began to sing.
Rodare did not know the song, but he knew that
the healer was invoking an ancient power far
beyond his understanding.

"Cean toran emanu seatu cora imitu somase."

Raphael glowed more brightly as he sang. Rodare
felt the warmth and caress of the power that the
healer invoked begin to fill his body. He had never
experienced the power of a healer. He found
himself enjoying it, despite the fact that its rays
were not meant for him.

"Cean toran emanu seatu cora imitu
somase...Cean toran emanu seatu cora imitu
somase..."

Over and over, Raphael repeated the Words. Each
time he repeated the song, he grew brighter. In
time, Rodare could not see the healer, nor could he
see his partner. So bright was the Healing Essence
that he could no longer see anything in the room,
save his own form and the ceiling of the temple
high overhead.

Minutes turned to hours as Raphael continued his
song.

"Cean toran emanu seatu cora imitu somase."

Rodare felt ancient wounds from battles long
forgotten begin to heal. He had never allowed
himself to see the healer, and he had simply
learned to accept the aches and pains not healed
by the Symphony as part of the price of being a
Gatherer. His arms, legs, shoulders, and chest
began to flow and swell with the energy of the
healing. After a while, he began to feel better than
he had in a very long time. He wished that Anshar
could feel the relief that he was experiencing. Deep

down, however, he knew that his partner's wounds were much more serious than his.

After a couple more hours, Raphael stopped singing. He lowered his head in prayer, dimmed the glow of his Essence, and began to breathe deeply.

"He will sleep for some time. We should talk, brother. He will be fine here for a while. Let us visit the Parliament of Trees."

"Thank you for all you have done for him."

"He is very ill, but there is much that can be done for him. Come, let us fly together."

The Parliament of Trees was a large consortium of immense oaks, birch, pine, poplar, elm, bamboo, and spruce elemental tree structures that grew in the center of the Healing Temple. Each tree was more than 1,000 feet tall. Early in their lives, angels were taught that the Parliament acted like a battery of life force and healing energy for the Healing Essence of the Celestial World. The Parliament covered some eight square miles and Raphael often frequented a small grove of poplars that grew near its edge. He often recharged himself in this area. He also used it to deliver very bad news.

After a few minutes, they reached the poplar grove and Raphael softly alighted upon the lush, grassy carpet that grew on the floor of the Parliament. Raphael beckoned for Rodare to join him. Even Rodare knew that the healer never allowed himself to settle upon the floor of the temple. He braced himself against the trunk of a particularly large poplar and waited for the healer to speak.

"There is a malady that befalls your kind that is very rare—very, very rare."

"What is it?"

Raphael sighed deeply and looked Rodare squarely in the eye.

"It is called the First Darkness. It is so rare that in all my time here at the temple, I have only seen it perhaps a handful of times."

"What is this First Darkness?"

"When Gatherers are created, each of you is given the power to perform awesome, almost impossible tasks. You are the strongest warriors in our world. However, the core of your strength is not limitless, and, over time, even your legendary strength can begin to fail.

The First Darkness is a disease that has its roots in the basic fabric of our universe. Each being is created from the Essence. The Essence is formed from the particles of consciousness emanating from the Creator's thoughts. As he thinks, so are we created. In order for balance to exist within our world, he realized that light must be balanced by darkness. Thus, even the greatest of us is created with the seeds of light and darkness. Among lesser beings, humans, elementals, demons, and so forth, this darkness creates death and rebirth. We do not die and we are not reborn in that way. We are Immortals.

Over time, the energy of darkness grows within us, and our only saving grace from being consumed by this force is the Symphony. The Gatherers are given souls at the time of their birth, unlike many angels who are born without souls. Unfortunately, billions of years of battle and mayhem take a toll upon the soul of a Gatherer. The darkness feeds slowly upon the chaos of battle and mayhem. Over time, even the blessing of Symphony cannot heal the scars laden upon the soul caused by these forces. In short, the work that you do damages your soul and ultimately darkens you."

"What is going to happen to him?"

"If there were anything more that I could do for him I would, but I am sorry to have to tell you that he is never going to be the same again. Anshar is going to go mad."

"So let me get this straight...he is going to live, but he will go mad?"

"That is correct. I have stabilized his condition to some extent. When he awakens, he will be lucid for a time. I have added a bit of Essence to his being that will extend this period of lucidity for another 1,500 to 2,000 years. After that, however, he will begin to lose his sanity quite rapidly. Before that, however, his Celestial vitality will slowly drain away. Over the next few years, his wings will decay and fall away. He will lose a major portion of his stature. He will age over time. In short, he will begin to resemble an old, human male."

Rodare stared in silent terror as the healer outlined the fate that would befall his beloved partner. He heard the words, but he refused to believe them. In the billions of years of his life, he had seen many wondrous things. He had met beings who were capable of fantastic miraculous feats. He knew a man who could consume the energy of an entire supergiant star in one day. He had seen a woman give birth to 600,000 children, all the size of small asteroids. Both he and Anshar knew the Word that could give life to rocks and other inanimate objects. He had laughed intimately with the Creator himself. Rodare knew the far and wondrous forces of this universe. He had triumphantly faced odds in the heat of battle that would have crushed the soul of a lesser being. He refused to believe that nothing could be done. If worse came to worst, he would speak to the Creator himself on his friend's behalf.

"You said that this was a rare condition. You have seen it before?"

"Yes."

"What happened to those angels? Why have I never seen or heard of this condition among our brethren?"

The archangel Raphael tensed his wings and extended himself to a height of 20 feet. He rose a few feet higher off the ground and drew a deep breath. He forced himself to smile and then looked directly at Rodare.

"You will have to speak with the Creator in order to get an answer to that question. I am not permitted to speak of it."

"Not permitted? You are the healer! If you can't speak of it, then who might I ask?"

The archangel Raphael sighed deeply and smiled at Rodare.

"As I said, you will need to speak with the Creator."

"Will he cure Anshar?"

"The Creator is all-powerful. He can do anything he wishes. Though there are some things that he chooses not to do, that is his right as Creator of all things."

Rodare unfurled his massive wings and rose to meet the archangel at eye level. He looked deeply into Raphael's eyes, as if trying to discern every last kernel of information that he could. He knew that Raphael spoke the truth. He knew that he had only one choice left.

"May I see Anshar now?"

The archangel closed his eyes and focused. After several tense moments, he opened his eyes and spoke.

"He is awake. Please, follow me."

The archangel flexed his wings and, in one smooth, fluid motion, propelled himself toward the examination room. Rodare had never seen a being move with such grace and power. As he watched Raphael move through the temple, Rodare wondered if he could best the archangel in battle.

Suddenly, the archangel stopped in midflight. He turned slowly to Rodare and spoke carefully.

"There is one thing that I must tell you before you see him again. It is the only thing that the Creator permits me to speak of in regard to the First Darkness."

Rodare tensed his wings and tried to calm himself. He was not sure that the news could get any worse.

"Tell me, healer."

"Anshar will go mad, irretrievably so. But as he succumbs to the Darkness, he will slowly turn to the evil side of his nature. He will become a killer."

"I cannot believe that. Anshar is a warrior. He is one of the most honorable beings I have ever met. He would never wantonly take a life. Gatherers are incapable of murder."

"You must understand, brother. When the First Darkness consumes him, he will no longer be a Gatherer. He will become someone you could never recognize."

Rodare recoiled at the thought of losing his partner to evil. He could not believe that the Creator would allow such a thing. Then suddenly, a cold chill gripped his being and he began to feel light-headed. He knew what he had to ask the healer, but he was terrified of what the answer might be.

"Will I suffer the same fate, healer?"

"I do not know, brother. I can tell you this, the longer you continue to battle, the more susceptible you are likely to be to this malady. But that would mean betraying your Oath of Loyalty to the Creator. I must implore you to speak with Him."

The archangel did not wait for Rodare to respond. In the blink of an eye, he raised his wings and moved to the examination area.

Within seconds, they arrived at Anshar's side. He had indeed awoken.

Rodare rushed to his side.

"I will leave the two of you for now," the archangel said.

Before either of them could look up, the archangel had disappeared.

Neither of them spoke for several minutes. Rodare looked at Anshar and tried his best to smile. Anshar was sitting up under his own power, but there was something different about him. His skin had already lost its luster. The evanescent glow that marked the presence of the Celestial Life Force had begun to fade. He did not look older yet, but the spark of eternal youth and power was no longer evident on his face.

"How do you feel, brother?" Rodare asked quietly.

"I feel very weak. Where am I?"

"We are in the Healing Temple. You have been treated by Archangel Raphael."

"He saved my life. I wish to thank him."

Rodare sighed and grasped Anshar by the shoulders.

"We have much to discuss, but now it is imperative that we see the Creator at once. Can you fly, brother?"

Anshar struggled to stand. He drew a deep breath and flexed his wings. He drew another breath and willed himself into the air.

"I believe so."

Rodare was relieved to see his partner fly. If he could fly, there was still hope. Rodare rose into the air beside his partner.

"Follow me, brother."

All angels instinctively knew how to reach the Creator. Regular intake of the energies of the Symphony created a bond between all Immortals. The Creator, the greatest of all Immortal beings, emitted a powerful resonance that allowed all of his servants to find him easily. Since they were already deep within the heart of the Celestial City, Rodare knew that they would soon be with the Creator.

Chapter Twelve

The Creator Speaks

Rodare flew quietly as he approached the Celestial
Throne. The Creator was surrounded at all times
by a number of mighty Seraphim. These beings
maintained the vast power of the aura surrounding
the Presence. Surrounding the Creator with their
might, these angels emitted a near-blinding aura
that could only be tolerated by the most powerful
beings. Rodare knew full well that entering into the
Presence was dangerous under even the most
congenial of circumstances. He was very concerned
that Anshar might not survive the attempt.

Anshar struggled to keep up with Rodare. His wings beat the air in painful bursts of effort that left him nearly drained with each passing second. Anshar knew that the throne was nearby; otherwise he would not have even attempted the journey. He did his best not to let Rodare know the true extent of his weakness. His chest throbbed with pain. His eyes strained to see the horizon ahead. Each breath that he took burned his lungs. The searing vapor of the cool Celestial air, normally calming and soothing with its honeyed aroma, burned the very fabric of Anshar's delicate lung tissue.

Angel physiology was quite different from that of humans. Each wing structure was intimately grafted onto the body as an extension of the lung itself. The extraordinary filament system that lined the alveolar system of the lung extended into the fabric of each wing. The wings protected the lung tissue with a redundant outgrowth of dense epidermal tissue that firmly anchored each wing to the body.

Breathing was possible through the body of the wing alone. Each wing allowed the angel to breathe no more than one or two times per hour—less during times of rest or sleep. However, during stressful times, such as battle or prolonged flight, angelic respiratory rates could approach near human levels of eight to ten times per minute. Large, highly evolved angels such as the Cherubs and Seraphim possessed up to 64 pairs of long, elaborate wing structures. Each pair allowed them to take the essence of the Celestial air into the body and process the energy independently. As a result, they needed to take even fewer breaths than their lesser evolved brethren.

The angels of the Celestial Throne stood at over 20 miles high. Their wings towered over an area 50 miles in circumference. Each of these massive entities took in the eternal wellspring of power and energy from the Celestial Presence. These angels did not breathe. In fact, they had no need for breathing, heartbeats, or other physiological functions associated with the maintenance of life. In essence, they lived within the Well of Life itself. It is said that one of the Seraphim of the Throne initiated the Symphony each Celestial Day, but no one knew which of them performed that function. Indeed, so closely interlaced were their presences in the Celestial World, it was believed that they all initiated the Symphony in unison.

The Creator's Throne filled the Celestial City with the very light that ignited the stars. In the beginning, the Creator lived in perfect peace and harmony, alone within the expanse of reality that he defined as existence. Over time, he called into being his thoughts and created the first of the Demiurges, the great vessels that would carry his mind into the far reaches of reality. Michael was the greatest of these entities and, to this day, the archangel Michael stands alone as the greatest of all the entities in the Celestial World, save the Creator himself.

The archangel Lucifer was created as a twin fire to the furnace that was to become Michael. His fall greatly saddened the Celestial World and none but the oldest of the Demiurges within the city spoke of him. The Creator was often seen weeping after he ordered the destruction of Lucifer's vessel as he was cast out of the city. For many millennia, no one saw the Creator except for Michael, and, during this time, it is said that the Creator secretly sent him to Lucifer and attempted to coerce him into returning to the city.

Lucifer refused to heed his brother's pleas and hardened his heart toward all who refused to stand by his side in defiance of the Creator. Lucifer could not tolerate the presence of the gift of free will that the Creator had given to the humans. Even the oldest of the Demiurges had to fight for millions of years to acquire even the slightest glimmer of this precious gift. Seeing the humans flaunt and ignore the enormity of its power set his mind reeling with confusion as to why the Creator would grant them such a gift. They could do anything that they could imagine.

He swore that he would tempt and confuse their race at every available opportunity in order to prevent them from ever seeing the raw power of the Gift. Hearing this, Michael urged the Creator to form a Legion of Gatherers to resist the hordes of Fallen Ones that descended upon the souls of humans at the request of Lucifer.

Anshar and Rodare were among the first to be recruited for this task.

The Seraphim surrounding the throne were appointed as the leaders of the Gatherers. Their proximity to the Presence and their sheer power allowed them to perceive and anticipate challenges to the lower worlds far in advance of other angels. Anshar and Rodare had always received their orders from the Seraphim. However, they relied on their faculties of far perception, a kind of telepathy, to allow them the ability to communicate with their masters from anywhere within the universe. Today, however, they would need to meet them face to face.

Rodare saw the blinding expanse of Celestial Light that marked the end of their journey. Anshar could also make out the energy of the Presence. He drew near to his partner and steeled himself for the coming meeting.

"This meeting could prove dangerous for you, brother," Rodare said quietly.

"I am well enough to see my Creator," Anshar replied.

"I fear that your courage may be stronger than your body. I have seen how you struggled with this flight."

"I had thought to hide that from you. I see that you are not to be so easily deceived."

"I could speak with the Creator on your behalf...discover what he will do to save you from this evil."

"I will speak for myself!"

"If you insist, brother, I will remain by your side."

"Thank you. I do not mean to be irritable, my friend, but I believe that I am dying, and I do not understand all that the healer said regarding this illness called the First Darkness. I need answers."

"Our Creator will grant those to us, my friend...or we will die in the attempt."

The Celestial Throne could only be approached through formal prayer. Both Anshar and Rodare knew the routine and both summarily folded their wings, descended to the floor of the Celestial City, and bowed their heads in deep prayer. Just beyond their repose, eight large Seraphim of the Presence hovered above them. The Seraphim received the energy of the prayers, contemplated their worth and sincerity, and relayed them to the Creator. Most prayers from the lower worlds never completed the journey to the throne.

Fallen ones from millions of lower worlds fed upon the energy of prayer as a main food source. Only the strongest and most sincere of prayers from the lower worlds survived the deluge of attacks from these entities. Once they survived, certain angelic beings, called Messengers, took the prayers directly past the gates of the Celestial City to the hands of the Seraphim. Since Anshar and Rodare prayed directly at the very feet of the Seraphim, no Messenger intervention was necessary.

The energy of their prayers took the shape of two gold-colored crystalline balls. Each ball floated up to the hands of one towering Seraphim who gingerly took the glowing objects and spoke a massive Word of Power into the vessels.

"Bor ena ana enso!...Bor ena ana enso!...Bor ena ana enso!"

The ground beneath their feet shook as the Seraphim repeated the Words. Soon, several of the remaining Seraphim of the Presence joined in and repeated the Words. The thunderous din created by the Words shook the ground vigorously. Despite the heaving and swaying of the ground beneath their forms, Anshar and Rodare knew that they dare not move. In fact, they dared not speak or think in any way, for to do so might ruin their chances of securing an audience altogether.

"Bor ena ana enso!...Bor ena ana enso!...Bor ena ana enso!"

The Seraphim repeated the Words of Power for what seemed like hours. Neither Anshar nor Rodare had ever approached the Creator in such a manner so they did not know what to expect. After a few minutes, the chorus subsided and the massive waves that shook the ground around them ceased.

The light of the Presence dimmed and a cool breeze began to blow around the angels' bodies. Moments later, Anshar and Rodare felt themselves being lifted up and carried by an impossibly gentle yet powerful force that formed from the essence of the breeze. The Seraphim parted and allowed their forms to pass into their midst. Anshar looked at Rodare and saw that he was surrounded by a soft nimbus of golden light, which also formed a protective bubble around the angel's form. He quickly glanced at his form and saw that he, too, was surrounded by the nimbus of protective light.

Within moments, they floated into the midst of the presence and ascended to a glimmering orb of flame that hovered in the middle of the throne. They could not open their eyes to see clearly and, out of fear and concern, they instinctively covered their eyes tightly. Anshar felt a soft touch on his right shoulder, just above the point of attachment of his wing.

"I have seen your pain, my son...Come, tell me how I may serve you."

The voice descended upon Anshar like a torrent of love and overwhelming warmth. He had spoken to the Creator before, but never directly in his presence.

Anshar wanted to weep, but he knew that he must retain his composure.

"Father, I have long been your faithful servant. I will continue to serve you as for as long as I am capable. But now, I fear that I may be dying. I need your help. What is wrong with me, Father?"

Anshar dared not open his eyes or remove himself from the praying posture that he had adopted at the foot of the throne. Even with his eyes closed, the light was almost blinding.

Rodare retained his position next to Anshar and dared not open his eyes. He, too, was almost blinded by the Light of the Presence. He remained silent as his partner fought for his life.

"The healer has told you of your condition?"

"Yes, Father. I do not understand."

"When I created your kind, I knew that certain inevitable risks were to be taken during the course of your battles. These risks were to be balanced by both your power and your longevity. However, I could see that there would come a time in which even those strengths would be overcome by certain inevitabilities."

"Inevitabilities, Father?"

The Creator's voice bathed Anshar with a light and warmth that he never thought possible. His body swayed with pleasure at each syllable that the Creator spoke. It was all he could do to form his questions properly.

"When a warrior confronts evil, one is forced to expend a certain amount of power in defeating it. Over time, each confrontation with that force begins to take a toll on the warrior. You and your kind were created to be my greatest champions in the lower worlds, but even you were not designed to withstand this force forever."

"This evil force...that I have fought for you, my father...will it destroy me?"

Anshar was close to tears. He felt a warm rush of power fill his wings and he longed to soar upward toward the Presence. He knew, however, that the energy he would encounter in so close a contact with the Creator might well destroy him.

"All things—including you, my son—must follow the patterns of Creation. You have lived for billions of years...far longer than most of the stars and galaxies in the heavens. You are one of my most beloved creations. I am very sorry to say, my son, that your time has come."

"Father, do you no longer require my service?" Anshar asked pleadingly.

"You and your partner are my greatest
warriors in the lower worlds. I could create a new
partner for Rodare to replace you. But that one,
too, in time, would come to a cruel end. It is the
way of creation, my son."

Rodare could barely hold his thoughts in check. He
knew that he had fought alongside Anshar for
billions of years. He knew that eventually, he, too,
would succumb to the darkness if he continued in
battle. Tears filled his eyes and he felt anger begin
to grow in his heart.

"Father, we are your servants, spare us this fate.
Please restore us!" Rodare shouted.

Silence filled the space surrounding the nimbus of
light that carried the angels. They floated along in
the soft breeze and dared not move as they waited
for an answer from the Creator.

"There is a way...but it will require much sacrifice.
Many humans in the lower worlds may die in order
that you might live."

"I have given my life to protect all who serve you,
Father. Is there no other way?" Anshar replied.

"The balance of the universe is a very delicate
thing, my son. Change one life, and millions of
others are affected. Your life as an angel is coming
to an end. However, you can, should you choose,
attempt to begin a new life."

"A new life? In what form, Father?" Anshar
questioned.

"Though it has never been attempted before, I will
give you the chance to enter into a human form. In
this form, you may attempt to achieve immortality
and return to the Celestial World as an Immortal.
In an Immortal form, you will not die and you
would retain all the powers and abilities that you

have amassed during those lifetimes. You would also retain those abilities that you attained as a Gatherer."

"Father, why would this risk the lives of humans in the lower worlds?" Anshar asked.

"The First Darkness has already begun to consume you, my son. You have a few short millennia in which to accomplish your task before the madness that accompanies this force consumes you. As it consumes you, you will have no choice but to cause much suffering. It is the way of things."

"And if I do nothing, Father, what then?"

"You will die in madness, my son."

"Is there no other choice, Father?"

"None that I may allow, my son."

Silence once again filled the space within the throne as both angels silently pondered the weight of the news that the Creator of Heaven and Earth had just visited upon them. Anshar knew that the words of the healer had been true, but hearing the finality of the Creator's declaration gave the enormity of the words new weight.

Rodare saw his future flash before his eyes. He did not wish to suffer the same fate as his partner. He could no longer restrain himself.

"Father, what of my fate? I do not yet suffer from this darkness. What is to become of me?"

"Rodare, my son, you have more time than Anshar. The darkness has not yet caught you in its grasp. There is a way that you might escape its grip. But it would mean that you must leave my service and depart from the higher worlds."

"But, Father, I have always lived to serve you.
I could not bear to leave you or my brethren."

"I will give each of you the answers that you seek,
and then I will conclude this audience. Anshar, you
will be granted the space of 10,000 human years
in which to complete the process of incarnating
into a human form. You must gather 108 human
souls, fashion them into the soul of a Gathering
Angel, and place this soul into that of a human
female.

This female must then give birth to a form that is
capable of carrying the soul to term. Following the
birth of the soul within that body, you may begin
life as an Immortal. I will grant you a world within
the astral plane from which you may perform this
task. I caution you, you may not directly gather
these souls yourself; rather, you must find a
suitable vessel to carry out this task for you. Your
presence in the astral world will cause enough
damage.

Your vessel may accomplish this task during the
course of a series of otherwise normal lifetimes. If
in your mission you fail to complete this task in the
allotted time, you will die, my son.

Rodare, I grant you leave from the service of the
Gatherers. You may enter into the lower worlds.
You may choose the world you wish to enter and
there you may live your life as an Immortal. In this
way, you may avoid gathering the force that
poisons you during battle and live your life in
peace. It is the only way to stop the progression of
the madness.

You may not alert innocent humans to your
presence and you may not assist Anshar in the
performance of his quest.

Both of you would be wise not to attempt to
circumvent my edicts in this manner. Do you
understand?"

Anshar and Rodare spoke in unison.

"Yes, Father."

"So let it be done."

Chapter Thirteen

Edna

Edna Bowles hated working at the Circle One. Unfortunately, after dropping out of high school two years ago, she could find little else to do to fill her time. Her parents had cut her off long ago, especially since she had taken to the odd habit of stealing their jewelry in order to feed her rather expensive weed habit. In her mind, they just didn't appreciate how much the good stuff really cost these days. At 35 dollars a gram, a bag of ChemDog was no easy fix. After they changed the

locks and left her stuff on the back porch, she
felt obligated to leave home and strike out on her
own.

Edna volunteered for as many overtime shifts as
she could get. She lived in a two-bedroom
apartment near the Circle One and walked to work
every day. She met Tala, her roommate, at a rave
on the West side and they became friends almost
immediately. Edna needed a place to sleep and
Tala needed someone to help pay for rent and
utilities. The fact that they were both connoisseurs
of fine cannabis only sweetened the deal. Two
months and a good, steady job later, Edna felt that
she was just starting to get her life on track.
Almost.

Five weeks ago, Edna met Ronald, who was the DJ
at the rave that she and Tala attended in Midtown.
When he singled her out to come into the booth,
Edna felt that she might have found true love.
Ronald didn't talk much, but he was a master at
spinning CDs, albums, and even the occasional
DAT tape into his mixes. After the party, she went
back to his place and they made love for hours on
his fur-covered couch. Later that morning, she left
for work and gave him her number. He never
called but she did remember his address. She
wanted to walk back to his place 100 times and tell
him just how big a jerk he was. But, that was
before she missed her last period. Using a condom
with such a gorgeous guy just somehow didn't
seem to fit the moment. She didn't plan to keep
the baby, but she wanted to scare the hell out of
him just to get even.

Today wasn't going to be the day, however. Edna
had just finished her third ten-hour shift in three
days and she simply wanted to go home, light up a
big bong of ChemDog, smoke until she passed out,
and sleep for the next 20 hours. Tala was out of
town for the weekend and she would have the
place to herself.

Edna had only two more hours left on her shift.
She didn't mind working the late shift, even though
sometimes the sheer boredom of it all made her
wish smoking Dog on the job were a real option.
The local cops kept her company and one of them
actually thought he had a chance of getting into
her pants, even though he was old enough to be
her father.

Edna had worked at the Circle One for more than
eight months and she knew most of the regulars
who shopped there. In that part of town, very few
people stopped for gas late at night and most
people only came in for beer, snacks, and
cigarettes. No one had walked in for more than two
hours and Edna was beginning to think that she
might be in for a wonderfully rare slow night.
Then, he walked in.

Ronald wore a very large, tattered T-shirt, a
Yankees baseball cap, and a pair of Levis. His
sneakers were covered in mud and he didn't look
at Edna as he pushed his way into the store. Edna
held her breath and tried to act calm. Her heart
pounded inside her chest and she felt that at any
minute, she might leap over the counter and run to
him. She didn't understand how she could be so
stupid, but in her mind, being 19 gave a girl
certain privileges.

Ronald didn't look up as she staggered toward the
counter. Strangely, he walked with his hands
buried deep within his pockets and he said nothing
as he reached the counter.

"Hey, can I help you?" Edna was proud of her
ability to feign nonchalance.

Ronald did not answer.

"Look, guy, I don't know how you found out where
I work, but I have been meaning to talk with you."

Ronald did not look up, he did not answer, and he did not seem to notice Edna's questions.

"Ronald, I know you remember me, or at least you should. What do you want? What are you on?"

Ronald shifted his weight nervously, lifted his T-shirt, and placed his hands into his pants. Moments later, he pulled out a Ruger .30-caliber Blackhawk handgun. Edna had never seen such a large weapon. Instinctively, she stepped on the silent alarm on the floor near the cash register and then backed away from the counter.

"Look, man, I don't know what you're on, but we should talk."

Ronald pulled the trigger twice. The first bullet struck Edna in the center of her chest, shattering her sternum and collapsing her lungs. The second bullet pierced the right side of her neck and ripped a hole into her carotid artery. Edna fell backward onto the floor and died instantly. She never got the chance to tell him about the baby.

Ronald then turned the gun on himself. He heard the sound of the sirens as the police approached the store. Seconds later, two local cops burst into the Circle One and ordered Ronald to drop his weapon. Ronald smiled, squared off on the policemen, and began to fire.

In the hail of gunfire, Ronald managed to hit both officers in the head. Both officers managed to connect with clean, well-grouped shots to Ronald's chest. Within moments, all three men lay on the floor of the Circle One.

High overhead on the ceiling of the store, a reddish-gray mist swirled and then descended into the bodies of the older of the two policemen, Ronald, and Edna. The mist disappeared into each body in turn, only to emerge seconds later bigger, brighter, and seemingly engorged with new life.

After leaving the third body, the mist gathered itself into a large red phosphorescent ball of energy, passed through the ceiling of the building, and disappeared high into the night sky.

Chapter Fourteen

The Fragment

Mitchell drove the Jaguar slowly as he approached the Morton house. He had wanted to go back there for some time now in order to complete the spiritual aspect of his investigation. The energy traces that he had detected during his first visit were intriguing and he wanted to check them out without the prying eyes of his dear friend Gerald.

Mitchell brought the car to a complete stop
some 500 yards south of the main entrance to the
home, where he would be just out of range of the
main security cameras that he had spotted earlier.
With any luck, he could take his time and leisurely
investigate the grounds without hindrance.

Two hours earlier, he had called Patricia Morton
and made arrangements to meet her at the
mansion. Fortunately, he had been able to clear his
schedule for the afternoon and arrive an hour
early.

The forest surrounding the Morton estate was alive
with an almost bewildering variety of plants and
wildlife. Thomas Morton loved to hunt and he
stocked the area surrounding his home with deer,
wolves, rabbits, and pheasant from two
neighboring states. Mitchell walked a few yards
into the forest and soon spotted a clearing under a
copse of small pines and a thick patch of
blackberry bushes.

The air was fresh and still with the clinging scent of
pine and ripening berries. If it were not for the
annoyance of a few swarms of gnats, the spot that
he chose would have been perfect for a quick
picnic.

Mitchell sat down in the clearing, crossed his legs,
and began breathing deeply. Without thinking, he
removed his large bronze medallion from the
protective sleeve that he kept hidden away in his
undershirt. The medallion glowed with a deep,
blue-white light. As his breathing deepened,
Mitchell felt the familiar tug of his astral form
leaving his body. His breathing slowed to an
almost imperceptible four breaths per minute.

His body tensed in response to the rising of his
astral form and assumed a defensive rigidity
almost as a reflex. In his astral form, Mitchell was
much freer to explore and investigate the area
than when in his physical body. If someone were

to stumble upon his body, they would only see a man meditating in the woods. In his astral form, however, he could assume a much more formal spiritual appearance.

In most humans, the astral body was a loosely congealed amalgam of mental, etheric, and bioelectrical energies that functioned primarily as a vessel for dreaming, near-death experiences, and the occasional sexual escapade with other wandering astral forms. However, if one chose to develop that form during certain very rare, secret, and powerful spiritual alchemical processes, the astral body could flower and grow into a formidable asset.

In the physical world, Mitchell stood at just over six feet one inch. At 215 pounds, he was large enough to be mistaken for a professional athlete, even as he approached his fiftieth birthday. In his astral form, he stood at over eight feet tall. His skin glowed with a bluish-gold hue, and his aura, the energy form that surrounds all living things, extended some 12 feet beyond the perimeter of his astral body. He wore a deep royal blue robe that had been fashioned over a series of lifetimes to fit the demands of the spiritual work placed upon him by his Order. The robe was emblazoned with a large golden orb that seemed to pulse with a life of its own. In the middle of the orb lay the form of a large red dragon, with eyes that glowed with the same light as the golden orb.

Mitchell rose swiftly into the air and began to survey the area around the mansion. Within minutes, he picked up the faint trail of the red mist that he had seen a few days before. The odd metallic smell burned his astral senses and, for a moment, left him feeling slightly nauseated.

He spoke a brief Word of Power and expanded his senses into the adjoining timeline around the time in which the mist entered the area. His field of view exploded into a cacophony of rainbow colors that coalesced into a crystal clear series of images.

Each image floated silently in the space in which it was created. All events in time and space are recorded upon the fabric of space-time in which they are created. These events are fragments of energy that may be retrieved through various energy manipulation techniques. Many lifetimes ago, Mitchell had learned to gather these fragments and read them as easily as one might read the morning paper.

The first image showed the Morton boys playing in the yard. Thomas Morton sat watching the boys from the tall overlook that adjoined the back of the mansion. Mitchell grabbed the image, stretched it, and expanded it to several hundred times its normal size. At this level of detail, he saw something that startled him.

Thomas Morton did not move as he watched the boys. Just to the right of his physical form, however, a faint reddish form began to shape and writhe unbeknownst to Morton. The form slithered silently around Morton's chest and swiftly surrounded his entire body. After a few seconds, the energy form slowed its rapid rotation, focused on Morton's head, and slammed into his eyes with the fury of a tornado striking a wooden barn. Morton staggered and reeled for a moment, as if he were struggling to resist his unseen attacker. After a few moments, Morton righted himself, smiled, and walked into the main house. The time fragment began to shimmer and then quickly dissolved.

Mitchell grabbed the fragment immediately next to the one that he had just played. In this fragment, Morton emerged from the house brandishing the weapon that he had used to kill his sons. Mitchell watched in awe as Morton first shot his children and then turned the weapon upon himself. The red mist emerged from Morton's body, traveled into the bodies of the two boys, and then emerged engorged and swollen with energy. Mitchell froze the image for closer examination.

Mitchell stretched the time fragment and examined it closely. Carefully, he focused on the red mist and gradually zoomed in on its engorged form. Pulsing within the engorged misty form, he could clearly see three shimmering gemlike structures. Each structure was multifaceted and multicolored. Mitchell examined the detail of each crystalline form. There was only one conclusion that he could draw. The red form climbed into the sky over the yard and approached a glowing opening in the fabric of space that formed in the sky. The mist sped up as it neared the opening and, in an instant, it was gone.

Mitchell spoke a word of dissolution and willed the scene away. He drew in a deep breath of astral essence and descended back into his body. He then forced his lungs to take a deep breath of the clear afternoon air. Leaving the physical form drew a small amount of life force from the body, and each breath that he took when he returned from the astral sojourn refreshed his form.

Mitchell spoke a silent Word over the glowing medallion and placed it back into his undershirt. As quickly as he spoke the Word, the light of the medallion faded and the bluish-gold light cooled and dimmed. He rose to his feet, walked briskly to the car, and resumed his journey to the Morton home.

Chapter Fifteen

The Ride

Patricia Morton loved horses. Before her husband died, the family often took long trail rides through their property. Her favorite steed was a young black mare that Thomas had acquired from a stable in Kentucky. She had named the horse Tina, and at least three times per week, she rode her through the property and sometimes deep into the neighboring Sandhills. She carried her cell phone with her on these journeys so that Thomas could reach her. She didn't know why she carried it today. Some habits were hard to break. Suddenly, the haunting sound of Luciano Pavorotti's voice broke the still trance of Tina's gait.

"Nessum dorma! Nessum dorma! Tu pure, O, Principessa..."

She had programmed Pavoritti's version of "Nessun Dorma" from Thomas' favorite opera *Turandot* as her ringtone. She hadn't bothered to change it. Patricia had been startled by the sound of her own ringtone. Looking down at the number, she could see that Maria, her housekeeper, had just called.

"Yes, Maria, what is it?"

"Mrs. Morton, Dr. Gibson is here to see you. Shall I tell him to wait or would you like to reschedule him for another day?"

"No, tell him to meet me at the stables. I would like to continue my ride, if he is up to it."

"I don't know if the doctor knows how to ride, Mrs. Morton."

"Then he will have to learn. Show him to the stables, Maria, and I will meet you there in 15 minutes."

"Yes, Mrs. Morton."

Patricia sighed heavily and pulled gently on Tina's reins. She didn't really want to speak with anyone today, or even for the next 10 days. However, she had promised to answer some questions regarding her husband's death and she was a woman who liked to keep her word.

Fifteen minutes later...

"Welcome to my home, doctor. Thank you, Maria, I will take it from here."

Maria bowed slightly, smiled, and walked back toward the main house.

"Well, doctor, it would appear that we have some things to discuss. Do you ride?"

"My wife and I used to take the kids for rides in the stables near our home in Arizona before we moved. I have ridden a few times, and, for the most part, I am comfortable on a horse."

"Very good, then we will ride as we talk. Do you see a steed that you like?"

Mitchell looked around the stable and marveled at the variety of horses the Mortons had collected. Most were quarter horses of different colors and ages. There were eight chestnut-colored French Trotters that had gathered in a corner near the northwest corner of the large main stable. Close to that group, Mitchell spotted a group of six American Paints. One stood over 16 hands high and was a stunning midnight black with splotches of pearlescent white. Mitchell knew which one he wanted.

"I like the Paint over in the corner near the Trotters."

"Oh! You know something about horses?"

"Only what I read in *Encyclopedia Britannica*. You have an excellent selection of horses here."

"Thank you for your kindness. You chose Midnight. He is one of our best jumpers. You will like his spirit."

"He is not too spirited, is he?"

"No, doctor, he is just perfect for you. Come let us saddle him up and we will have our talk."

Patricia walked with Mitchell to the main barn and secured a black saddle.

"This one is guaranteed to keep you riding for hours, doctor. The seat is deep and comfortable and extremely well padded."

Patricia placed the saddle on Midnight and began to secure it. The saddle had a rounded skirt, padded stirrups, and nylon-reinforced leather cinch straps that provided extra security and strength. Mitchell also noticed that it included a very well-padded fleece underskirt that helped to provide extra cushion for the horse's body.

"This is an excellent steed, Mrs. Morton. Thank you for your hospitality."

"You are most welcome, doctor. Please, call me Patricia. It would mean a lot to me."

"Of course."

Mitchell mounted the horse, grabbed the reins, and righted himself in the saddle. Midnight looked back at his new rider, snorted briefly, and bent down to sample a new tuft of dandelions that grew near his left front hoof.

"Shall we go?" Patricia queried.

"Let us ride toward those hills off to the right, shall we?"

Patricia quickly mounted her horse, gave her a gentle nudge, and trotted off. Mitchell nudged Midnight, took a deep breath, and gave chase.

Patricia did not intend to conduct an interview with Mitchell unless he could catch her. She had not told him that, however.

She removed a small riding crop from her saddle and gave Tina a swift slap on the rump. The horse snorted, reared its head, and broke into a swift gallop. Patricia looked back to see if Mitchell was keeping up.

Midnight was indeed a wonderful horse. Mitchell could sense the horse's thoughts as they rode. He knew that the animal could sense his inexperience and was, for the most part, doing all the work of holding his new master in the saddle.

Mitchell projected his thoughts into the horse's mind and asked him to catch up with Patricia. Midnight looked back at Mitchell, grinned, and projected a loud thought string outward.

"What's in it for me?" Midnight asked.

"What would you like?" Mitchell asked while trying to stay in the stirrups and hold onto the reins at the same time.

"I would like apples, fresh red apples, daily."

"Done, my good friend," Mitchell replied.

"I have your word then."

"Yes, I will convey your wishes to your mistress and convince her to give you the best red delicious apples that she can secure."

"Very well, we have some running to do. Hold on please."

Suddenly, Midnight broke into a fast gallop. Mitchell did his best to hold onto the reins and attempted to at least appear to know what he was doing. The horse was doing all the work. Mitchell was truly just along for the ride.

Patricia sped up as she sensed Mitchell's approach. She huddled down close to Tina's neck and focused on reaching the nearby thicket of pine trees some 200 yards ahead.

Mitchell sensed Midnight's thirst for victory. The horse veered to the right of a small boulder and increased his pace as he closed in on the Trotter.

As they approached the thicket, a small stream appeared. The stream was no more than eight feet across, but it ran directly in front of the thicket of trees toward which Patricia was headed. She must have known that the stream stood between them and the finish line.

"Don't worry, my friend, I love this part," Midnight said confidently as he approached the stream.

Midnight broke into a full gallop and easily overtook Tina. Within seconds, he approached the stream, took a deep breath, and cleared it with more than three feet to spare.

Tina quickly followed with Patricia Morton in tow and completed a beautiful jump that led her to Midnight's side a few seconds later.

Midnight stopped just short of the thicket and began to catch his breath.

"You have surprised me, Dr. Gibson. You ride well."

"You gave me an excellent steed. He truly did all the work."

"Remember my apples," Midnight said quietly.

"Oh, does your horse like apples? We just got a few bushels of gorgeous Red Delicious apples from a client of mine in Washington. I would love to make a gift of some of them to this beautiful animal."

"How did you know? Midnight loves apples, especially red ones."

"I thought all horses loved apples."

"Your gift is generous. Please bring them by and leave them with Maria. She will make sure that Midnight gets them."

Patricia Morton shook her head and dismounted Tina. She grabbed the reins and began to lead the horse through the thicket of pine trees.

Mitchell quickly dismounted Midnight and followed Patricia into the thicket.

"Thank you, my friend," Midnight said quietly.

"You are a wonderful animal, sir. The pleasure is all mine."

"You were right, he is a wonderful jumper."

"He is our best. He was Thomas' favorite horse."

Patricia stopped briefly and removed a white handkerchief from her jeans. She wiped a tear from her eye while she looked longingly at Midnight.

"I know that this is hard for you. Your husband has only been gone for such a short time, but we must speak about what happened."

"I'm sorry, Dr. Gibson, this is so hard for me. I thought the ride would take my mind off things, but the past is all around us here. What questions can I answer for you?"

Mitchell took a deep breath and lazily pulled a small clump of dandelions from a thick patch that grew a couple of steps away from where they walked. He fed the flowers to Midnight slowly and rubbed the horse's head as he ate.

"I recognize the pain that you are going through, Patricia. Losing a spouse is one of the hardest, if not the hardest losses a person can suffer. I believe, however, that your husband's death was not as clear-cut as it might have seemed."

"What do you mean? The police said that he killed himself and my children. I do not believe that there needs to be anymore said about it, doctor."

"I understand what the police report states. But the reason that the police have asked me to look into the case resides in certain skills that I bring to the table, beyond those that I possess as a forensic psychiatrist."

"I have looked into your record, doctor. You are a highly respected physician in your field. I have no doubt that you possess formidable skills in many areas of medicine."

Mitchell sighed deeply again, stopped in his tracks, and began to smile. He glanced briefly at Patricia's aura and spotted the deep golden energy that he had seen on his first visit with her.

"Thank you, Patricia, but the skills that I refer to are not limited to the field of medicine. Patricia, have you ever had any experiences in your life that you would call supernatural?"

Patricia did not look up at Mitchell as she
spoke. Her voice did not change, nor did her
demeanor shift in any way. She did, however,
begin to laugh uncomfortably.

"When I was a child, I once saw a man in the
window of a department store that my parents had
taken me to for Christmas shopping. He wore a
thick coat and a furry hat that covered his ears. I
remembered this because Christmas in our country
is very warm. I must have been about five at the
time. Anyway, I pointed out the man to my mother
and she looked at the window. She saw nothing.
She scolded me for making things up."

"Who do you think the man was?"

"I think he was a ghost...a spirit...maybe..."

"Why do you think that?"

"Because, after a few moments, when I looked
back at the window he was not there."

"Has this happened to you at any other time,
Patricia?"

"Only one other time. When I was 12, I went
horseback riding with my father. We owned a large
stable and he loved to ride. We would often ride
for hours in the countryside. One day, while we
were riding along the river near Corrientes, we
stopped to let the horses drink for a few minutes.
While the horses were drinking the water from the
river, I looked down into the water and I could
swear that I saw people swimming under the
water. One of them even waved at me and smiled
before swimming away. I remembered what my
mother had told me about the man in the window
and I never told my father what I saw."

"Do you think you made it up...that you were
imagining things?"

"No, never. I saw these things as clearly as I have ever seen anything. I have not thought of these things for decades, doctor. Why do you ask? What does this have to do with my husband's death?"

"Patricia, I believe that you have certain gifts, abilities that are dormant within your mind that could be very useful to you in your life. These gifts are rare and they do not appear in very many people. Have you ever met anyone who can see things the way that you do?"

"You mean psychics, clairvoyants?"

"Not necessarily...everyday people...people like yourself who do not advertise their abilities, so to speak."

"I don't like to talk about such things, doctor. My family raised me to be very devout in my Catholic faith. We do not seek to traffic with the supernatural. It is unholy."

Patricia's aura flared gold and white briefly. Mitchell eyed the flare quietly and did not mention it to Patricia. Suddenly, a strange and wonderful idea occurred to him.

"There is someone that I would like you to meet. I know a great holy man who lives not too far from here. He might be able to help you seek the benefit of exploring your gift...as a service to humanity."

"What is his name, doctor? I have heard of no such man and I have lived in this area for many years."

"He keeps to himself pretty much and he doesn't venture out of his home often. I can assure you, he is a very holy person, with great spiritual gifts, not unlike your own."

"How long would a journey to his home take?"

"Not long...perhaps thirty minutes. He lives just outside of Burlington, on Old Glencoe Road."

Patricia paused to gather her thoughts for a few minutes. She reached into her pocket and retrieved a few cubes of sugar. She fed a couple to Tina and slowly walked over to Midnight and shared a couple with him. Both horses greedily munched on the delicious treats and snorted their approval. Their joy made Patricia smile.

"Alright, doctor. I will meet this holy man you speak of. Perhaps I could secure a blessing from him. I could certainly use one. What is his name?"

Mitchell grinned a big toothy grin and stroked his chin briefly.

"His name is Rodare."

"A strange name for a man...I have never heard such a name...where is he from?"

"I will let him tell you that."

Chapter Sixteen

The Training

Salva waited by the door as she watched the old man approach the house. She did not recognize the young man walking with him. He was handsome, tall, and she found herself feeling attracted to him almost immediately. She was sure that she did not recognize the two dogs that

walked submissively by the old man's side.
Then she realized that Melvina was not with the
group.

The old man led the dogs to a fresh carcass that
had been laid by the fire. The other dogs seemed
to have sated themselves on the flesh of some
large and interesting animal that they had found in
the neighboring forest. They hardly seemed to
notice the two new arrivals.

Within moments, the new dogs tore away at the
blood-drenched flesh and soon became oblivious to
the foreign nature of their new surroundings. One
could almost say that they seemed happy.

"Where is my sister?" Salva shouted.

"She is with us, my dear. My apologies for a most
unfortunate oversight," the old man replied.

The old man then waved his hand over Gerard and
uttered an imperceptible series of words. Gerard's
form shimmered briefly, disappeared, and was
almost immediately replaced by Melvina's familiar
body.

Melvina looked down at her hands, touched her
chest, and ran to Salva. Both girls began crying
and embracing each other lovingly.

"How did you do that?" Salva asked as she
brushed the tears away from her eyes.

Melvina took her sister's hand and clenched it
tightly. She knew that the old man was much more
than he appeared to be. She knew that he was
likely not an old man at all. She also realized that
Salva had to be protected from the secrets of this
place at all costs. However, after the display that
she had just witnessed, she was not sure how she
would accomplish that.

"The time has come for the two of you to know the nature of what I do and why you are here. My power will not last much longer and I will need your help if I am to survive the ordeal that faces me."

"I guess you have made my job much easier, old man. We need answers and we need them now. What is this place? What are you?" Melvina asked.

The old man turned to Salva and smiled.

"Salva, go into the house and prepare the evening meal. After we eat, I will explain everything."

Salva turned quickly, kissed her sister on the cheek, and walked back into the house.

Melvina was not sure why Salva was so willing to follow the old man's dictates without question or comment.

"Why does she follow your commands so readily?"

"She is my servant, as are you."

Melvina felt a strong sense of rage and powerlessness begin to boil within her chest. She had seen a long display of the old man's power. The memories of her life as Gerard were still fresh within her consciousness. She did not know how far she could push him for answers or what his response might be if she overstepped the limits of his patience.

"You promised me that you would explain everything."

"Let us eat. I need to gather my strength. I will keep my promise to you then."

Salva had prepared a large pot of boiled meat stew that simmered in a broth of vegetables, spices, and herbs that she had gathered from the field nearby. A fresh pan of bread baked in the oven, which the old man had fashioned in the center of the cooking area. The food smelled delicious. After the transition she had just made, Melvina found herself famished.

After they had eaten, the three of them sat down in the main living area of the cabin. The old man seemed to be restored by the meal and Melvina thought she could see a dim glow of light around his face.

The old man stood in the center of the room and looked longingly at the two girls. He did not speak for a few long seconds. He stared first at Salva, and then at Melvina, and soon broke his silence.

"My name is Anshar. I am dying and I need your help."

"Why do you need our help? You have all these crazy powers. You live here in the middle of nowhere and you seem to be able to get along just fine without anyone or anything," Melvina replied.

"How did you change my sister? I saw this with my own eyes," Salva added.

"I am not as I appear. The form that you see before you is not my true form. I am an angel."

"If you are an angel, where are your wings? And, by the way, angels are immortal. They cannot die. You said you were dying. Your words don't make sense," Melvina quipped.

"Angels are not immortal. By human standards that would, of course, appear to be the case. We do, however, live for billions of years. If you will allow me to do so, I will show you something that will answer many of your questions. Please, follow me outside."

Anshar walked quietly to the door and disappeared. The girls looked at each other, shook their heads, and followed him outside.

He walked away from the house down the path toward the river. The trees hung low in the background and seemed to stare at the unlikely trio as they passed. He did not speak and motioned for the girls to follow. After a few minutes, he stopped near a large clearing.

Melvina was sure that she had not seen the clearing before.

The sun shone brightly in the sky overhead. Anshar stood erect, opened his eyes wide, and stared directly into the heart of the orb. Almost immediately, his body began to grow in size. His shrunken old form melted away and a new glowing figure emerged. His flesh began to glow with the color of brilliant midday sunlight. His muscles and limbs stretched outward and he grew to a height that seemed almost impossible. The very fiber of his muscles rippled with power and the mixture of light, physical beauty, and the seemingly improbable process of transformation left both girls speechless.

Anshar's wings materialized from his back and spread out over a vast area. Within seconds, he floated aloft, carried by the Celestial Light that emanated from his body. He smiled at the girls as he looked down at them from above.

Melvina and Salva crouched on the ground below, frozen in awe. They stared at the now fully transformed figure of the old man and said nothing. Neither girl could find the words to express the overwhelming sense of shock and wonder that overtook them.

Anshar floated serenely in the space above the opening for several minutes. In his primordial form, he could clearly hear the Symphony. He knew, however, that the humans below could not hear the rapturous sound, even if he chose to try and share it with them. After a few long moments, the Symphony ended.

Anshar descended to the grassy floor of the clearing and stood in his angelic form. Slowly, his primordial form began to recede. His body began to shrink. The primordial glow of energy that surrounded him faded, and his wings disappeared in a flash. His muscles and sinews shriveled. His face grew smaller and smaller. Within a few seconds, he resumed the familiar visage of the old man.

Melvina and Salva stared at the old man for several minutes before they could find the words to speak. Salva found her words first.

"You *are* an angel. You really are an angel."

"Why do you choose to look like this if you are an angel?" Melvina asked.

The old man righted himself and pulled his robe close to his body.

"I am dying, as I said. I can take my true form for brief periods, but the process leaves me drained. During those moments, I take in energy from the sun and replenish myself."

"Why are you dying?" Salva asked.

"I have a disease, a very rare disease that strikes only angels of my clan. I am one of the oldest of my kind and I have lived longer than the stars in the sky. This disease leaves me barren and weak, unable to perform my appointed tasks. The Creator fashioned this place that you see, this land, the house, everything, so that I might have a chance to live."

"This place? How can this place be of any help? There is nothing here," Melvina responded.

"When I initially learned of this malady, I came to this place by order of the Creator. Because of my long service to him, he allowed me a chance to live. In this place, I can access the human world through you, Melvina."

"That is why you sent me there?"

"What is he talking about, sister? Where did you go?" Salva asked.

"You should tell her, my dear. She deserves to know now."

"I don't really understand it all, but I was just born into the world as a man, the man that you saw before I was transformed back into this body. It is a very long story, sister, but I died in that life and brought two people back with me."

"But you were only gone for a few hours..."

"A few hours for you perhaps, but for me, it was a lifetime."

"Perhaps I should explain. Melvina is my Gatherer. She leads souls back to me from her contacts in the human world. Over time, I collect the souls and use them to help cure my illness."

"You collect souls...you collected me...us...that is awful!"

Salva began to back away from the clearing.

"This whole thing is crazy. How can human souls cure your illness?" Melvina questioned.

"I use the souls to create a vessel...a vessel that will hold my true form in the human world. Once I am incarnated into that form, I will free you and leave this place."

"Sister, you are working with him! You brought me here!"

"I didn't know anything about this place. I didn't know this old man, angel, whatever. I only meant to protect you. You have to believe me!"

Salva shook her head and refused to look at her sister. She burst into tears, continued to back away from the clearing, and soon broke away and ran down the path as fast as she could.

Melvina began to follow her but the old man raised his hand and motioned for her to stay.

"She cannot go anywhere now...at least not anywhere that I cannot control. She will be fine. We, however, have some work to do."

"I still don't understand any of this. If you are an angel, why don't you just heal yourself and go back to Heaven, or wherever you came from?"

"I sought the counsel of the best healer in the universe, and he has done everything in his power for me. I should be dead by now, but the Creator has given me grace. That is why I need you."

"You said that I have been gathering souls for you for a long time. I assume that my sister is human. Who am I? How did I get here?"

"You are human as well, but you are a very special class of human. When I came to this place, I found that there were many of my kind already here. The Creator had not told me of this. There were a small number of them lying about in varying degrees of filth and madness. Some of them I knew. I had even trained a couple of them when I was in Heaven. In our world, an angel may disappear for eons at a time while completing a mission. I had always assumed that such disappearances meant nothing.

The creatures were pitiful. They did not know me. They did not know themselves. They could not fly. They could not care for themselves properly. One of them attacked me, perhaps in a mindless blind rage. The being tore at my flesh and bit me until I bled from a hundred wounds. I barely escaped with my life. Fortunately, I was able to use a Word of Power and transform them into dogs. In that form, they consume less energy and are infinitely easier to control."

"That explains the dogs in this place, and what you did to Lady Evans and Lea. What about me? What am I? Where did I come from?"

"After I took care of my brethren, I rested for a time. While I rested, I wept. I wept for more than 30 human years. I wept for my lost life. I wept for myself. I wept for my brothers. Sometimes, I wept for no reason at all. After I stopped crying, I knew that I did not wish to die. I found strength in assuming my true form from time to time. I found strength in singing while I took in sunlight, and then I discovered a plan.

I knew that the Creator had given me an opportunity to heal myself, but he forbid me to enter the human world. About 300,000 years ago, my partner and I completed a mission in which we freed a soul held captive in an astral slave colony. I remembered talk of a special breed of slaves that possessed a rare mixture of powers that brought a high price on the market. Certain demons traded these slave souls to human sorcerers in exchange for sacrifices and promises of servitude in the lower worlds. The sorcerers then took the various powers that the souls possessed and used them in the human world. This process irreparably damaged the slave souls and left them bereft of

memory or the ability to incarnate properly
into the human form. Demons would then use their
shells as sexual playthings or as sport in their
arena games.

I pulled myself together, made my way back to the
slave market, and began to inquire about the
powers that the slaves possessed. Over time, I
learned that some of the slaves were gifted with
the power to gather souls, much like that of the
angels. Those human souls could lead others into a
particular world in other dimensions. The ability
was dormant, of course, and the slaves could not
control the power consciously. However, with the
right guidance, I reasoned that I could find one of
them that might be able to help me. Then, I found
you."

"I was an astral slave...a thing traded like a horse
or a cow?"

"Yes, that is how I found you."

"How did I get there? How long was I there before
you came along?"

"When humans create children that are
subsequently lost to abortion or disease before
they are born, certain entities sometimes take
those souls into slavery. Usually, they only concern
themselves with the most gifted and powerful of
those souls. There is probably no way to ever find
out who your human parents were."

"Can you tell me anything more about me? Did I
have a name?"

"You were not given a name. You were never
born."

"How long have I been your slave? How long have
I been working for you?"

"If it is of any consolation to you, you have been helping to save a life. You have led many humans away from desperate and miserable lives in the underworld."

"How long have I been with you?"

"I found you 9,391 years ago. In my estimation, my time is running short."

Melvina took a deep breath and sat on the ground next to the old man. She looked at him and touched his face. The answers to her existence did not bring her peace. They did not calm the fires of anguish and confusion that raged through her soul. What she did realize, however, is that in all the universe, this angel was her only true connection to what she might call reality.

"What happens to me after you get what you want?"

"I will set you free."

"To do what? I don't know anything else. I don't know anyone else, except my sister, and she isn't really even my sister. I need something more."

"What more can I give you? I have told you all that I know of your life."

"I don't want to be a leaf blowing in the wind anymore. I want to have power, like you. I want to control my own life, my own destiny. I want to be able to live and not die anymore. I remember two of my deaths now, and I am sick of it. I want it to stop."

"But death is the way of things, my dear. Even I cannot stop it."

"I have seen you use Words or something like that. You make things happen. I want to learn how to do that. You owe me that after all I have done for you."

"And what would you do with these Words if I were to teach them to you?"

"I don't know. I would use them to have power...to take control of my life...anything, I guess...at least I wouldn't be weak anymore. I could use them to have power and take control of my life."

"Words of Power are the greatest gift that the Creator gives to those in his service. We use them in all that we do. We do not share them with humans."

"You owe me. I have served you for almost 10,000 years. I don't even remember everything that I have done for you. I don't even know how many souls I have brought to you in this place."

"You have brought me 590 souls. I need 27 more."

"If you help me learn these Words, I will work with you, willingly, and without resistance."

"You cannot resist. I own you. Your offer means nothing."

"What if I just kill myself?"

"You were dead when I met you."

"Wouldn't I be a better Gatherer for you if I had some power? Wouldn't I be able to bring you souls more quickly if you taught me how to really use this gift that I seem to have?"

"Perhaps you have a point. Perhaps some measure of training and power might speed up this process...perhaps..."

Anshar's breathing became labored and raspy. For a moment, he turned pale and began to fall forward. Melvina caught him in her arms.

"What happened? Are you going to be okay?"

"As I said, I am dying. I do not know how much time I have left. A week, a year, a century. In my current condition, I cannot tell you more. The souls you bring me give me strength."

"I just brought you two new ones. You turned them into dogs."

"They have not been processed. I cannot use them as yet. Give me a few moments, I will recover my strength. After that, we can begin your training."

Chapter Seventeen

Old Glencoe Road

Old Glencoe Road was one of the most beautiful areas in Burlington. During the spring, tall, stately dogwoods lined the winding corridors of the

highway for miles and draped the area in a
blanket of pink and white flower petals that danced
from tree to tree. Just behind the dogwoods,
groves of loblolly and longleaf pine trees dotted the
open forests. Patricia sat quietly in the passenger
seat and said nothing during the drive. Mitchell
listened to the last movement to Mahler's Second
Symphony as they drove. The notes of the
haunting chorus filled the car and seemed to add
an air of solemnity and peace to their journey.
Patricia did not seem to notice the music.

Mitchell turned off the main road and onto a steep,
rocky trail that seemed almost unfit for modern
traffic. There were signs that other vehicles had
traversed the terrain, but one had to be very
careful in watching every turn and stone along the
path. Mitchell had driven this road many times and
he knew it well.

After a few steady and cautious miles, Mitchell
brought the Jaguar to a stop. Just beyond the point
in the road where they had stopped loomed a large
iron gate. The gate was closed and there was no
sign of any human attendant.

"This is where we stop and wait for the gate to
open."

"There is no one here."

"Believe me, there are plenty of people here. You
just have to know where and how to look."

Mitchell smiled and honked the horn on the Jaguar
twice. After a few long moments, the large iron
gate began to swing open. It moved slowly at first,
but after a few moments, it swung wide and
allowed them to pass.

Mitchell eased the Jaguar through the gate and
slowly drove onto the manor grounds, which were
covered with dogwoods, pines, and a curious
admixture of roses, elms, and oaks that seemed to

have been planted in some sort of symbolic pattern. The trees and flowers were perfectly manicured and the entire area bristled with wildlife. Curiously, there was no house in sight.

"Where are we going? I do not see a house of any kind."

"Patience, Patricia. It is just ahead."

Mitchell parked the Jaguar. He got out of the car and motioned for Patricia to join him on the grounds. As they walked, Patricia looked around the area and attempted to make sense of the seeming lack of human presence. She loved being out interacting with nature and she loved the peace and serenity that she sensed around the place. An estate with a gate, gardens, wildlife, and no manor home bothered her. She knew all of the families of means in the area. If the holy man lived on a large estate, she would know him and his family.

"I can see the anxiety on your face. I will answer your questions in a moment."

Mitchell closed his eyes and began to breathe deeply. He spoke a silent Word and his body immediately began to shimmer. His outer garments began to glow and, in an instant, they disappeared. They were at once replaced by the royal blue robes that signified his station within the Order. He turned to Patricia, smiled, and extended his hand toward her.

"You will need to take my hand."

"I don't understand any of this, doctor."

"Soon, all of your questions will be answered."

Patricia drew a deep breath, took a furtive step
forward, and took Mitchell's hand. Mitchell nodded
quietly, smiled, and began to speak another Word.

"Eanakenonei!"

He reached into a pocket of his robe and removed
the large medallion that usually hung around his
neck. He spoke the Word directly into the
medallion and, within moments, it began to glow.
He then grasped the medallion in his left hand,
placed it against an invisible, horizontal flat
surface, and pressed down. A blinding flash of light
enveloped the area. A few moments later, they
both stood in a giant hallway.

"Where are we?"

"We stand in the hallway of the manor."

"How did we get here? How did you do that?"

"Time and space are not the simple creations that
most people believe them to be. Within our reality,
many subdomains of reality share a coexistent
space with our world. If you know where to look
for these subdomains, you may find them. Once
you find them, it is then only a simple matter of
knowing how to knock."

Mitchell turned to face Patricia, placed his right
hand against her face, closed his eyes, and blew a
soft puff of air onto her body. In a flash of light,
her clothes were transformed into a simple white
tunic. Her shoes were nowhere to be seen.

"There are certain protocols one must observe
when seeing the holy man. First, you must bow at
the waist and keep your head down until he speaks
to you. Second, only raise your head when he
instructs you to do so. Finally, under no
circumstances should you attempt to touch him."

"There is a lot you must answer for, doctor, before I take another step with you."

"I understand your frustration and confusion, Patricia. There are many forces at work here. In a moment, I will ask you to close your eyes. Do not open them until I instruct you to do so. When you reopen them, you will understand things much more clearly."

"I certainly hope so, for your sake."

Patricia glanced around the room, drew a deep breath, and instinctively folded her arms across her chest.

Mitchell drew the symbol Crian in a circular pattern over their heads. In a flash of light, the space around them began to shimmer and pulse. Windows appeared out of nowhere. Ornate chairs, desks, and tables sprang into existence. Large bookshelves over 12 feet high expanded into the room as though they had been stored in bulky envelopes. The sun shone brightly through the windows.

"You may open your eyes now, Patricia."

Patricia opened her eyes. She took a deep breath and tried to allow her vision to become accustomed to the light. The room was beautiful, breathtaking even to her cultured eye.

"Where are we?"

"Allow me to answer that question for you, young lady. My name is Kahlia."

Just behind a large desk three feet directly in front of Patricia stood a stunningly beautiful woman. Patricia had not seen her a few seconds before she spoke.

"How did you get in here?" Patricia asked.

"Actually, I have not left this room for more than four decades," Kahlia replied.

"What is this place?" Patricia queried further.

"It is my master's home."

Kahlia stared intently at Patricia and smiled. Standing at over five feet ten inches tall, she was an imposing figure. Kahlia wore only a simple light blue tunic, which draped her lithe form very tightly. Her long black hair flowed down her back and filled the expanse of her body with impossibly curly locks of raven-colored hair. The color of her skin was a perfect mixture of ivory and mahogany.

"How can you not leave a room for four decades?" Patricia asked.

"My master's work requires much patience and focus. We often remain secluded in this space for long periods of time. Except for the rare treat of the occasional visitor, we seldom interact with outsiders."

"Outsiders? How do you get food, water, supplies?" Patricia asked.

"I suppose he hasn't told you who we are," Kahlia replied.

"No, he has told me nothing."

"I see why you chose this one, Mitchell. Her soul does indeed show promise," Kahlia replied.

"I am happy to see you again, Kahlia. May we see the master?"

"I'm not going to see anyone until someone answers my questions. Who is this woman and what is this place? Why am I here?"

"You have entered the domain of Master Rodare. I am Kahlia, keeper of this manor. I am an Immortal."

"What do you mean 'Immortal'?" Patricia asked.

"I died over 800 years ago during a plague that swept my village. My family, my friends, my entire parish were wiped out by the Black Death. I was thrown into a pile of bodies that were to be burned. I believe that I lay there for over a week before I woke up. Luckily, I arose on a rainy evening, long after midnight. I was able to slip away into the forest before anyone knew that I was gone.

I wandered for days before the master found me. He explained to me that I had passed through the first death and had emerged as an Immortal. He told me that I no longer needed to eat, drink, sleep, age, or die. He told me that most humans go through the first death and are required to reincarnate into a fresh new body before returning to life. In the case of True Immortals, we die, and regenerate after a fashion, without the need for reincarnation. Some of us can be killed, with difficulty, but even those unlucky few will regenerate if the body is allowed to remain mostly intact. Most of us cannot be killed. I have served my master for over 800 years. He protects me."

"If you cannot die, then why do you need protection?" Patricia asked.

"There are those, human and otherwise, who would seek to use my blood and organs to regenerate themselves. My regenerative powers allow me to regrow all of my organs at will. I have no wish to be used in that manner. My master ensures that none approach me for those purposes. His power allows us to remain hidden from the world so that we may complete our work, undisturbed."

"What is your work?" Patricia asked.

A booming voice materialized in the background.

"I believe I should answer that question, Kahlia."

In a blinding flash of light, a large winged form appeared hovering near the ceiling overhead. He was clothed only in a simple golden tunic. He allowed himself to float above the room for a moment, and then he gently descended to the marble floor.

"My name is Rodare. It is wonderful to see you again, doctor."

Rodare extended his arms and embraced Mitchell warmly. He then turned to Patricia.

"And this must be Patricia. You are welcome in my home, madam."

Rodare's presence filled the air with the scent of cinnamon, honey, and rose petals. Patricia did not know why, but she was overwhelmed with a sense of awe, joy, and longing. She desperately wanted to fling herself into the angel's arms, but she remembered Mitchell's warning. She dutifully bowed and remained in place. She answered quietly and did not raise her eyes to look upon the being.

"Thank you for the honor," Patricia replied.

"The Creator has asked me to train her. I need your help, master," Mitchell said.

"She will need the tour, of course. Please rise, Patricia," Rodare replied.

"I will be happy to show her around, master," Kahlia said.

"You have not yet learned to fly. How will you show her the mountain areas?" Rodare asked.

"I can levitate. You showed me how."

"Only up to a few thousand meters, and the effort leaves you exhausted for days. Besides, you have never attempted it with a human in tow."

"I understand, master."

"Mitchell, you will remain here with Kahlia while I personally show your charge the other side of her beautiful city. I believe the Symphony will be starting within the next couple of hours. You may enjoy it here if you like."

"I would be honored, master," Mitchell replied.

Mitchell turned to Patricia and took her hand.

"You must go with the master now. He has many important things to show you. You will be safe with him."

Patricia nodded quietly. Rodare reached out for her hand and Patricia glanced quickly at Mitchell. Mitchell nodded, smiled, and motioned to her reassuringly.

Patricia took Rodare's hand. In the next instant, they disappeared in a flash of light.

"Would you like to go get a steak, doctor? I really need to get out of this place," Kahlia asked.

"Lawry's off the strip?" Mitchell replied.

"We should be back in time for Symphony,"
Kahlia said.

Mitchell reached into his robe and took out his
medallion. He began to speak a Word but Kahlia
interrupted him.

"Permit me."

Kahlia grabbed Mitchell's hand, closed her eyes,
and spoke a Word.

"Soreie-sotnal."

She then made a single slashing motion and cut
through the air in front of them. In the opening,
Las Vegas Boulevard appeared in front of them.
They both climbed through the opening and
immediately stood in front of the Tuscan Casino,
directly across from Lawry's Restaurant.

Mitchell looked at their clothing and realized that
they needed to make an adjustment. Two elderly
couples stared at them in disbelief and quickly
walked toward the front entrance of the casino.

"Permit me."

Mitchell waved his hand quickly above their heads.
Kahlia's tunic was transformed into a beautiful red
Versace evening dress. Mitchell's robe was now an
off-white Hugo Boss linen jacket, light brown shirt,
and matching brown linen slacks.

"I always liked your taste, doctor. You should have
married me, you know."

"Are we going to go over that again, or can we just
enjoy a juicy cut of prime rib?"

"Why not both?" Kahlia replied.

Chapter Eighteen

Actus

Melvina saw that Anshar was dying. She knew that
she would only have a very short time to learn

everything that he had to teach her. His voice grew weak and faint with each passing word. His skin color had lost much of its luster. He struggled to draw the diagrams and geometric shapes that accompanied each Word. She knew that he was only imparting the bare essentials of the knowledge that she would need. If they had the time, she knew that he would give her all that he had. However, time was not an ally in this part of her life. She didn't even want to think of how her "life" would have turned out if Anshar had not rescued her.

"How long will it take for you to teach me all I need to know?"

"If I were at full strength, perhaps a couple hundred years."

"What about now?"

"To be honest, I can teach you only a small fraction of what you need to know in order to truly tap into your dormant potential."

"Is there a way to speed things up?"

Anshar allowed himself to consider an action that he had long considered unthinkable. He had only sparingly taken his true form during the period of isolation he had endured in the astral realm. He placed his mission before all else, except the maintenance of his present form. He looked at Melvina and smiled. He knew the outcome of his decision. On the rare night that he had allowed himself to sleep, that one idea had robbed him of much-needed rest. However, he knew that the girl's suggestion held a kernel of deep truth.

"There is an element of danger for both of us if we commit to this path. If I do this, we may both die."

"I would rather die than live in limbo."

"Are you certain?"

"What is the plan?"

Melvina planted herself at Anshar's feet. She looked up at him with an unwavering glance and fixed her eyes squarely upon him.

"First, I must explain to you the reason for this journey. Thus far, I have attempted to impart to you the theory and application of the use of Words of Power. As I said, normally, this method would require only a couple hundred human years. For an angel, this would be the equivalent of a long afternoon. Unfortunately, I don't have two hundred years of life force left in me. We will have to switch tactics and do this the way angels do."

"What does that mean exactly?"

"I will need to take you into the Actus region of the sun. Once we are there, I will need to teach you how to absorb the raw information factors that empower the Words."

Melvina looked at Anshar and shook her head. She knew that he was a powerful being. She knew that as a Gatherer, he had held the very power of Creation in his hands. In his present state, however, she wondered if he were capable of the feat that he proposed.

"I realize that you are probably skeptical of this idea. But it is our best hope of completing your training. I will need to clearly outline what is to be done so that you will understand."

Before Melvina could speak, Anshar rose to his feet and assumed his full angelic form. His wings spread out further than she had ever seen and his countenance nearly blinded her. She knew that he was expending a tremendous amount of primordial life force for this endeavor.

Anshar raised both his hands, looked up to the sun, and shouted aloud.

"Itak-onse-soren-onse-piasnot-nor-onto-bo!"

The sky began to shimmer and glow with power. The orb of the sun began to spin and gyrate. Brilliant pincers of light began to pierce the sky and hurl themselves toward Earth. After a few moments, the sun began to move in the sky. For the first few moments, it only appeared to cover a small fraction of space. After a few more seconds, the sun appeared to be hurtling toward Earth at an alarming pace.

Anshar began to weave a complex geometric form in the sky directly above his head. He then spoke another series of Words that made the sky seem to sizzle with orange and gold light.

"Bereeis tonak itsos-nonatis!"

Melvina stood frozen in time and space and she witnessed the orb of the sun slowly descend from the heavens and float above the angel's head. She could clearly see the brilliant yellow and orange tongues of flame that enveloped its surface. The orb floated peacefully overhead as though it were a ripe fruit neatly plucked from the Tree of Heaven. There was no heat. There was no blinding light. There was no pain of any kind associated with its close proximity to her face.

Melvina began to cry. She didn't know why, but tears seemed to fit the moment.

"There is no time for tears, child. We have much to do."

Anshar grasped the disc of the sun and shaped it into a ball of energy a little over a foot in diameter. He then blew a delicate wisp of air over the figure.

Instantly, a grid of arcane letters formed over the ball.

"The Words of Power that we use are part of the fabric of creation. The Creator imbues each galaxy, star, and planet with its own special sound. These sounds interact with each other and create more complex sounds. Each sound is unique to the universe. The sounds themselves are not mere groupings of notes and melodies. They are the basic units of divine creative power. In other words, the sound that a star emits is the power that projects it into existence.

As the sound of the star is projected, ostensibly from the Creator, the star itself is literally sung into existence. The confluence of all the sounds of all the stars, planets, and galaxies that make up the universe is called the Actus Signal. Each star has a special region within its core that receives and processes the Actus Signal.

During our training, all angels spend time within the Actus Signal of the Great Central Sun. This allows us to absorb and control all of the Words of Power associated with controlling the known universe. You could never survive such an experience. But, your local star, the sun, is small enough that we just might be able to get you into its Actus Region. Once you are there, you would be empowered enough to control the Words associated with this region of space. That should give you more than enough power to complete our mission."

Melvina sat frozen in awe of Anshar's power. She knew that he was probably expending the vast majority of his reserves on the feats of the last few moments. She also knew that he was probably capable of just about anything right now. She knew she had to be careful with both her words and actions. He could vaporize her with a single errant thought.

"You brought the sun down from the sky! How is that even possible?"

"I will replace it when I have completed my task. Does this plan trouble you in any way?"

"Only one small problem, how will I survive being in the sun? I mean, you are an angel. I don't have that particular asset."

"There are many sentient races living inside your sun. Many of these races are humanoid. I will extend my life force to shield you and provide life support while we are en route. Once we reach the orb itself, there are pockets of reality that are easily molded by your thoughts. These areas can be made to provide you with adequate life support."

Melvina took a deep breath. She knew that too many questions beyond this point would only weaken her nerve.

"Let's do this before I chicken out."

Anshar smiled and took her hand.

"You should close your eyes until I tell you to reopen them. You are not accustomed to rapid space flight. The journey can sometimes try the sanity of a human."

"No problem there."

Anshar approached Melvina and grabbed her firmly with both hands. Melvina had never been held so intimately before. Without realizing it, she felt herself becoming intensely excited by the experience. In his full angelic form, Anshar's energy was extremely erotic. Melvina closed her eyes. She felt her body leave the ground, but she also felt her internal energies begin a journey of their own.

Anshar's warmth began to caress her body in ways that she could scarcely imagine. In his full angelic form, he was over two feet taller than she was. In a strange way, however, the discrepancy in size only served to heighten her arousal. Anshar had asked her not to open her eyes. After seeing what he was capable of, she did not intend to contravene his orders.

Strangely, she could feel the sting of the Celestial winds as they passed by. She did not feel the cold, but she could feel the movement of space beyond the powerful yet protective wings of the angel. Anshar had placed her body directly next to his and, as they flew, she could feel the ripple of his muscles and the warmth of his life force sustaining him. Each time his wings moved to propel them through space, their bodies were pressed together very tightly. The combination of Anshar's angelic scent and the rhythmic movement of their tightly pressed bodies was almost more than Melvina could take.

Anshar said nothing as they flew, but Melvina knew that he was fully aware of everything that transpired between them. Melvina slowly worked her way down, closer to the lower part of Anshar's body. She desperately wanted to explore what it meant to be a woman. She might never get another chance with him. She didn't even know if it would be possible. She wanted to try.

Anshar remained silent as they flew. She did not know how long it would take for them to reach the sun. She only knew that she would take advantage of the time as it presented itself.

Within moments, Melvina had positioned herself so that she could take full advantage of Anshar's lower anatomy. She kept her eyes closed tightly, but every fiber of her being longed to inspect his body in excruciating detail.

Anshar wore only a loose-fitting gold tunic. His inner wing structures provided secure protection and warmth for her body. As his outer wings moved, his inner wings tensed and throbbed in rhythm. They also shielded her from his view.

In his form as the old man, Anshar was wrinkled and wizened to the point of extreme senility. In his full angelic form, Anshar was a perfect male specimen. His skin was golden brown and his muscles were taut and exquisitely developed. Melvina ran her fingers over his stomach and torso. Her fingers tingled as she embraced the angel's flesh. Anshar's skin emitted a faint golden-blue light that seemed to seethe with erotic force and power. Melvina's breath came in short gasps as she willed herself to raise her arms and embrace him more fully. She ran her hands over the wide expanse of his chest and grasped the larger muscles of his shoulders.

Anshar seemed to slow in the speed of his flight as she pursued her explorations of his form. She could not sense if they were nearing the sun as she had not opened her eyes. She began to contemplate far more delicate and important schemes in her mind.

Melvina began to untie her tunic. On most days, a simple twist of the side knot was more than enough to send the garment tumbling to the ground. Today, however, she could not seem to loosen it. She was tempted to tear the garment off and rip it from her body.

Slowly, she unleashed the tunic and wrapped herself around Anshar. She grasped his buttocks and thighs and pressed herself against him tightly. She drew a deep breath and reached down for his manhood.

She could not believe its size. She grabbed it and tentatively stroked its length. His organ grew and pulsed underneath her hands. It was larger than she imagined. Melvina took slow, deep breaths and decided to take the ultimate risk.

She felt Anshar begin to slow down in flight. She hoped that he had the same idea as she did.

"We have arrived."

"What? You're kidding me, right?"

"We have reached the Actus region of the sun."

Melvina shook her head and tried to clear her mind. She had almost totally forgotten the true reason for her trip to the sun.

"We must move very carefully within this region of the sun. All of your thoughts receive tremendous power and acceleration while you are here. I have learned to control my emotions and perceptions. You have not learned to do so as yet. This could prove to be a problem if we are not careful."

"What do you expect? I am still human."

"This mission has nothing to do with your humanity. You must focus your thoughts and your senses if this process is to work properly. My power has created a bubble of space-time that contains a small portion of the Actus region in this area. When you open your eyes, you will see what I mean. You will be able to breathe normally."

"Can I open my eyes now?"

"Yes, you may."

Still angry that Anshar seemed not to notice her advances, Melvina opened her eyes. She expected to be at least half blinded by the glare and intensity of the light. The scene that unfolded in front of her caught her totally by surprise.

As far as the eye could see, a vast expanse of
unimaginably complex golden geometric shapes
floated in the space around her. Each shape
seethed and pulsed with life and power. From time
to time, huge tongues of gas and flame penetrated
the forms and infused them with additional power.
The shapes defied simple explanation. Some of the
forms were small, no more than three to four feet
in height. Some of the forms were intermediate in
size, 10 to 12 feet in height. The width of the
shapes varied from form to form. However, most
of them were no more than a few feet wide.

A few of the forms were truly monstrous. These
shapes loomed over the solar sky and seemed to
dominate the very life pulse of the orb itself. These
forms stretched across miles of solar sky.

"What are these things?"

"You are witnessing the primordial form of Words
of Power. Each of these forms contains the raw
essence of a single Word. On your planet, humans
have learned to absorb the essence of a Word
through certain hidden solar practices. My people
taught these practices to your kind long ago. The
have only mastered a small fraction of the
potential of the Word as they have seen them only
from a distance. These powers have been hidden
away by the major Orders in your world."

"What is an Order?"

"An Order is a grouping of humans who have
dedicated themselves to the dissemination and
preservation of divine knowledge. There are two
primary groups. The Red Order seeks to further
the spiritual evolution of your world through the
use of divine knowledge. The Green Order seeks to
use this knowledge to further their own selfish
desires for money, fame, and power. There are
other smaller factions in your world, but they are
of little consequence in comparison to the larger
groups."

"Why have I never heard of any of this? Why
are there so many secrets? Everyone should know
how to do this."

"Very few humans are prepared to hear the truth
of their relatively limited existence. The sun is a
vast source of information, knowledge, and power.
Even so, it is yet only a small fraction of the power
hidden within the universe. We must hurry if we
are to complete the task at hand."

"What do I need to do?"

"The Words that you see before you are very
ancient. Each one is controlled by a different race
of entities. These entities all dwell on the orb that
you call the sun."

"I don't see anyone but you and me."

"Do not worry. They are all around us. They
assume that I will guide you in the correct manner.
They are correct in this assumption."

Anshar looked intently at Melvina and began to
cough. Every time he coughed, he expelled a
bright red ichor that filled the space around him.
He clutched his chest tightly and doubled over.
Each time he coughed, huge gusts of heat and
flame bathed Melvina's body. She was not
seriously injured, but she realized that without
Anshar, she would quickly perish in this place.

"What is wrong?"

"We do not have much time. I must show you how
to empower yourself. First, you must focus on your
own survival."

Melvina tried to calm her thoughts. She tried to
focus on the calm, cool breezes of her homeland.
She saw herself sitting by the lake while fishing
with Salva. Somehow, the thoughts seemed to

steady her senses. As she focused, a small grouping of Word forms began to cling to her body. They glistened with light and power as they touched her skin.

"Very good. You have attracted the Words for survival. Now, reach out and touch them with your hands."

Melvina extended her hands and allowed the Words to embrace her form. The energy of the Words tingled to the touch. One by one, the Words melted into her body. As they entered her form, they released a surge of energy that caused her body to writhe and pulse with power.

Anshar coughed again and released an even larger cloud of red ichor. His angelic form was only partially visible now. The red, inky fluid almost completely obscured his outer form.

"Now, you must open your mind to this place. Remove all the barriers that you have created to receiving power. As you do this, you will first attract lesser Words. As you open your mind more and more, you will attract greater Words. The greater Words are the larger and more powerful forms that you see around you. As you absorb these Words, the energy of the forms will restructure your mind and soul energies. In essence, the Words themselves will teach you everything you need to know about their use. All you need to do is open yourself to them."

Melvina steeled herself to the task. She knew that the lesser Words that she had already absorbed were sustaining her life force. She looked up into the solar sky and flung her mind wide open.

At first, nothing happened. After a few moments, she saw a small grouping of intermediate and larger Words begin to approach her. The Words

moved slowly at first, but, within moments,
they penetrated her mind with a force she did not
think possible. The Words tore at the very fabric of
her being. She screamed in agony. She was not
sure how her body managed to endure the pain
that she was experiencing.

Word after Word penetrated her form. Melvina
closed her eyes and allowed the Power to wash
over her. She was not sure that she would live
through the next few minutes, but she was sure
that she would not give up. She could no longer
see Anshar nor the solar sky. She could not feel
her body. She could no longer feel the pain of the
Words as they tore through her frame. She knew
that she was still alive and that the Words had
found a place within her consciousness.

She felt the intensity of new thoughts, energies,
and forms racing through her mind. She instantly
understood concepts and ideas that she never
thought possible. Lightning surges of intense pain
ripped through her skull and planted themselves
into her spine. Her body jerked and heaved like a
leaf in the wind. Melvina held her ground and did
not allow herself to move from the spot where
Anshar had placed her.

After a few minutes, she felt a very large energy
form approach her mind. Unlike the others she had
absorbed, this form felt bigger and more
menacing.

The form felt dark and malevolent in its presence.
Melvina forced her mind to open further to receive
its contents. Instinctively, she used the power of a
newly acquired Word to protect her consciousness
and physical form enough so that she could look
upon this new Word.

As she opened her eyes, Melvina saw a deep red
energy form attempting to penetrate her body. The
form stretched as far as the eye could see and she
realized that she was already surrounded by its

wake. Her mind cried out for Anshar, but she could not see his form anywhere.

The force attempted to take her forcefully and rip away the last vestiges of her resistance. Melvina reacted without thinking.

"Moriestia!"

As soon as she spoke the Word aloud, the force recoiled and retracted like a frightened animal. The shape shrunk and folded in on itself and tried to assume a near-human form.

Melvina thought that she could make out the faint outline of a wing in the morass of the form. The thought of what that implied sickened her.

"Anshar?"

For a moment, the dark red mist glowed gold and yellow. Melvina saw a hand reach out from the mist and attempt to grab onto hers. In her mind, she knew that it was Anshar's. A weak voice escaped from the mist.

"Run!"

The voice was very faint. The words were almost imperceptible, but the voice was familiar. It was Anshar, or what was left of him.

Melvina's mind began to race. She knew that Anshar could no longer help her in his present form. She also knew that she would die if she attempted to stay in her present form for too long.

Melvina closed her eyes and focused on the shore of the lake back home. She focused on Salva and tried to imagine hugging her. Suddenly, a Word sprang from her lips and her body began to tingle.

"Ennn-al-iitiuk!!"

A round vessel of light began to form around her. The colors were not unlike that of a rainbow. The vessel began to envelop her and she felt a welcome surge of power embrace her consciousness. Melvina felt her body rise from the floor with the rainbow vessel. It rose slowly at first, but with time, she gained speed. In the background, she saw the red mist begin to regain shape and take flight after her. She willed her vessel to travel faster. However, the faster she flew, the more the red mist closed in on her.

Melvina searched through her mind for a Word that would help her escape. The Words swirled and leaped in her mind like living things. Each Word seemed to have a life of its own. One after another, the Words presented themselves to her consciousness and attempted to help her form a solvent plan. One after another, the plans exploded and died within her mind.

Melvina looked back and saw that the mist was only a minute or so behind her. The reddish-black mass roiled and seethed like an angry thunderstorm tearing through the night. If she were going to come up with something, she had to do it now. She had only seconds in which to respond. Elaborate plans had no place here. Suddenly, one small but intensely simple idea sprang from a relatively silent Word. She had no choice. Melvina smiled as she looked at the red mist and closed her eyes. Then, she spoke.

"Workir-nsa-itl-a!"

A large vortex of spinning light opened before Melvina. She felt her body begin to shrink. As her body shrank, it fell rapidly into the vortex. The red mist tried to follow but the vortex snapped shut before it could enter. She felt a strong force begin to squeeze and mold her form. Within seconds, the vessel of light shrank to a gossamer-thin gold orb and disappeared within her body. The squeezing force strengthened and she began to cry out in pain.

She felt a large set of hands embrace her body. A rushing gust of humid, warm air hit her in the face and she coughed in disgust.

"Congratulations Mrs. Gonzalez! You have a new baby girl!"

Melvina heard a voice booming in the background near the hands. She knew that she was safe.

"What will you name her?"

"My husband and I have already picked out a name for her. We will call her Patricia."

Melvina smiled to herself. She knew that for a while at least, she was safe. She looked up at her new mother, closed her eyes, and fell asleep within the confines of the pink wool blanket that had been wrapped around her.

Chapter Nineteen

The Elevator

Jahil Andware was a wonderful chemistry professor. After graduating from high school, he accepted a full scholarship to MIT and graduated in four years. He completed his master's and doctoral work in physical and theoretical chemistry four years later. He then worked for the Department of Defense for over 27 years in its Research Division and retired with a tidy pension. He married his college sweetheart, Shara, and fathered six children. They moved to Greensboro after he retired and he took a job teaching high school chemistry at a local private school just to keep himself occupied. He had played football in high school and had also played middle linebacker for MIT during his freshman and sophomore years. However, a torn ligament in his right knee ended his football career.

He loved teaching chemistry. Two of his students had won awards in national science competitions. He was only four years from becoming fully tenured in his new position. His only regret in life was that none of his six children showed any interest in or aptitude for science.

Jahil did not understand why he had spent the last three nights wrestling with thoughts of killing himself. He was happy with his life and he was a very devout Muslim. He carried out his prayers five times per day and, each time, he felt renewed and hopeful. He never realized how easy it was to secure weapons online. He found a very reasonably priced, privately owned, fully transferable H&K MP5. The weapon was correctly stamped MP5, with the flapper mag release installed and nice black refinishing done by Terry Smithson himself. The original "cut" H&K 94 barrel was later replaced with an unfinished new original MP5 Pakistani barrel, which has the three-lug adaptor and the Navy threads; this work was done by a former Navy Seal. The steel barrel was unfinished and contrasted with the solid black receiver.

The weapon included a Vollmer-manufactured plastic body that fit over the clip-on lower trigger pack. The MP5 package also included the standard wide fore-end, both the fixed A2 and collapsible A3 rear stocks with multiple 30-round magazines, and a cloth sling. Jahil purchased 600 rounds of ammunition. He used his school credit card so that his wife would not notice the purchase right away. The gun and the ammo had arrived earlier that morning.

Except for the unfamiliar obsession, he felt fine. He packed the materials in a large, black Swiss gym bag and threw them into the back of his black 2010 Volvo V70. He kissed Shara tenderly before he left for work. His children had already left for school earlier and he had made a special effort to hug each of them. His youngest, Johari, had a slight fever and he almost insisted that she stay home for the day, but her class was scheduled to go to the local zoo and she did not want to miss her chance to pet the rabbits.

Jahil arrived at work twenty minutes later. He eased the Volvo into his parking spot, turned the motor off, and walked to the rear of the vehicle. He removed the gym bag, slung it over his shoulder, and grabbed his briefcase. He whistled confidently as he walked toward the west entrance of Saint Mark's school.

Saint Mark's was founded in 1796 and was the oldest private Christian high school in North Carolina. There were over 568 students in attendance and 95 teachers. All of Jahil's children attended the local public school. Academically, he had no difficulty with Saint Mark's School. He had been nominated for Teacher of the Year on three separate occasions. He won the award in 2009. However, he did not agree with their strict religious philosophy and narrow opinion of Islam. Despite his wife's objections, he did not allow his children to attend the school.

Jahil walked into the science building and waved to some of his former students. He turned down the hall and quickly reached the elevator that led to his third-floor laboratory. The elevator was large and could easily accommodate twenty students. On most days, especially in the morning, the elevator was packed. Students hated taking the stairs, especially to the chemistry lab.

Before he could close the door, a swarm of students jammed into the elevator. Jahil found himself wedged into the corner of the elevator near the controls. When the unit reached full capacity, a buzzer began to sound and Jahil closed the door. Jahil towered over most of the students. Standing at over six feet five inches and weighing 230 pounds, he was usually the tallest person in the room.

He smiled as the door closed. As the elevator rose, he quietly armed the MP5 while it lay in the bag. He waited until the unit reached the third floor and pushed the stop button. The students looked at him expectantly. Jahil said nothing. He turned off the lights in the elevator. He then pulled the weapon from the bag, released the safety, and began firing into the crowd of students. He could not see the students, but he figured that as long and they made noise, he would keep firing.

Several of the students screamed and tried to hide on the floor under the bodies. Jahil quickly emptied the first clip of ammunition, reloaded, and resumed firing. Within a few moments, he no longer heard any screams. He separated some of the bodies from the heap, reloaded the MP5, and began firing again. After emptying the magazine, he reloaded the weapon, placed the muzzle against his chest, and pulled the trigger. The machine fired automatically and discharged 10 rounds into his heart before he fell onto the mass of bodies. Jahil died within seconds.

Moments later, a thick red mist rose from his body, seeped through the ventilation shaft overhead, and floated outside. As the mist floated, the main body of the mass began to thicken. The mass fell to Earth just outside the elevator shaft and onto the floor nearby. Dozens of students had heard the noise in the elevator and anxiously waited for the

doors to open. The red mass drew screams of
awe and terror as the students gathered around it.

Tommy Burleson opened the elevator door. A
thick, bright pool of blood flowed from the elevator
and soaked his new sneakers. Tommy saw the pile
of bodies, tried to draw a deep breath in an
attempt to scream, and fell to the floor
unconscious.

As the students watched, the red mass continued
to bubble and congeal. Within a few moments, the
mass disappeared in a hiss of steam. In its wake, a
large, nude body covered in dark patches of
reddish-brown fluid lay still. A few moments later,
the body began to twitch and move.

There was no chemistry class that day.

Chapter Twenty

The Tour

Rodare had moved into Greensboro before the
area was settled by humans more than 9,300
years ago. He set up the manor as a retreat from

life, and as a laboratory. He wanted to find a
cure for Anshar's illness and he needed privacy in
order to carry out his work. He had done well by
himself for thousands of years. The pain of his
separation from Anshar hit him harder than he
ever thought possible. He relished the solitude and
the intensity of the work of finding a cure.

Rodare realized that at some point in the future he
might suffer from the same malady. He searched
most of the known worlds within easy reach of
Earth. Even the greatest physicians and healers
that he could find had never heard of the First
Darkness. He found a few mages who had heard of
the malady, but none had so much as a
symptomatic remedy. He had already spoken at
length with Raphael. The Celestial Healer did not
know of a cure, but he hoped that, through his
research, he could find a solution to the problem.

Rodare relished the thought of showing Patricia the
spiritual world in and around the manor. He had
not left the manor very often and the chance to
stretch his wings for the first time in decades was
too good to pass up. He actually felt himself
becoming excited and anxious about the whole
affair.

Rodare lifted his body easily into the air over the
manor. Patricia was a very light load for the
Gatherer. Most humans never really looked at the
world around them. He glanced at the golden
essence within her aura but was not quite sure
what to make of it. He knew that she might have
the Sight, but anything deeper would require
further research.

"Mrs. Morton, I will be showing you a number of
places that you probably haven't notice during
your stay in our fair city."

Patricia did not hear the angel's voice at first. She
was completely taken over by the warmth and
power of his body. His wings completely shielded

her from the cold of the afternoon air. His cinnamon smell overtook her senses in a way that she never anticipated.

"I don't know what to say. This is all so shocking to me."

"I must say that I am sorry for your loss. Your husband's death was senseless and shocking."

"Thank you for your kind words. I am recovering, but it is all very overwhelming. What is this 'tour' that you are supposed to give me."

"Each part of this world is covered by areas of reality that intermingle with what you recognize as normal space. Within these areas are dwelling places that give rise to much of your mythology. Nothing exists within the world of what you call 'imagination'. All things have a place in the world, if you know where to look."

"What are you trying to say? Are you going to show me the things that go bump in the night?"

"In a manner of speaking, yes. First, you will need to place this ring on your finger."

Rodare pulled out a large, ornately designed brass ring. The body of the ring was cut into a flowery metal pattern. The side panels were inlaid with a carefully crafted arrangement of small diamonds that resembled a fleur de lis. The ring sparkled and shimmered with a life force of its own.

Patricia was sure that the large ring would not fit her finger. When the angel placed it on her right ring finger, the item shimmered, pulsated, and slid perfectly into place as though it had been crafted specifically for her. As the ring settled onto her finger, Patricia felt a pleasant pulsation of energy and warmth creep over her body. The energy of

the ring crept into her brain and filled her
nervous system with crackling tendrils of electric
energy.

"You may notice a change to your senses in a few
moments. Do not be alarmed. Allow yourself to
gradually become used to the sensations."

"What is this ring?"

"An enhancement...essentially, the ring opens part
of your senses to the world around you. It also
enhances the dormant energy hidden within your
subconscious. Think of it as a doorway into the
hidden realm of yourself."

"I suppose you're going to tell me that God gave it
to you."

"This ring was created by the archangel Chamuel
for the Celestial Order of the Red Dragon."

"What is that?"

Rodare climbed higher into the air and then
sharply to the left. He held Patricia tightly as he
flew. He smiled at her curiosity. He liked her
without knowing why.

"I cannot tell you more than this about the ring at
this time. Look down at the city below, tell me
what you see now."

Patricia bristled at being dismissed so casually. She
was used to having her questions answered. She
realized, however, that she was flying high over
the city that she lived in while being cradled in the
arms of an angel. She wanted to protest but it did
not seem quite appropriate.

She looked down at the city of Greensboro beneath
them. As she had flown into the city on dozens of
occasions, she expected to see the familiar

landscape filled with trees, lakes, rivers, and country estates that she had come to love. Instead, a totally different scene filled her vision.

Directly below her, the city of Greensboro was nowhere to be seen. She did not recognize the landscape at all.

"What is this? I don't recognize anything that I am seeing below me.
Where are we?"

"You are looking at the Torisian Republic, a diamond island located in the Pacific Ocean off the eastern coast of Asia. Physically, it is considered a pleasant place to live, with few hurricanes and no earthquakes. They have four seasons a year, and it is said that their rice is best eaten in the fall season."

"How can this be? Are we not flying over Greensboro?"

"Yes, that is true. As I said, however, there are areas of space-time that overlay our fair city. These areas coexist with us in space-time but are slightly out of phase with our reality. They exist alongside our world but are not part of it. We call it the spiritual world."

"What is this Torisian Republic?"

"The government is constitutional, and making war on other countries is banned by law. Because of the shape of the island, the symbol of the country is the diamond, which appears on everything from currency to a baseball team that employs the best players in the world. When the team wins, citizens are known to throw themselves in the river.

Everyone in the Torisian Republic has a guardian spirit watching over them, known as a roku. Rokus can take almost any form and are only as strong as the will of the person they are attached to. There are two basic levels of roku, the first level being the strongest and the second the weakest. A special level is acknowledged above all the others for the most powerful roku. The system of ranking rokus is banned by the government, but still in active use by ordinary citizens. A new visitor to the Torisian Republic may find themselves attached to a roku if their willpower is strong and their need great. Your ring will protect you from any such attachments while you are with me."

"If I were not seeing this with my own eyes, and traveling with you, I would swear that I was dreaming all of this, making it up."

"Yes, I suppose you would."

Rodare flew past the Torisian Republic and banked to the right. After a few moments, he slowed his pace and pointed downward.

"Directly below you is a region called Pleneica, a small country in Eastern Europe behind the former Iron Curtain.

Pleneica is an absolute dictatorship, with all power invested in a ruthless dictator. Pleneician life appears to be entirely based around crime and subterfuge; the entire population of the country consists of saboteurs, spies, and secret agents.

The dictator controls the nation through the use of the Office of Central Control, through which he is able to spontaneously organize heavily armed mobs of Pleneicians.

The culture of Pleneicians reflects the central position of spying and crime. Notable flora and fauna of the country include the Pleneician creeper, a man-eating plant that is revolted by acts of kindness, and the Pleneician carrier pigeon, which may or may not be a vulture.

All tourists to Pleneicia inevitably find themselves imprisoned, though conveniently, all diplomatic staff in the country also reside in prison. The borders of Pleneicia are perpetually surrounded by mile-long lines of natives attempting to leave the country. It is not known how much Pleneicia has changed since the fall of the Iron Curtain, except that in Pleneicia, the Iron Curtain was represented by a massive curtain made of iron.

"Pleneicia sounds like a revolting place. And this is right next to Greensboro?"

"Yes. Using some illegal technology, some of your worst criminals migrate from Pleneicia into Greensboro. The Order seeks to discourage such passage, but the criminals are persistent."

Rodare stopped in midflight. He extended his outer wings and enclosed his inner wing structures tightly. He spread his primordial light outward in sharp bursts of energy.

"Patricia, I need to show you something very special. Please close your eyes."

"What is it?"

"Takaamahara. It is a very important place in the spiritual world. You might say that it is one of the capitols. The city emits an array of primordial light forms that are blinding to visitors. You must adjust your sight in order to avoid being blinded. I will do this for you."

"Why must we visit this place?"

"It is the home of the Order. At some point in time, once you are fully trained, you will need to visit this city for an extended time. You will need to become aware of its customs, laws, and energies."

"Takaamahara is the oldest city in the spiritual world. No one knows when it was built, but it has been the seat of power in our world for over 100,000 years. The city did not make contact with humans until the late 1600s. The inhabitants of the city are tall, over 12 feet in height, and are blue in color. Their bodies glow with blue light and they are extremely long-lived. They made contact with life beyond our solar system thousands of years ago and have enjoyed an advanced level of civilization and culture since that time. There has been a large degree of alien interbreeding with their royalty, establishing a unique seat of power in the country.

This sector of the population has the ability to transform their bodies into light, and often visit Earth in various forms. They are said to have established most of the religions and technology of this world.

The combination of alien technology with their own accounts for much of the advancement of their culture. The natives of the city all have the ability to shift time with their minds. They also have the ability to alter space just by thinking about it."

"If they are so powerful, why don't they help us solve some of the problems on our world?"

"That is a very good question. The natives of this city believe that humans are a primitive race. They have plans for you, but they are not willing to share those plans. They prefer to allow the Order to do their bidding."

"And I am supposed to work with these people one day?"

"Yes. They are your rulers in every sense of the word. This race has an agenda in relation to your people. Over time, the population of blue-skinned hybrids has begun to dwindle, the consequence of alien females being scarce and Takaamaharan

women being rarely strong enough to bear
blue children. Human women are now being
'recruited' to bear their young."

Patricia drew a deep breath and closed her eyes.

"I think I have seen enough. Please take me
home."

"There is much more to see, Patricia."

"Perhaps another time. You are right, we humans
have a difficult time seeing past our limited
perspectives of reality. This is all a little too much
for me."

"As you wish."

Rodare descended toward the manor. Within
moments, he penetrated the outer perimeter
defenses and landed softly on the front lawn.

He retracted his wings and called for Kahlia. She
appeared instantly.

"Master, we have a development."

"What has happened?"

"Anshar has appeared on Earth."

"Where?"

"Here, in Greensboro."

"Have you informed the doctor?"

"Yes. While you were away, we stepped out for a
bite to eat. Gerald called him before we could
complete the main course. He is heading down to
the station as we speak."

"Take Patricia to the house and await my orders. I will go to the station."

"Yes, master."

Chapter Twenty-One

Anshar Returns

Detective Gerald Holmes had worked in Greensboro for a long time. As a policeman and detective, he had seen hundreds of crimes. He had also seen hundreds of criminals. He had hoped that

he would get a break in the strange grouping
of serial murder-suicide cases that had gripped the
city. He had done his best to keep the stories out
of the paper—at least, any potential connecting
ties between the stories. When he got the call
about the shootings at Saint Mark's, he was
appalled. However, he was relieved that there was
somewhat of a break in the case.

The man found naked and covered in blood on the
floor next to the elevator was a godsend. For the
first time, there was a potential suspect who might
help to break the cases open. Gerald did not
believe that such a large number of people with no
prior record of homicide or criminal behavior could
all of a sudden resort to such violent behavior.

Mitchell didn't quite know what to make of Gerald's
call. Gerald had just learned the details of the
massacre minutes before he'd called. He was still
almost out of breath from giving the myriad orders
necessary to secure the scene and keep the press
out. The suspect was large, over seven feet tall. He
was well built, nude, covered in blood, and
completely cooperative—not unusual for crimes of
this type; not common, but not unusual. Then, he
mentioned the wings.

Gerald met Mitchell at the door leading into the
precinct house.

"I knew someday that I would get a case for you
that would stump you." Gerald flashed his pearly
whites at Mitchell and waited for a response.

"Where did you place the suspect?"

"He is in the corner holding cell. We put a sheet
over him and led him down the hall. We saved as
much of the red fluid covering him as we could.
But get this, the boys at the lab just paged me and
gave me a prelim on the results. You are not
gonna believe this. It's not blood."

"What is it?"

"Some sort of acellular goo that seems to defy explanation. It doesn't look like anything they have ever seen...but that's not the strange part."

"You're referring to the wings?"

"You're damn right. Our forensics team did a quick once-over on the guy before we washed him down. Seems that the wings are real. They are attached to the guy's chest. They seem to be growing out of his lungs into his back. I think I'm gonna need a drink after this."

"I would like to talk with him as soon as possible."

"I was kinda hoping you would say that. We can go there right now. I will need to escort you."

Mitchell flashed his consultant's badge and walked past the metal detectors near the entrance to the cells. Gerald swiped his ID over the electronic sensor and stepped back. The tall, brown metal doors swung open and creaked to a slow halt.

There were 10 cells in the passageway. Each cell was no more than ten feet wide and eight feet deep. Each cell held an iron cot draped by a thin mattress. There was a small stainless steel sink and a commode built into the wall.

The two men walked quickly as they passed the cells. This part of the jail had been emptied over a week before the new prisoner was brought in. The county had scheduled the area for renovation.

When they reached the cell, Anshar was floating quietly about three feet above the floor. He had draped a sheet around his torso and his feet were bare. His aura was faint but he still exuded the power and strength of a Gatherer. Gerald had placed one guard at the end of the hall and two by the door. He wasn't taking any chances.

Both men looked at each other and shook their heads. The vision of an angel floating naked in a jail cell was almost overwhelming. Gerald spoke first.

"Is that what I think it is?"

Mitchell said nothing. He opened his vision to wide aperture. Most of the time, he kept a tight seal over the powers of his third eye. For the most part, the physical world gave him little reason to use the full powers of his gift. Furthermore, the strain of absorbing large amounts of energy from the physical world through this third eye often left him weak. Early on in his medical training, he had learned to shut down his third eye in order to maintain a sense of sanity.

The winged being exuded a bright reddish-gold light that permeated the energetic space of the room. The light was bright enough that he was sure that even those without sight could see it clearly.

"I believe that we are looking at an angel, detective."

"I can see that. I've been puzzled by that fact since we first brought him in. You see, he didn't have wings when we first picked him up. Turns out, they grew out while we were transporting him."

Mitchell walked into the cell first. He stared directly at Anshar. He was not sure why an angel of the Host would be present at the scene of a mass murder. He was not sure why such a being would be covered in what appeared to be a primordial sludge known as ichor.

He quickly realized that the detective would never believe the extent of the spiritual truths that surrounded his fair city. The obvious realities of the angel's presence, however, changed the dynamics of the situation immensely.

"Gerald, please ask your men to leave."

"Are you kidding me? We have no idea what this being is capable of. He is a suspect in at least half a dozen murders, maybe more."

"If he wanted to leave this cell, he would have done so by now. Your men would be dead within seconds if he chose to harm them. Your weapons cannot kill hm."

"Then why is he still in the cell?"

"That is what I need to find out. The presence of your men only complicates matters."

"Are you sure?"

"Look, Gerald, we've known each other for a long time. You're going to have to trust me on this. Look at him."

Gerald shook his head and bit his lip. He was way out of his element and he knew it.

"Okay. Twenty minutes, and then I'm calling them back in."

Gerald summoned his lieutenant to the door. He gave the young man some quick orders and, within seconds, the hallway and the cell were clear. They were all alone with the angel.

"Thank you, my friend. There are a couple of things I need to tell you before we start our interrogation. Let me finish what I have to say before you respond."

"Shoot."

"One, I am going to do some things that will seem, well, a bit unnatural. Two, I am going to ask you to put on a protective talisman."

"Can I speak now?"

"Yes."

"You're not gonna hypnotize me and make me quack like a duck are you? Cause I've seen you do some strange things over the years."

"No, I will not hypnotize you."

"Allllllright...can I ask my next question?"

"Shoot."

"What is a protective talisman?"

Mitchell grinned and reached into his pocket. He retrieved a small ancient relic he had received from his master over 400 years earlier. The relic resembled a small Buddha statue hanging on a leather cord.

"This is a protective talisman. I don't know what kind of forces we may be dealing with here, but I don't wish to take any chances."

"What about you? Don't you need some kinda protection too? You don't have a gun or nothing."

"I am fine."

"I thought angels were the good guys."

"I can hear both of you quite clearly." Anshar descended to the floor as he spoke.

Mitchell spoke a brief Word and donned his robe. His archangel medallion glowed brightly on his chest. He then turned and faced the angel. Anshar smiled as he stared at Mitchell.

"A magus...I am impressed. And what might your name be?"

"My name is Dr. Mitchell Earl Gibson, Magus Second Order, House Josiphitis, Third Domus, Ordo Rosae Draconis."

"Impressive. I am Anshar, Commander General of the Celestial Gatherer Host."

"Who is the human standing next to you?"

"I am Detective Gerald Clark Holmes, Greensboro PD, son of Thomas and Helen Holmes. We need to ask you some questions."

"Gerald, allow me." Turning back to face the angel, Mitchell continued, "Clearly we cannot hold you against your will. Therefore, you remain here by your choice. I respect that. Can you tell me why you are here?"

"I have killed many of your kind during my sojourn on this planet. I accept whatever punishment you choose to levy against me."

"So you confess to killing those kids at Saint Mark's?" Gerald asked.

"I do not recall the incident clearly, but it is likely that I did."

"We found over 17 dead bodies in that elevator. Do you know what kind of penalty that crime carries?"

"Yes. I suppose you will either imprison me or attempt to kill me. In either case, I will submit to your law."

Mitchell looked at Anshar and shook his head.

"Something is not quite right here. An angel of the Host does not kill innocents. Why have you done this?"

"It is a long story. I have been ill. I have only recently regained my faculties, though I am unsure as to how long I will retain my lucidity. I recall many of the people whose souls I have taken. I can tell you that they are not innocents."

"Innocents?...Nobody deserves to be slaughtered against their will," Gerald replied.

"I am a Gatherer. I gather the souls of the dead and bring them into the Celestial City. I have done so for billions of years...before your race crawled out of the seas of this planet."

"That does not give you the right to take souls indiscriminately before they pass from this life!" Mitchell added.

"Those souls were destined to cause the deaths of thousands. Mr. Morton, for instance, is an excellent pilot in his spare time. Two years from now, he would have had a heart attack while flying his Twin Engine Cessna and crashed into a fully loaded Boeing 747 bound for Atlanta. More than 150 humans would have died.

Jonathan Thaler, one of the children on the elevator, was destined to discover a rather potent mutated strain of Pseudomonas aeruginosa during his work with a military laboratory. That discovery would have been paired with an accidental release of the bacterium during a training exercise in Richmond Virginia. 350,000 humans would have died before the contagion was secured. Shall I continue?"

"How do you know these things?" Mitchell asked.

"I am an angel of the Host. Certain incidents in this world are revealed to my kind eons before they are born."

Suddenly, a bright flash of incandescent white light filled the room. Mitchell shielded his eyes and quickly extended the fabric of his robe around Gerald. Seconds later, Rodare appeared.

Rodare extended his wings aloft and looked upon the inhabitants of the room. He stared at Anshar for a few moments.

"I am happy to see you, brother," Rodare said.

"I am happy to see you as well, my brother," Anshar replied.

"Two angels? I have gone my entire lifetime believing I would only see these beings in my afterlife. Now I find that my hometown is crawling with them," Gerald said.

"Master Rodare, how did you find us?" Mitchell replied.

"Kahlia told me about the call. I came as quickly as I could."

Rodare reduced his size and enclosed his outer wings into his body. He descended into the cell and stood next to Anshar.

"This space is far too crowded. Allow me," Rodare said.

Rodare spoke softly and, within moments, the room transformed into a large cathedral. The ceilings were more than eight stories tall and the windows surrounding the area were made of gold and purple stained glass. The floors were made of glossy dark brown mahogany.

"Do not worry, doctor. The guards outside will continue to see us as we were," Rodare said as he nodded to Mitchell.

Gerald stared up at the ceiling high overhead and said nothing. He wished that Mitchell would hypnotize him.

"You know this angel, master?" Mitchell asked.

"We were partners long ago. Yes, I believe I know him quite well."

Rodare moved toward Anshar and embraced him. Enclosed in a crimson and gold light, the two angels flew aloft for a few moments.

"It is good to see you again, my brother. I feared the worst. I thought you were dead," Rodare said.

"I thought of you often, my brother. I feared that the Darkness had overtaken you as well."

"I have been looking for a cure. I made a vow when we left the Celestial City that I would not rest until I had secured a cure for our kind."

"Did you find something?"

"Yes I have. Almost."

"Explain yourself."

"Her name is Kahlia."

"I will explain further after you tell me why you have murdered these innocents."

"Look into my mind, brother. You will see the truth of my actions."

Rodare nodded and extended his senses into Anshar's mind. He saw the lives of all the victims parading before him. He saw their actions and their destinies. He saw their hopes, dreams, fear, nightmares, and their secret thoughts. He saw why each of them had been chosen. He saw the meaning behind the madness.

Rodare withdrew his senses, sighed, and allowed himself to sink to the floor. Anshar descended slowly beside him.

"Did he tell you why he murdered those people?" Mitchell asked.

"Yes, he did," Rodare replied.

"He has agreed to give himself over to our law. He is a murderer," Gerald added.

"Your jails, your law, could never hold him. He is not human and you do not have the facilities to accommodate our kind. Besides, should the Darkness return, he could release himself from any facility you care to name and start the killing all over again."

"I am not an animal, my brother. I have restored myself, after a fashion, to a reasonable facsimile of health. I am capable of taking responsibility for my actions," Anshar said.

"You cannot speak for the madness that lives within you. Taking souls that were destined for individual lifetimes and stuffing them into your being is not a permanent solution. We have no idea if they will remain secure within your form. They could free themselves at any time," Rodare added.

"You mentioned that you had discovered a cure. Tell me of this Kahlia?" Anshar asked.

"What do you mean cure? What does Kahlia have to do with any of this?" Mitchell asked.

"Kahlia is an Immortal. She is one of a unique breed of Immortal Humans. She is immune to disease, physical injury, and aging. Her body can repair itself from any injury or infirmity. I have protected her for many centuries. I love her as I would one of my own kind. Over the past forty years, we have perfected a technique that would allow me to use her cells to fashion a healthy vessel for those of my kind who become afflicted with the Darkness."

"This is the work that you referred to?" Mitchell asked.

"Yes. We were just about to start a search for those of my kind afflicted with the Darkness when you and Patricia visited us, doctor."

"Do you really believe that this 'cure' can work for me, brother?"

"Kahlia has agreed to provide us with a supply of her own tissue for the process. No harm will come to her during the procedure and she will regrow the tissue within hours."

"You are describing a process known in our world as cloning. If you are successful in this work, you will create thousands of copies of an Immortal being inhabited by a potentially dangerous disease. How do you know if Kahlia's unique healing ability will stop a Celestial-level disease?" Mitchell asked.

"My understanding of both the disease and cloning are thousands of years beyond your comprehension, doctor. Granted, you are an Adept and a physician among your people. But I have been a Gatherer billions of years longer than your soul has been alive. Your incarnations have not prepared you to even begin to understand the questions that you are asking."

"I meant no disrespect, Master Rodare. I only wish to point out that if you are wrong, you will have effectively spread the disease that you describe to the far corners of the universe."

"Can I ask a question here?" Gerald interjected.

"Speak, detective," Rodare replied.

Gerald cleared his throat, shuffled his feet briefly, and tried to clear his head. He never imagined that his world would be turned upside down by the revelations of the day. He wanted desperately to understand how he could explain the crimes that had hit the area in a way that did not make him sound crazy.

"How am I going to explain this to my superiors? Angels, Celestial diseases? Killing people before their destiny can cause harm in the future? I don't know if I can believe any of this and I am standing here with two angels and a guy that I don't even know anymore," Gerald said.

"There are no easy answers, my friend. I have a suggestion that will help ease all of our minds.

Master Rodare, you propose that we use the cells of an Immortal human to quell the spread of a potentially dangerous Celestial disease before we know the consequences of your actions. Master Anshar, you claim to have sequestered the souls of a large number of humans before they can cause the deaths of innocents in our world.

I propose that we take this matter to the Order. They have jurisdiction over these matters and their rulings are upheld by the Celestial Court," Mitchell replied.

The entire group became silent. Anshar looked to Rodare and both angels nodded to each other. They knew that eventually this matter would reach the ears of the Celestial Court. Mitchell's suggestion was an inevitability.

"You do realize that we could simply ignore the dictates of your Order. We answer only to the Creator," Anshar said.

"This is true. But if the Order finds that your actions might endanger this world, they have the full authority of the Celestial Court behind them. You would have to fight large numbers of your own kind to defy them. You answer only to the Creator, but there are laws in our world that even you cannot break," Mitchell replied.

"What is the Order?" Gerald asked.

"Long story, my friend. I will fill you in later."

"If we are to settle this matter, we should do so immediately. I have waited a long time for this cure. I do not wish to wait any longer," Anshar stated.

"I agree. I have worked for centuries trying to find a cure for the First Darkness. I believe that I have done so. I will present my work to your Order, doctor. I believe that they are evolved enough to understand the implications of my discoveries," Rodare quipped.

"Very well then, we will leave at once. However, before we do so, we must make one stop," Mitchell said.

"Where?" Gerald asked.

"Kahlia is crucial to the working of this cure. She has a right to attend the proceeding before the Order. Patricia is my charge and I have been meaning to present her before the Order. We may as well bring both of them along," Mitchell replied.

"Then we must return to my home. Permit me."

Rodare raised his right hand and emitted a brilliant ball of light. Within seconds, the ball filled the room and covered all four participants. A moment later, they disappeared.

Chapter Twenty-Two

The Order

The Annals of Tigus Andrachus

The Sorcerer Tigus Andrachus had a vision. He was the greatest magic worker of his kind. Sadly, he was forced to use the vast majority of his power just to keep the peace in his world. Vast factions of dwarves, elves, human mages, fairies, trolls, demons, and other unnamed races all fought for control of the globe. Tigus led a small compendium of wizards who had dedicated themselves to giving the human race a chance to evolve and grow. In his vision, Tigus saw the human race leading all the races in the galaxy out into the vast reaches of space. He saw lightships that stretched for miles across the void filled with mages, fairies, trolls, demons, elves, and all the unnamed races.

Tigus did not know how he would overcome the centuries of distrust and the history of violence that marred the past attempts at unifying the users of power. He had traveled across the globe speaking with various spiritual leaders, most of whom supported his efforts in theory. Few among them trusted their fellow magic users to work together. Few among them trusted any alliance beyond the needs of the moment. Cooperation among the races was not seen as particularly valuable. Magic was a power that was hard won by the chosen. Any power attained within a race was jealously groomed, guarded, and protected by those who knew of its existence and benefited from its presence.

All magic users believed that magic in and of itself was not a force to be tamed and corralled. Tigus disagreed with this philosophy. During one of his journeys into the astral world, he encountered a pocket of subspace that was populated by a strange race of beings. All the beings spoke one language. All the beings in the domain were powerful magic users. Tigus had traveled through the pockets of subspace more than most mages. He had found that most of the areas of subspace were dark, desolate, and empty places. He had discovered a race of submissives who did anything he asked. He particularly liked their women.

He wanted to explore the strange and unique race of magic users that he had encountered. A single race in which all inhabitants were magic users was unheard of. Tigus spent decades among the people

of this race. As far as he could determine, they had no name for themselves. They did, however, have a name for just about everything else. Tigus discovered that this unusual race had stumbled upon the infinite power of the Primordial Word.

According to their ancient legends, the Primordial Word was the greatest power source in all creation. All creation had been spoken into being by the force of the Word. Everything that had been created drew its power from the constant emanation of the Primordial Word.

This race believed that the Creator, in his infinite wisdom, had given all sentient beings the power to discover these Words. All aspects of reality were sustained by the Creator's utterance of this Word.

The Word itself was actually composed of trillions of individual syllables. Each syllable empowered a different aspect of reality. The syllables, when spoken aloud, provided the user with the ability to control the very fabric of time and space. Certain Words allowed the race to move through time and space simply by speaking the proper alignment of sounds. Every place that existed contained a unique sound. By uttering the sound of two places simultaneously, the people had discovered a way to travel instantaneously. The first sound uttered was the place of origin. The second sound uttered was that of one's desired destination. By uttering the primordial name of an object, that object could be summoned into existence from this air.

Certain Words gave them the power to look into the future. Other Words gave them power over life and death itself. Tigus befriended a mage among the people named Bona. Bona lived in seclusion in a cave high above the largest city on the planet. Bona realized that his people possessed a great power and he knew that they must be protected from discovery by outsiders. The Words gave them the ability to see dangers before they manifested. The Words gave them the ability to protect themselves from anything they could imagine. The

Words could not protect them, however, from their mind-numbing boredom.

The power of the Words gave the people of his land near ultimate control of their world. Over time, they wanted for nothing. Bona saw a reality in the arrival of Tigus that he had never seen before. His people needed a way to evolve. If they continued life in the way that he envisioned, he saw that they would simply lose the desire to create and build anything. Eventually, they would fall into a sort of sleep wherein they could create all they ever needed simply by thinking about it. Bona knew that if that happened, his people would begin to disappear and would soon be a forgotten race. He knew that they needed a new challenge in order to forge any kind of meaningful future for themselves.

Bona liked Tigus and the two men soon developed a friendship. Bona was a master of the Word and he taught Tigus everything he knew of the Word. Tigus learned quickly and was soon more powerful than he ever dreamed. Bona knew that Tigus would enjoy the power. That was part of his plan.

Bona devised a plan that would allow his people to evolve and, at the same time, spread the power of their magic out into the universe. Bona presented his plan to his people. They used their magic to examine the veracity of Bona's vision. After much intense debate and discussion among the race, they decided that Bona had seen true. His vision for the race was seen to be powerful and far-reaching. They decided to accept his magnum opus.

Bona's plan was as simple as it was brilliant. Bona proposed that his people transform themselves into pure energy and take on the form of pure Words of Power. In this form, they would then spread across the vast reaches of space and seed themselves among the lower races. The Words would plant themselves into the unconscious and subconscious energy matrices of these races. For millennia, the recipients would be unaware of the presence of the Words.

Over time, the race would slowly supplant the recipients' subconscious mind with knowledge in the use and understanding of the Words. As the recipients evolved, the race would then effectively have created new species of beings with the Power of the Word. The new species would be an amalgamation of their race and the lower races. The race could use the untapped unconscious resources of the lower races to continue their growth and evolution while, at the same time, helping the lower races to evolve.

Tigus liked the plan, but he knew that the races in his domain would never accept it. He knew that the lower races would never accept what he saw as a benevolent parasitic relationship. So, Tigus made a choice that forever changed the face of reality. He invited the ancient race to inhabit the races of his domain without their knowledge. The lower races had neither the skill nor technology to plumb the depths of their subconscious energy resources. The Ancient Race, as he came to know them, could begin their influence over the younger races without any interference for millions of years before anyone even thought of discovering their presence.

The Ancients wasted no time in implementing their plan. They transformed themselves into pure energy using their most powerful Words. The Ancients then lifted themselves into the heavens and began scattering themselves among the lower races. They drifted from star system to star system, replicating and multiplying their forms as they went. As they spread, they quietly planted themselves into the unsuspecting subconscious minds of every sentient being they encountered. Human, demon, angel, elven, fairy, dragon, amoeba—none was immune to their touch. As they began to populate among the angelic Host, their actions captured the notice of the Celestial Court.

The Celestial Court consisted of three immensely powerful Arch-Seraphim who presided over the entirety of creation. They were appointed by the Creator and had total autonomy in decisions regarding the day-to-day activities of all races. They decided the ultimate fate of all beings and their decisions could only be overturned by the Creator himself. The Celestial Court's power was supported by an army of over 10 billion Gatherers and Seraphim granted to them by the Creator.

The archangel Michael reported the actions of the Ancients to the Court and asked that they render a decision as to the legality of their actions. The Court deliberated for over twenty years before reaching a decision. They saw the hand of the Creator at work in the actions of the Ancients and decided to allow them.

When their verdict was announced, a number of angels refused to accept it and openly plotted rebellion against the Court. Within months, a war broke out over the issue and the Court ordered the archangel Michael to quell the rebellion. Michael's brother, Lucifage, the Seraphim Lightbringer, had chosen to lead the rebellion and pleaded with his brother to join him. Lucifage had spoken with both Tigus and Bona and had attempted to dissuade them from supporting any further expansion of the Ancients into Celestial or mundane space. His efforts had, however, fallen on deaf ears.

Michael spoke with Lucifage at length and warned him that any action taken against the edicts of the Court would lead to war within the realm. Despite his brother's protests, Lucifage gathered an army of followers from the ranks of the dissenters and on the morning of Celestial date 09:81:602.7, Lucifage led his army to the gates of the Celestial City. Michael awaited them with 3,000 legions of Gatherers and Seraphim warriors. Michael's warriors easily suppressed the rebellion and dragged Lucifage and his generals before the Court.

The Court wasted no time in ordering Lucifage and his followers to incarnate down into the lower worlds and live among the lower races until such time that they understood the necessity of the Ancients' plan. Billions of rebel angels were cast down into the astral and physical worlds. For a time, there was peace among the peoples of creation.

The Ancients continued their spread among the lower races. At first, none of the races noticed their presence. It is said that the Dragon races were the first to become aware of their presence. The Dragon races were among the oldest living species in the universe. They had mastered the oldest elemental magic and were always actively looking for new ways to extend their power. When their young began to spontaneously speak Words of Power and manifest spectacular feats of magic with no training, the Dragon Elders knew that something wonderful had happened to their people.

The Red Dragons, masters of the element of fire, were the first to amass a large number of these new mages. The Red Dragon Elders jealously guarded knowledge of the presence of their gifted youth and tried to hide them from the other races. However, as they grew, the youths refused to be caged and hidden away. The Red Dragon Elders did not have the power to control their movements and soon, the youths began to travel among the stars.

Tigus watched with joyous anticipation as the young Red Dragons spread among the stars. He watched them begin to use the Words and spread the knowledge to other worlds. They were careful, however, not to spread the knowledge to Dragon races that had not yet awakened. They carefully watched and observed millions of Dragon races, waiting for the signs that a few among them would begin to awaken to their gift.

Approximately 6,000 years after the
awakening of the Red Dragons, the Green Dragon
race began to notice the emergence of uniquely
gifted youth among their ranks. The Green Dragon
Race comprised masters of the element of Earth;
they were not as beneficent in their actions as the
Red Dragon race. The Green Dragons had long
sought a way to dominate the other races. They
interpreted the emergence of the gifted and
powerful youth as a sign from the heavens that the
time for their ascendancy had finally come. Using
the Words, they quickly realized the presence of
the power of the Red Dragons. They also realized
that war with that race would ultimately lead to
their own destruction.

The Red Dragons quickly noticed the power of the
fledgling Green Dragons. They realized that war
empowered by the might of Primordial Words
would ultimately threaten the delicate web of the
matrix of reality itself. Tigus and Bona met with
leaders of both factions and forged a pact. Both
sides would agree to the formation of two Orders.
Each Order would allow the other to grow and
flourish so long as their activities did not cross
paths.

On those occasions when their goals crossed
paths, the elders of each Order decided to settle
their disputes in a unique way. They would choose
a leader from their most powerful Adepts. When
disputes arose, the most powerful Adept from each
Order would be called into combat against the
opposing house. The Adepts could choose the field
of battle as well as the time and place. The battles
would be witnessed by all who wished to attend
from either side. All battles were to be fought to
the death. The Order sponsoring the victor Adept
would rule the matter in dispute.

Disputes that could not be settled in this way were
to be presented before the Celestial Court. The
rulings and edicts of the Court in these matters
were considered final. Any Order resisting those

edicts risked facing the wrath of the Celestial Army, led by Archangel Michael.

Under this organization, the Celestial Order of the Red Dragon and the Celestial Order of the Green Dragon grew in size and power. The Orders divided themselves into a house system based on skill, mastery of the Word, and longevity. The oldest and most powerful mages of each Order gathered into House Josiphitis, named after the founding Master Josiphitis. The remaining houses listed in order of descending power and status were House Jeres, House Timaras, House Honoris, and House Zagasel. No one knows why both Orders agreed to accept the same House names.

Other races awakened to the power of the Word, but none ever equaled the mastery and skill attained by the Dragon Races. The Dragon Orders maintained the uneasy truce they had forged under the watchful eyes of the Celestial Court. They recruited the most gifted and talented Word mages from all the races they encountered and, in time, both Orders contained the most powerful mages in existence.

Tigus appointed himself de facto leader of the Red Dragon Order. Bona presided as the head counsel for the Green Dragon Order. Both men had long ago transformed themselves into Immortal Beings of Light. This feat alone earned them the respect of both sides. The men did not see themselves as opponents. Rather, they saw themselves as elder statesmen, dedicating themselves to maintaining the peace between the two factions.

After several million years of watching over the Green Dragon Order, Bona decided that he wanted to explore new dimensions of reality. Tigus tried to talk him out of his decision, but Bona was resolute. Bona's absence created a power vacuum within the Green Dragon Order. Soon, power-hungry Elder Green Dragons fought among themselves for leadership. Tigus knew that if he interfered, the stability of the system that they had worked so hard to build would be threatened.

Leazar, a very old and very powerful Green Dragon from House Josiphitis emerged as leader. Archmage Leazar was a brutal and powerful dragon who sought to change the status quo among the Dragon races. He vowed to one day unite the Dragon races under his rule and crush the power of the Red Dragons. He had not yet attempted to bring war to the Orders, but all members of the Orders were aware of his growing threat.

On planet Earth, the first Word mages emerged only 4,300 years ago. Both Celestial Orders had stationed sentries throughout the known worlds; they were trained to detect the presence of new mages. The Orders wasted no time in establishing a base of operations on Earth. As the numbers of Word mages grew, the Orders slowly took over the financial, spiritual, and political power bases of this world. Backed by the power of the Orders, the mages soon found themselves running the planet. Their presence, however, remained unknown to the denizens of Earth.

The Annals of Tigus Andrachus,

Celestial Record Number 89.20.22.1.6.11

Chapter Twenty-Three

Reunion

Kahlia relished the fleeting moments when she could leave the manor and explore the world outside. She did not know anything about Patricia, but she had lived long enough to recognize a gifted soul when she saw one.

Patricia didn't say anything to Kahlia as they waited. She didn't know why Kahlia had called the angel "master." She didn't know why or how she had been dragged into the world of angels, magic, and secret dimensions. She had not even had any real time to mourn the loss of her husband. Somehow, she knew that there was more to the story of her existence than she had been led to believe. Her relationship with Mitchell rekindled a burning desire that had smoldered within her soul. On the one hand, the strangeness of the events of the day could easily be explained away by hypnosis and suggestion. The instantaneous transportation that Kahlia had accomplished to bring her to the manor was another thing altogether.

"Kahlia, who are you and how do you know the doctor?"

"Mitchell and I go way back. We have known each other for more than 80 years."

"That is not possible. You don't look a day over 30. Mitchell can't be any older than 50. You could not have possibly known each other that long."

"You may not believe this, but I am hundreds of years old. Mitchell is at least two hundred years old. I met him in 1867, just after the end of the American Civil War. He served as a doctor in the Union Army. I met him shortly after he returned home from duty."

"You're telling me that Mitchell is hundreds of years old. You're also telling me that you are hundreds of years old. People don't live that long. How is that even possible?"

"Most people die after living only a few decades. Some people die after living a few years and aging rapidly from diseases like progeria and cancer. There are some people that nature cannot kill.

There are some people that learn to outsmart death itself. You might say that Mitchell and I are exceptions to the rules of life and death. By the way, there are a lot of people like us living in the world."

"If that is true, then why have I not heard about any of you? Why is your presence not earth-shattering news?"

"We go to great lengths to keep that from happening. The most powerful and wealthiest people on this planet are Immortals. They take on different personalities from time to time, kill them off, and adopt new personalities. They have been doing this for thousands of years."

"So you are telling me that they own the newspapers, television, and media outlets. They control the flow of information in the world so that if they wanted to hide these facts, they could with the push of a button?"

"Or the muzzle of a gun...mortals are easily persuaded to do whatever we need them to do when death is added to the equation..."

A brilliant flash of white light punctuated the room. Within moments, Anshar, Rodare, Detective Holmes, and Mitchell appeared within the nimbus of light.

"Kahlia, my dear, have you been entertaining our guest?" Rodare asked.

"She is a most inquisitive human. There is something about her though. She has a beautiful aura."

Patricia had only recently been introduced to Rodare. She was mesmerized by his beauty and power. She was even more perplexed by the arrival of yet another angel. This one seemed vaguely familiar.

"Permit me to introduce both of you to my partner, Anshar. He is a Gatherer."

Kahlia stepped forward and took Anshar's hand. She smiled briefly and allowed herself to examine him from head to toe.

"So this is the great Anshar that you have told me so much about...he is a cutie...can we keep him?"

"Mind your manners, my love."

Patricia stared at Anshar with a look that could chill one's soul to the bone. Her breath came in deep gasps and she could not bring herself to speak. She didn't understand her reaction to the stranger. Every fiber of her being wanted to run from the room and disappear into the forest outside. She forced herself to stand quietly and greet the angel.

"I am pleased to meet you, Anshar." Patricia extended her cold hand in greeting and forced herself to smile.

Anshar stared at the beautiful woman who offered her hand to him. He looked at the glow of her aura and forced himself to peer deeply into her eyes. Within moments, he knew. Blinding torrents of raw emotion flooded his heart and mind. Part of him wanted to rush forward and embrace the woman. Another part of him wanted to strip the flesh from her bones with a sharp knife. Strangely, he felt that he would find pleasure in both actions.

"You don't remember me, do you?" Anshar questioned.

"You know this woman?" Mitchell queried.

Anshar did not look at Mitchell. He did not remove his gaze from Patricia.

"Should I know you?" Patricia's heart began to beat faster. She forced herself to remain calm. She did not know how long she could keep up the charade.

Rodare recognized that Anshar had a connection to Patricia. He also knew, however, that their meeting with the Order was of paramount importance. There was no time to ferret out the particulars of their past relationship.

"Kahlia, Patricia, we must leave at once," Rodare said.

"To go where? This is just getting interesting...why don't we crack a bottle of wine and get comfortable...really comfortable..." Kahlia loved to reduce any moment down to its sensual basics.

"We must attend a meeting of the Order as soon as possible. There is no time to waste," Rodare replied.

"You have got to be kidding! With all due respect, master, don't you remember why I am hiding out here with you in the first place?"

"What is she talking about, Master Rodare?" Mitchell questioned.

Rodare drew a deep breath and walked toward Kahlia. He took her arm and glared at her.

"Master, you are hurting me." Kahlia squirmed and tried to free herself.

"Master Rodare, what is going on?" Mitchell asked.

Rodare drew another deep breath and began
to sweep a broad geometric shape in the air above
his head. He ignored Mitchell's question.

Mitchell removed his archangel medallion from the
protective cover of his robe. He rubbed it three
times. A bright sheath of blue and red light erupted
from the medallion. Before anyone could move, the
light bathed the entire room. Glowing rivulets of
hardened steel-like bars of energy formed from the
light.

"You dare imprison angels of the Host?" Rodare
shouted.

"Neither one of you seems to want to answer my
questions. We are going to stay here until I get
some answers. I am not comfortable going before
the Order until I get some answers," Mitchell
replied.

Rodare looked at Anshar. Both angels knew that
they could not leave the room as long as the
Demiurge Bridge of Light held them in place.
Mitchell's move had caught both of them
completely by surprise.

"I didn't know you had it in you, doc. Nice move!"
Kahlia exclaimed.

Kahlia sat down on the floor and crossed her legs.
She levitated several feet off the ground and
smiled.

"I can save you the trouble, doctor. You are
looking at the only living being who has ever said
no to the Order and lived to talk about it."

"That is not possible! No one refuses membership
into the Order!" Mitchell replied.

"I did. Actually, I said no to both sides, the Red and the Green. That's why I stay here. They can't find me while I live in this domain of subspace."

"Is this true, Master Rodare? Do you know the penalty for hiding an Adept from the Order?" Mitchell asked.

"I am aware of the laws of your precious Order. The whole idea of its existence annoys me. They serve no purpose, either side, other than to build upon their own bases of power. Kahlia has the right to say no if she chooses," Rodare replied.

"Then why do you wish to expose her now?" Mitchell asked.

"I have no choice. If I continue with my work and expand my experiments to the rest of my kind, the Order will learn of my actions very quickly. Now is the best time to get this out into the open. Anshar's life depends on this. We have no time to waste."

"Why should she be forced to go if she does not want to join this group?" Patricia replied.

"Patricia is right. If the woman does not wish to go, then why should we force her?" Anshar added.

Mitchell raised his hand and formed a soft arc of blue light in the air.

"This discussion is pointless. Why didn't you tell me any of this before now? If we take Kahlia to the Order, they will imprison her. You both know that. If we don't take her, the Order will find her and we will all have to answer to the Celestial Court," Mitchell said.

Silence fell over the room.

"We have two fugitive Immortal beings in one room. We also have a Gatherer of the Host and an Adeptus Major of the House of Josiphitis. Yet all we are able to accomplish is idle chatter and a foolish Mexican-style standoff. If I didn't know better, I would think that this was a pissing contest. But, we all know that angels don't pee," Kahlia remarked.

The silence deepened.

Gerald had been curiously silent throughout the afternoon. He looked at the group and began to smile. His eyes glistened with supernatural power. His body began to glow.

Patricia was the first to spot the change. "What is wrong with the detective?" she asked.

Everyone turned and looked at the transformation beginning to take place in the body of the detective. His clothes began to shimmer and fade. Where his uniform once was, a glowing black and red robe emerged. In a matter of seconds, he grew two feet in height. His ears elongated and his skin turned green. A thin layer of silvery-white fur formed over his skin. His eyes turned red and his teeth broadened. His muscle structure thickened and, within moments, a new being emerged from the form of Detective Gerald Holmes.

Rodare released his wings to full power. Anshar attempted to follow suit but his power was not such that he could control its use to a great degree. Mitchell quickly formed a protective ward around Patricia and Anshar when he saw the angel's distress.

"Who are you, creature?" Rodare demanded.

"I am sure that none of you has had the pleasure of meeting me. I have waited a long time to reveal myself to you. Masquerading in this pathetic human form has been revolting."

"Who are you and what have you done with my friend?" Mitchell shouted.

"The detective existed only as a useful illusion. He was not a real person in the true sense of the word. I needed to get past the barriers of this place and find a way to get both Gatherers into this room."

"Creature, I have given you fair warning. Tell us who you are and why you have invaded my home!" Rodare repeated.

Before Rodare could move, the being pointed a long, pointed finger at Anshar, Patricia, and Kahlia. A thin pincer of green light illuminated the room. The light beam easily crushed the ward that Mitchell had erected and, within seconds, Anshar, Kahlia, Patricia, and the creature disappeared from the manor. Mitchell and Rodare were thrown back against the wall and knocked completely unconscious.

A few seconds later, a small sliver of paper manifested on the floor of the manor on the spot from which the trio had disappeared. One word in bright green letters appeared on the paper—Leazar.

Chapter Twenty-Four

Six Hours Later

Rodare struggled to his feet. After billions of years of battle, he thought that he had seen everything. He had never been caught off guard in such a manner. He looked around the room and saw a large, black, charred remnant where his left rear wall used to be. Crumpled immediately below the wall's structure lay Mitchell's form. Rodare rushed to his side and placed his hand over the doctor's chest. He perceived a faint life pulse, but a human physician would have pronounced him as dead. Rodare peered into the body and saw a thin cord emanating outward into the expanse of the room. He followed the cord with his vision and saw that it extended into the sky above the manor. Rodare immediately knew what he needed to do.

He gathered Mitchell's body into his arms and extended his wings. Within moments, he crashed through the skylight above and flew toward the sky. Rodare looked down at the buildings below and spotted Mitchell's home. He spoke a brief Word. Seconds later, four copies of his angelic form stationed themselves in the sky a few feet above the home. They were invisible to the naked eye. Kathy had just gone outside to retrieve groceries from her car. She saw the Gatherers materialize above her home. She knew that something was wrong. Luckily, the children were not at home.

Kathy dropped the groceries, ran into the house, ran a bucket of water, and hurriedly carried it into the meditation room. She mumbled a quick series of incantations over the water and plunged her right hand into the bucket. The water flashed and roiled with a brilliant blue and red light. Kathy threw her clothes off and quickly donned her robe. She placed her feet into the bucket after burning two protective runes into the water. Seconds later, her soul form was flying in the sky next to Rodare.

"What happened?"

"We were attacked by an Elder Dragon. I believe that it was Leazar. Patricia, Kahlia, and a friend of mine have been kidnapped, Mitchell has been injured. We must retrieve a new soul for him before it is too late."

"How could such a thing happen? Your home is heavily shielded. You are a Gatherer. My husband is a senior Adept. Kahlia is an Immortal of immense power. Who is this Leazar?"

"We do not have time to discuss this. If we do not rejuvenate him quickly, he will not recover from this attack. Do you understand?"

Kathy shook her head in disbelief. She had stood by Mitchell's side through hundreds of battles and soul journeys. She could not believe that an Elder Dragon had taken the time to attack an Earth dwelling in such a manner. Such an attack was a breach of all the rules agreed upon by both major Orders. When this was over, she would see to it that someone paid—and dearly.

Rodare encircled the three of them within the aura of his mighty wings. He gathered his senses and looked for the thin tapered form of the life cord that Mitchell had left for him to find. He saw the cord piercing the cold atmosphere several miles above his head. He drew in a deep breath and hurled himself toward the cord. He uttered a Word and a large portal opened above his head. The light from the portal shimmered and moved like a living thing. Rodare willed the three of them through the opening. As he followed the cord through the opening, he entered a field of intensely brilliant light. Rodare recognized the field. Mitchell had led him into the Prima region of the sun.

Rodare took another deep breath and forced a stream of dense primordial particles into the aura protecting their bodies. The intensity of the light was almost blinding, even to his vision. He made the field of his aura thick enough so that the light would not harm Kathy or Mitchell.

The life cord soared into the deeper realms of the Prima region. The region was densely covered with billions of glowing human forms. Each of the forms was nude and lay curled into the fetal position. Rodare could clearly see that each of the forms was different, though some of them bore a striking resemblance to each other. Some of the forms were blue. Some were florid red. Others were bright white and gold with iridescent sheets of glowing light wrapped around the main form like a cocoon.

Rodare and Kathy followed the life cord without speaking. They knew that if they did not find its destination soon, the trip would be for nothing. Rodare focused all of his powerful senses on the course of the life cord.

The life cord winded its way through the Prima field. Soon, it slowed its course and paused above a large gold and white shielded form. Rodare looked at the form. The life cord circled it and merged with the shield.

Rodare gently placed Mitchell's still form into the cocoon-like light form. Kathy stood quietly and tried to control her emotions. She had never witnessed the process of rejuvenation before, though she had heard a great deal about it.

Thin ribbons of light swirled around Mitchell's form. Within seconds, his body disappeared into the cocoon. Rodare spoke a loud series of Words and asked Kathy to stand back.

"Enaliatiuk soran itso itun noris soran!"

The cocoon pulsed and heaved with energy. Soon, the form lifted from the floor of the sun and righted itself. Swirling gold rivulets of power wrapped themselves around the cocoon. The rivulets first formed themselves into complex mandala patterns. The patterns wavered, suspended in the light, and then gradually began to condense. Each mandala dissolved into a bright ball of light. Each ball floated into place and began to form a human structure. First, the torso structure appeared, then the head. Moments later, the balls of light formed themselves into arms and legs.

Rodare shielded Kathy's soul form with his wings. Shortly thereafter, Mitchell's new form burst into a torrent of light. Rodare and Kathy were flooded with a powerful stream of light and primordial particles. Strong currents of heat poured from the form; without Rodare's shielding, Kathy would have been consumed.

Soon, the heat and light subsided. Rodare removed his wings from around Kathy's form. Before them, shining in a golden bright light, Mitchell stood smiling. He drew a deep breath of primordial air and broke free of his cocoon.

"I am glad you found my signal."

"I, too, am glad. How do you feel?"

"Rejuvenated."

Mitchell realized that he was nude. He quickly summoned his robe.

Kathy burst into tears and flung her arms around him. They embraced for several seconds. Rodare joined in the embrace and encircled all of them within his wings.

"We are all that remain of our family. We must recover our friends, doctor."

"What just happened here? Will one of you just tell me what happened?"

"I will explain, my love. Leazar, a powerful Elder Dragon mage, attacked the manor and kidnapped Patricia, Kahlia, and Anshar. Anshar is an angel. He tried to kill both of us during the attack. I have never seen such power. My body was badly damaged but not beyond repair. I knew that Rodare would find me and help rejuvenate me.

All humans have light body forms stored within this region of the sun. These forms may be used to rejuvenate the physical body. Before I fell into total unconsciousness, I summoned my life cord and willed it to lead a trail to this form. Master Rodare did the rest."

Kathy began to feel the heat from the sun penetrate her soul form.

"I guess we can continue this discussion back home," Kathy replied.

"I don't know how Leazar could pull off such a feat. Implanting Gerald into the subconscious matrix of Earth...breaching the defenses of a senior Gatherer..." Mitchell replied.

"He could not have done these things without help...a lot of help," Rodare said.

"Are you thinking what I am thinking?" Mitchell questioned.

"I most certainly am. He must be operating with the help of a Gestalt. He must be using the combined forces of a number of Dragon Elders channeling their energies into his consciousness. If you will permit me, we must return to Earth," Rodare remarked.

"Are you sure you're well? I mean after what just happened, shouldn't you get some rest?" Kathy asked.

Mitchell smiled and took Kathy's hand. He hugged her and kissed her on the forehead.

"After a rejuvenation, my body is replaced with primordial light. I am still Mitchell, but my form is no longer human in the traditional sense of the word. I no longer need to eat, sleep, breathe, or drink water. I can assume any form that I wish."

"How long will you stay like this?" Kathy asked.

"There will be no change in our worldly relationship if that is your concern. If I do not wish it, the children will never notice the change, at least until they are much older. You know that I have already lived for hundreds of years. Now, I will live in this form for millions of years."

"I guess that makes me feel better...sort of... Let's go home," Kathy replied.

Rodare opened a portal in the solar sky. He gathered Mitchell and Kathy in his wings and, seconds later, they stood on the floor of his manor.

"We will need to come up with a plan. As long as Leazar has the power of the Gestalt to support him, we cannot fight him in the usual way."

"No human has ever gone against an Elder Dragon and lived, Mitchell. This is going to be dangerous, especially for Kathy."

"I know. My rejuvenation has helped me to see some things very clearly. I have a plan that just might help us defeat this monster and get our loved ones back."

Chapter Twenty-Five

The Reckoning

Anshar awoke in pain. He tried to stand but his
feet would not support the weight of his body. He
slumped back onto the cold wooden floor and felt
something warm scurry away from his feet. He
looked down at his legs and saw a cadre of large-
jawed rodents nibbling at Kahlia's thigh. As each
bite fell upon her sleeping form, the wound healed

and a fresh series of rodents descended upon her. Kahlia was oblivious to the feast that she had become. Anshar summoned a ball of primordial fire and incinerated the rodents. Patricia lay sleeping next to Kahlia. The rodents showed little interest in her body. Anshar looked more closely and saw the protective ring and medallion that she had tucked away beneath her clothing.

The room that had become their prison was bare. The walls were over 100 feet tall. As far as he could determine, they were composed of concrete. The floors were some variety of ancient wood that he had never seen. Large, jagged holes scattered the floor in numerous places. Anshar could hear the scratching noises below the floor that could only be made by the brethren of the beasts that he had just destroyed. Anshar extended his senses upward beyond the ceiling. He could see nothing. He could hear nothing.

Deep within his being, he could still feel the rush and cry of the madness that threatened to overtake him. He knew that the souls he had gathered were never meant to live within one body. He knew that each day he attempted to mold them into one consciousness, he would move one step closer to insanity. For now, however, he knew that there were other greater concerns to be addressed.

He looked at Patricia and a smile formed on his lips. His wings unfurled and, despite himself, he floated aloft. His eyes focused on her slumbering form and the promise her female body held within its wake. He was afraid that if he did not wake her soon, he would ravage her. He did not know if her human form could bear the force of his embrace. Only part of him cared.

He remembered Melvina, and the centuries he had spent grooming and shaping her soul to his service. He looked at the woman that she had become and he wanted to forget her betrayal. He wanted to forget the decades that he had spent searching for her soul before he fell into madness. He wanted to forget how he had tracked her to South America. He wanted to forget how the madness had willed him to follow her young body into the city where she now lived. Were it not for the madness, he would have taken her and returned to the astral subspace domain the Creator had given him. The madness diminished not only his power, but his ability to form coherent memory and thought. In its own way, the madness had helped to save Patricia's life.

Now that he was whole again, he wanted to start anew. He wanted to live a life with Melvina that bore some semblance of normality. He remembered all of the atrocities that he had committed in the service of his own healing. He balanced those thoughts with the atrocities that he had committed against the Corps of Gatherers that he had served for billions of years. For now, he had neither the time nor the luxury of self-pity.

He tested the limits of the expanse into which he had been thrown and then he rose toward the ceiling. A sharp, acrid smell pierced his nose and mouth. He extended his angelic senses a few feet above his head and opened his Celestial vision to full capacity. Crisscrossing the ceiling over the cell, he saw a green pattern of energy that crackled with arcane power. He recognized the pattern from the attack he had experienced before. He decided not to test the strength of the field, which draped itself over the full expanse of the ceiling. He descended to the floor and focused on the large space that loomed some 100 feet in front of the wall. The same arcane pattern covered the space. Anshar knew that there was no escape.

He descended to the floor and destroyed a new cadre of rodents that threatened to resume feeding on Kahlia. He summoned a Word and closed the holes in the floor with a layer of purple and red primordial fire. He heard one rodent after another test the limits of the shield. One after another,

they incinerated themselves until they realized
that no further feeding would take place in the cell.

Anshar examined the life force of both women.
Kahlia's aura was brilliant with fire and color. The
golden white of her immortal life force had started
to assert itself. Anshar knew that, within minutes,
Kahlia would revive herself. He could see that
some of her major internal organs had been
damaged, but they, too, were already beginning to
heal themselves. He decided to focus his efforts on
Patricia.

He saw that Patricia had suffered a concussion. He
examined her scalp with his vision and saw a tiny
hairline fracture creasing her scalp. Her face was
lined with a small film of blood that issued from
the wound. He did not see any broken bones or
internal injuries. He knew that he had been
seriously injured by the attack and that were it not
for his Celestial healing force, he would still be
unconscious. Kahlia's immortal life force had
protected her from the worst of the force. He
wondered how Patricia had escaped with so little
damage. Perhaps the ring was more powerful than
he thought.

Anshar extended his wings, held forth his right
hand, and spoke a Word of healing.

"Worshise-en-ton!"

A honey-colored mist emanated from his hand and
spread over the two women. After a few moments,
they both stirred.

Kahlia took a deep breath, opened her eyes, and
screamed in pain. The sound of the noise brought
Patricia to full consciousness.

"What happened?" Patricia asked as she touched
her scalp. She looked at Anshar and a wave of
anxiety and passion consumed her mind. She
willed herself to calm down.

"We were attacked," Anshar replied.

Kahlia stirred and rose to her feet. She looked at the cell, Anshar, and Patricia. She groaned and grabbed her right side with both hands.

"Whoever did this to me is really going to regret this day!" Kahlia said, summoning a defiant smile to her lips.

"Where are we?" Patricia asked.

"As far as I can tell, we are in a cell. The cell is large and filled with rodents. We are held in place by what appears to be some sort of arcane ward. I would not recommend touching the field."

Anshar extended his hand and made the warding field visible.

"So what's the plan? Do we stay here until someone or something comes to get us?" Kahlia asked.

"I am not sure. I need time to think. I am not familiar with this technology. Any wrong move on my part could destroy us all. For now, I recommend we stay put," Anshar replied.

"Where are we?" Patricia asked.

"I do not know. My senses have not revealed a location. Kahlia, can you get a bearing on our location?" Anshar queried.

Kahlia focused for a moment. She extended her mind as far out into the surrounding space as she could. Her perceptions folded and moved like a living thing. At first, they bounced off the warding fields and rebounded into her body. She recoiled at the power of the rebound, but soon redoubled her efforts. One of the benefits of her immortality was the power of sense. She could extend her mind for miles around her with little or no effort. If she wanted to, she could listen to a concert 200 miles away while sitting comfortably in the manor.

She knew why Anshar had not tried to move them with a Word. The warding field absorbed her power like a sponge. Any Word she attempted to summon dissolved into the field. Her senses had little effect on the field. As she attempted to penetrate the area, she expended more and more power. Soon, she found herself feeling exhausted.

"I can't get anything. Whoever erected this thing has put a lot of power behind it. I have never seen anything like this," Kahlia replied as she bent over, trying to catch her breath.

Moments later, a brilliant flash of light illuminated the cell. Twenty feet in front of them, Leazar appeared. Just behind him, Anshar could clearly see more than one dozen heavily armed demon soldiers. He knew that, in his current condition, he was no match for them.

Leazar examined the floor beneath them and smiled. "I like what you've done with the place. I'm glad to see that you're making yourself at home," he remarked.

"Why have you taken us, creature? Who are you?" Kahlia shouted.

"My name is Leazar, Grand Arch-mage of the Celestial Order of the Green Dragon. You are my guests."

"Guests? You must be mad. Why have you brought us here? Where is Mitchell?" Patricia asked.

"I suppose you would have a lot of questions. Unfortunately for you, I do not have the time to answer them. You are to appear before the Council of Elders immediately."

"What is the meaning of this?" Anshar asked.

"We have little time, but I will tell you this. You have a choice to make. Choose wisely and you will live."

"Why not simply kill us and be done with it? Why do you toy with us?" Kahlia asked.

"You and I both know that killing you is next to impossible. Besides, it would be a terrible waste of such a lovely body."

"What is this choice you speak of?" Anshar asked.

"I will allow the Council to answer that question for you, but I will let you in on a little secret. We didn't bring you here to kill you."

Leazar raised his hand and drew a large circle in the air over his head. The room crackled and hissed with power and the warding field fell instantly. Seconds later, the room dissolved into a cloud of vapor.

A broad, metallic platform formed beneath their feet and floated in midair, suspended by its own power. Surrounding the platform, a series of stadium-like seats began to manifest. The seats were covered in a lush satiny material and each one floated in the air.

The seats formed themselves into a conical structure as they appeared. At the bottom of the cone floated the metallic platform. On either side, totally surrounding the group, thousands of seats slowly appeared. Initially, each seat was empty, but each was soon filled.

Anshar determined that there were over 20,000 seats in the arena. Each seat was filled with a different being, each wearing a red and black robe

lined with a green sash. The beings made no
noise as they sat suspended in the arena.

Leazar smiled and looked up. "I present the
captives, my lords," he said.

"You have done well, Leazar."

The voice did not emanate from any single being.
Anshar, Patricia, and Kahlia heard the reply clearly,
but they were not sure of its source. The beings
seemed to speak as one entity. Anshar had never
seen a Gestalt with that kind of power before.

Anshar noticed that each of the beings seated
within the chairs were Elder Fire Dragons. He had
fought their kind on numerous occasions over the
millennia. Alone, they were no match for him. In
his prime, he could probably kill at least 1,000 or
more. He knew that he had no chance against a
grouping of 20,000 of their kind.

"We apologize for the rudeness of your capture,
but we had no choice. We wish to make you an
offer, angel."

"What is this offer?" Anshar replied.

"We are aware of your condition. We have
discovered a cure. We will offer it to you on one
condition."

Anshar could not believe his ears. He shuddered to
think of the possibilities of returning to full power.
He desperately wanted to cry out and rejoice, but
he remembered where he was.

"There is no cure for the First Darkness. What is
this cure that you speak of?" Anshar shouted.

"There is a rare flower that grows on one planet in
the multiverse. The planet is heavily shielded and
no one may enter its domain unless we will it. We

have created an elixir from this plant that will cure you. In exchange for this cure, we ask only one thing of you."

"How do I know that this cure you speak of will work? What is this thing you ask of me in return?"

The arena grew deathly quiet. No voice could be heard and the elders in the seats slowly began to disappear. One by one, all of the seats began to dissolve, except for one. The lone seat floated down to the bottom of the arena and landed next to Leazar. The Elder Dragon rose from the seat, smiled, and waved his hand. Leazar disappeared with his brethren.

The Elder Dragon floated several feet above the floor. As he floated, he began to glow. His robes dissolved and turned into a simple brown tunic. His dragon features dissolved and his face became human.

"We offer you this cure on one condition. We would like you to become the leader of our Order."

"What is your name? You are clearly not a dragon," Anshar asked.

The elderly man smiled and looked at Anshar for a few seconds before answering.

"My name is Bona."

Chapter Twenty-Six

Finding Faith

Kathy stood by quietly as she listened to her husband and an 11-billion-year-old angel plot strategy. They had returned to the manor hours before and had quickly returned home to make

sure everything was secure. It was shortly
after 6:00 p.m. and the children were just getting
home from school. They had decided to tell them
nothing about the events of the day.

The four guardian angels above the home floated
silently and kept a watchful eye for any sign of a
new attack. Neither Tiffany nor Michael had
developed their sight to a significant degree and
they were totally oblivious to the dangers that their
parents discussed. Mitchell decided to place them
in a sound hypnotic sleep after they had finished a
quick supper of baked chicken and beans.

Both Mitchell and Kathy worked feverishly to erect
a three-layer ward over the house. The ward was
reinforced with two Stones of Power, several
complex Words, and a fully charged 8,000-year-old
Egyptian oak wand that lay underneath a large
Sentinel oak tree in the backyard. They were
taking no chances on another sneak attack.

"Whatever we do, we must do it quickly. There are
only a few options that we can pursue that will
lead us to Patricia, Kahlia, and Anshar," Mitchell
stated.

"If we act rashly, we will not only lose time but we
will risk never finding them. The attack and
kidnapping were obviously planned very
meticulously by a large number of individuals,"
Rodare replied.

"With all due respect, Master Rodare, we have
been discussing strategy for over two hours now.
You believe that we should storm the main temple
of the Green Dragon Order and take them by
surprise. I suppose that in your Gatherer days,
that might have worked. But, neither you nor
Master Anshar have the power that you once
wielded. Unfortunately, even with that power, I
believe that we would stand little chance against
the forces that I sense we would be facing."

"How are you so sure that we are facing a Gestalt?"

"No one being could possibly have mastered the level of magic required to defeat two angels, a senior mage, and an Immortal human in a matter of seconds, not to mention the power required to bend reality and create a persona as convincing as Gerald's. I have never seen that kind of power. It fooled even you."

"You have a point, doctor, but I still have trouble believing that the Green Dragon Order would work together to that degree. They are not known for their willingness to cooperate with each other. That simply does not make sense to me."

"If we examine the facts rationally, there is no other conclusion. We are facing some new element within that Order that we have never seen before. They have their reasons for attacking us the way they did. They tried to kill us without remorse. Were it not for you, I would not have returned. They are up to something, and they sent Leazar as their messenger."

"Why do you not wish to listen to my suggestion?"

"I do not like it. You propose that we approach our Order with the idea to form our own Gestalt. You propose that they empower you, in your present condition, with the power to focus their will through your mind so that we can retaliate in kind against Leazar."

"Precisely!"

"We do not know if your present body can handle the pressure of all those minds. We don't know if anyone can handle that kind of psionic pressure."

"Leazar handled it."

"Leazar is an Elder Fire Dragon. He is millions of years older than you are and he is a warrior. He is descended from a race of Warrior Dragons bent on total domination of the entire multiverse. He is probably enjoying the power."

Kathy paced around the room and smiled at her husband and the Gatherer. A brilliant idea formed in her mind as she listened to their diatribe. She knew that as each moment passed, their chances of finding their loved ones grew faint.

"Why don't we ask Michael to help us?" Kathy queried.

"You mean the Demiurge, Archangel Michael?" Mitchell replied.

"Yes. He commands the entire Celestial Army. That is the largest, most powerful military entity in existence, is it not?" Kathy queried.

"The Celestial Army does not respond to personal requests. They are the main defensive force for Heaven and Earth. They only respond to commands given by the Creator or the Celestial Court. Why would they possibly wish to get involved in this matter?" Rodare asked.

"Without their help, you will never defeat Leazar. If what you fear is true, and Leazar has become part of a group psionic mind composed of an untold number of Dragons, no force in existence can stop them except the Celestial Army," Kathy said.

Mitchell and Rodare looked at each other and smiled.

"She is right. The answer was right under our noses. If we are facing a Gestalt, it will only be a matter of time before they attempt to confront our Order, even Heaven itself," Mitchell said.

Rodare shook his head and unfurled his wings. He did not like the idea of involving his old commander in this matter, but he saw no alternative. Even the combined forces of the Order could not long withstand this new threat. The balance of power in the known universe could possibly swing toward the unthinkable.

"Kathy, I salute you. Your wisdom has won the day," Rodare said.

"Thank you, Master Rodare. In my opinion, we must get word to the Demiurge as soon as possible. We can ask Master Djehuti/Thoth, the greatest magician in the universe, to help us find the group. Surely he will help you, Mitchell. After all, he was your teacher," Kathy added.

"My love, sometimes your ability to cut through the crap and see the bare essence of things amazes me. We don't have to do this on our own. We can ask for help. We do know people," Mitchell replied.

"This idea of yours is all well and good, Kathy, but it is predicated on one huge conclusion. How do we know that the Demiurge or Djehuti will see things our way? They could just say no," Rodare said.

"There is one thing that I have learned in all my years of working with both of you. Faith is our greatest ally," Kathy replied.

Silence filled the room.

"I guess we are going to make a little trip to Heaven," Mitchell said.

Rodare retracted his wings and reduced his size. He walked past the fireplace of the great room and sat on the black leather recliner. He pushed the controls of the chair and made himself comfortable.

"There is one other thing...I can't go with you."

"What do you mean you can't go with us?" Kathy asked.

"To make a very long story short, have you ever wondered why I am stranded here on this planet? Have you ever wondered why I live in this little town, cloistered away from my brethren?"

"We assumed that you had your reasons. We did not want to invade your privacy. There are a fair number of beings such as yourself living all over this world. We respect their need for privacy," Mitchell replied.

"Master Rodare, are you trying to say that you have been banished from Heaven? Is that the reason you live here?" Kathy asked.

"In a word yes...but not for the reasons you might think. When my partner, Anshar, became ill, I, too, inquired as to my likelihood of contracting the illness. Our healer, Raphael, assured me that I was in no immediate danger. However, that was almost 10,000 years ago. I have been working to find a cure for the First Darkness from the time that I came to this world. When I first settled in Greensboro, your race was still eating its meat raw and living in caves."

"Are you telling me that you could become the monster that Anshar was?" Mitchell asked.

"Possibly, but the Creator has given me time to find a cure. In the meantime, he has forbidden me to return to the Celestial City."

"You could have told us this a long time ago. Kathy and I have known you for decades. Why did you hide this information from us?" Mitchell inquired.

"I have suffered from this illness for longer than most of your ancestors have been in this world. I did not think that I needed to trouble you with that information."

Mitchell and Kathy looked at each other in silence. They realized that given the events of the day, they had little choice in their course of action.

"We need you, Master Rodare. This plan will not work without you. The word of a senior Gatherer will carry much weight with the Demiurge. Does he know of your illness?" Kathy asked.

"I would suppose that there is very little that the Demiurge does not know," Rodare responded.

Suddenly, the sound of the doorbell pierced the air.

"Ignore it, probably just a package being delivered," Mitchell said.

"Kinda late for a package..." Kathy replied.

Seconds later, the doorbell rang again...and again...and again...

"Persistent delivery man...we better go see if this is something we need to sign for," Mitchell said.

"I will go with you. Just to be safe," Kathy responded.

A few moments later, Mitchell peered through the glass pane that draped the outside of the large mahogany front door to their home. He drew a deep breath, shook his head, and looked again. He then turned to Kathy.

"You are not going to believe this."

"What is it, my love? Open the door and see what the man wants."

"That's just it. That is not a mail delivery guy."

"If you think it's safe, then let's see who it is."

Mitchell turned the lock and cautiously opened the door. As he did so, the visitor boldly stepped over the threshold and hugged Mitchell. Kathy stared at the man and refused to believe her eyes.

He was an older black man, perhaps 70 years old. He was no taller than five feet seven inches. His hair was thin and graying. His skin was thick and weathered. He wore a dark blue suit, black tie, and crisp Oxford shoes. As he hugged Mitchell, Kathy watched in awe.

After a few moments, the visitor turned to Kathy and smiled.

"Well Kathy, aren't you going to hug your father-in-law?"

"You can't be here. You died almost twenty years ago," Kathy replied.

"Well here I am—James Barnett in the flesh. Give us a hug, my dear."

Kathy hesitated and examined the man closely. She switched on her sight and focused on his aura. Seconds later, she knew why she was uneasy.

The visitor smiled and turned to Mitchell.

"She is quick, isn't she, Mitchell?"

"I wondered how long it would take her to figure out who you were," Mitchell replied.

"Well, Kathy, you can't blame me for wanting to have a little fun. I was listening to your conversation a few minutes ago and I thought I should drop by."

"You're...God?!" Kathy questioned slowly.

The visitor walked over to Kathy, held his arms out, and smiled again.

"Come give us a hug, my child. We have a lot of work to do."

Chapter Twenty-Seven

Bona

Anshar was not an easy being to surprise. However, during the last few days, he had been surprised several times. He stood with Patricia and Kahlia in the central meeting place of the most powerful clandestine organization in the history of the known universe. He knew that if they wanted any of them dead, they would already have been. He knew that if he tried to resist anything they wanted him to do, they would kill all of them immediately.

Anshar had heard of Bona. He knew the legends surrounding his power and the role that he played in the formation of the original Orders. He knew that there was only one person in existence who could dismiss Leazar so easily. He would not have believed it if he had not witnessed the dismissal with his own eyes. He did not understand why such a being would want him to lead the Order of the Green Dragon.

"No one has heard from you in a very long time. Why would you want me to lead this Order? I am sure that you know who I am." Anshar replied.

"You are the perfect being for the job, Anshar. Madness in an angel is rare. To find an angel who has overcome this madness, to some extent, and has fought his way back to sanity is very rare indeed. You are exactly what I have been looking for," Bona replied.

"Where have you been all this time?" Anshar replied.

"There really is no time to explain, my friend. Will you consider my offer?" Bona replied.

Patricia and Kahlia watched in awe as the events before them unfolded. Neither of them had ever seen the central chamber of the Green Dragon Order. Before today, neither of them had ever met an Elder Dragon and neither of them had ever heard of Bona.

"Will someone tell me what is going on here?" Kahlia demanded.

Bona waved his hand and two large couches appeared in the expanse. The couches were covered in fine Corinthian leather and studded with large emeralds and sapphires. He motioned for everyone to sit.

"I can understand how you must be confused by the events that have led you to me. Even for an Immortal, these things must be confusing," Bona replied.

"And to mortals as well!" Patricia replied.

"I, too, need clarification as to why you brought us here in this manner. You almost killed my friends. You imprisoned us. Leazar invaded my partner's home and destroyed part of the main library chamber. You have some explaining to do," Anshar replied.

Bona materialized a small marble stand next to the arm of his chair. He whispered a couple of Words and a gleaming silver tea placement appeared. Four sparkling silver cups draped themselves one by one around a large central teapot. Bright gold and blue arcane letters graced each cup.

Bona poured a cupful of tea into each of the cups. The aroma was thick and heady. Patricia immediately recognized the scent.

"Earl Grey?" Patricia asked.

"I love the taste. I created this brew not too long ago. I had almost forgotten how much I enjoyed the taste," Bona replied.

Bona took a teacup into his right hand, raised it, and allowed the steam to waft into his nostrils. He then sipped the piping-hot liquid without bothering to cool it. The heat of the boiling tea did not seem to bother him.

"You all should probably wait until this delicious brew cools down before you try it," Bona said.

"Enough of this waiting. Tell us why we are here," Anshar demanded.

Bona took another quick sip of the tea. He glanced at Anshar and placed the cup back on the tea service platter.

"Very well then. Allow me to tell you a story. It should answer your questions and help clear up this debacle. Before I start, I should apologize for the zealousness of my associate. I assure you, you are safe now."

"You want Anshar to lead your Order...why bring us along?" Kahlia demanded.

"If you will permit me to explain, I will answer all of your questions, Kahlia."

"How do you know our names?" Patricia asked.

"I created telepathy, Patricia."

Patricia shook her head and picked up a cup of tea. She allowed herself to breathe in the aroma before she tested the temperature. She sipped the tea slowly. It was the best blend of tea she had ever tasted.

"As I was saying, I need to tell you a story. A very long time ago, my people made a great pilgrimage. We left the shores of our homeland and ventured out into the stars. We were not the first race to do so, but we were the first to occupy vast regions of the universe. We spread to every galaxy, every nebula, every star cluster, and every planetary grouping in the known universe. But we did not use ships to make our voyage.

We were the first race to conquer death itself. We transformed the very essence of our bodies into pure energy and consciousness. We transcended the concept of mortality. Over time, we lifted ourselves beyond the bounds of time and space and became part of the fabric of the universe. Well, in a manner of speaking, we became the fabric of the universe.

Some of my people were not satisfied with our accomplishments. They wanted more. They wanted to evolve beyond the achievements of even our greatest ancestors. They wanted to control consciousness itself. That is when the true pilgrimage began.

We descended into the realm of consciousness itself. We took residence inside the conscious minds of every sentient being in the cosmos. It did not matter that these sentient beings were oblivious to our presence. We felt that our presence was a gift. We allowed a portion of our power to be used by any being evolved enough to discover clues to our presence. Of course, they could not discover the greater aspects of our purpose or the larger dormant potentials tied to our being. However, the power that we brought and the use of the Word was more than enough for most. Through our presence, magic entered the universe.

My people did not go to sleep in our new state. We thrived. We built civilizations based on the energy of pure consciousness within the deep energy reserves of the universal mind. We built vast cities that spanned light years of space. We built centers of learning that spanned billions of parallel universes. We conquered the matrix of space and learned to simultaneously inhabit multiple realms of time within the same space-time domain. But then, something happened.

We hit a wall. No matter how hard we tried, we could not extend our influence beyond a certain point in space-time. It was as though we were in some sort of cage. Yes, we occupied the known universe, but our growth became limited. We wanted to go beyond the universe. We thought that there was no limit to our growth. At first, we could not believe it, but our greatest explorers consistently relayed reports of the impossible. They discovered that the reason we could not breach the walls of this space-time construct lay in the fact that the universe as we knew it was part of a giant atom...one giant atom in an impossibly large molecule that seemed to be part of one impossibly large being.

Suffice it to say, billions of our greatest minds checked the accuracy of this discovery. The discovery was checked and rechecked billions of times over hundreds of millions of years. There was no mistake. The universe had played a gigantic joke on its greatest race. Despite all of our growth and power, we were no greater than a tiny atom in the multiverse. We, the gods of space and time, occupied no more of a place in the greater scheme of things than the smallest particle of matter.

Some of my people chose not to believe the discoveries. They were content with our might and influence. They chose to continue their exalted existence and explore the as yet unseen realms of the unconscious. Others were not so easy to appease. They saw the new discoveries as a threat to their sense of dominance and power. They saw the Atom, as it was referred to, as a threat to our existence.

What if the great being that created the Atom decided to crush it and destroy us all? What if the Atom was hit by some larger particle or energy source and was obliterated from existence? What could we do to protect our way of life and the beings we inhabited?

We were not willing to accept that the answers to these questions were far beyond even our vast levels of consciousness. We could not accept that something larger than us existed. The very thought drove thousands of the early explorers mad. We had never expected to experience disease or limitation within our own. We never expected to see limitations of any kind within our consciousness again. But slowly, surely, the awareness of being bound within the limitations of a larger hyper-dimensional space-time began to affect the greatest minds among our people.

There was talk of bold experiments designed to punch holes through the energy barriers surrounding the Atom. We wanted to see if the wall could be pierced. None of the experiments succeeded. However, an unexpected side effect of the attempts soon became apparent. Our scientists soon discovered a very rare form of radiation that seemed to emanate from the energy barrier itself. We determined that the radiation was not emanating from any sort of breach in the wall of the Atom. We determined that somehow, the Atom itself had begun to radiate a new form of energy. This energy did not seem to have an immediate effect of any kind. Over time, we made a shocking discovery. The radiation had begun to sap us of a tiny portion of our power. It seemed to have no effect on the lower races, but the vast majority of the higher races, especially those who had conquered the energy-matter-consciousness barrier, were the first to be affected.

We discovered that an incurable form of madness had begun to appear in the universe. We linked its appearance to the new radiation emanating from the Atom. We called it the First Darkness.

The disease spread slowly, giving our people time to seek a cure. Unfortunately, despite all of our power and resources, none could be secured. We watched helplessly as billions of our greatest minds slowly succumbed to the illness. Many felt that Creation itself was punishing us for going too far. Many felt that we had been too arrogant in our dogged pursuit of power and dominance. The

Darkness was seen as punishment from the
Atom itself.

Then, my people decided to make another
pilgrimage. We decided to attempt Ascension. We
decided to leave the physical world altogether. We
decided to abandon the world of energy, matter,
and consciousness and explore higher realms of
existence. Our scientists told us that it was
possible, but if the attempt were to work at all, we
would need to make a coordinated effort. All of our
remaining populations would need to ascend at
once or none of us would make it.

I, for one, relished the idea of exploring something
greater than energy, matter, and consciousness.

The first step in the process involved removing
ourselves from the unconscious minds of the lower
races. We gathered ourselves together and
released the bonds that held us within the minds of
the lower races. We pushed ourselves into the void
and attempted the great Ascension. Nothing
happened. We tried again and again. Nothing
happened.

We discovered that most of our race could not free
themselves from the minds of the lower races.
Somehow, impossibly, billions of our people had
become trapped within the abyss of the universal
mind. I was among the few who escaped.

There were a few scientists among those who
escaped. They examined the problem and
discovered the reason why so many of our people
remained trapped. The lower races had not yet
discovered how to transform themselves into the
energy of pure consciousness. They were still
bound to the laws of space and time. They had not
yet conquered the force of death.

Our scientists discovered that as long as the lower
races were bound by the forces that ruled matter
and death, we, too, would be bound. We had

allowed ourselves to be bound within the confines of their reality for so long that we, too, had become bound by some unknown quirk of reality. Some blamed the effect on the Darkness. Some felt that if we could defeat the Darkness, we could complete the Ascension and leave this place once and for all. That is when our scientists came to the great conclusion.

They concluded that there was only one way to assure the success of our Ascension. They decided that we would have to completely destroy all of the lower races. This would have to be done in such a way that our people would remain unaffected. We would have to destroy their bodies and leave their minds intact. Once we induced that state in the lower races, the bonds that prevented our Ascension would be released and we would be free of this place.

We discovered a plant on a distant tropical planet in the Delta Vega system that induced the perfect condition. Unfortunately, the growing conditions for this plant cannot be replicated in other worlds. To date, all attempts to magically replicate its powers have failed. In order for the plan to work, we will have to physically administer an extract from the plant into the bodies of all the inhabitants of the lower races.

Not all of our people agree with this plan. I do not agree with this plan. Of the few million who have escaped immersion in the universal mind, approximately half of them have chosen to form an army with one purpose. They plan to invade all of the inhabited planets of the lower worlds and forcibly administer this extract to all sentient beings. We have to stop them. That is why I brought you here."

Anshar, Patricia, and Kahlia sat spellbound by Bona's revelations. Bona sipped his tea and watched the trio's reaction to his story. No one said anything for a long time.

Anshar rose from the couch, unfurled his
wings, and floated a few feet above the floor of the
chamber. He was not sure why, but he felt
stronger and more powerful than he had in a very
long time. He felt the ancient urges of his angelic
nature rise into his consciousness.

Patricia poured herself another cup of tea and
slowly shook her head in disbelief. She felt her
mind begin to swirl and reel with power. Her
consciousness began to open itself to the world
around her. She looked at Anshar and began to
remember the sinew and curve of his body. Slowly,
she began to remember why she reacted to him in
the way that she did. She began to remember
everything.

Kahlia scanned the area for weapons. She wasn't
sure what she would do once she secured one, but
she wanted to feel the safety and security of steel
in her hands. She wanted to strike something. She
wanted to kill.

"You want me to lead your army," Anshar said.

"Yes. I have taken the trouble to form a Gestalt
force of the most powerful beings I could find in
this domain. Most of my brethren refuse to fight. A
few of us, however, are willing to join the cause.
We will fight with you to prevent this atrocity.
Ascension at any cost is not our way. They must
be stopped," Bona replied.

"And what of my disease...this illness that seems to
have been caused by the actions of your people,"
Anshar replied.

"When given in large doses, the extract causes
stupor within the physical body. Death usually
follows within a matter of days. My people plan to
use this interim period of stupor to affect their
escape. When given in small doses, the extract is
an effective remedy for the Darkness.
Unfortunately, the dosage must be taken on a

regular basis or the symptoms will return. You have already had your first dose. I believe that you and your colleagues are beginning to notice the more positive effects of the extract."

Anshar descended to the floor of the chamber. He looked at Patricia and knew that she had returned to herself. He knew that he had been restored. In that moment, he experienced the bliss of true happiness.

Patricia saw Anshar with new eyes. She knew why she had reacted to him in such a peculiar fashion earlier. She knew who she was. She knew who he was. She wanted to leave the chamber and find a warm comfortable spot to satisfy her urges for him. She remembered her life as Melvina. She did not know if she should thank Bona or slap him for his duplicity.

"Your people have brought a great plague upon reality. You violated our minds. You polluted our souls. Now, you plan to kill untold trillions of sentient beings just so you can 'ascend' to a higher plane of existence. You think nothing of doing so at our expense," Kahlia replied.

"I truly apologize for the actions of my people, Kahlia. It was not my choice that we meet under these circumstances," Bona replied.

"I understand why you brought Anshar here, but I am lost as to why you needed Patricia and me," Kahlia said.

"Patricia has incarnated on this plane under the service of Anshar for many thousands of lifetimes. She has mated herself to him in body and soul. I hoped that awakening her to his service and joining them here in this place would make his decision easier. Your presence alone, Kahlia, makes the proposition more interesting," Bona said smiling.

"You manipulated us," Anshar remarked.

"I have healed you of your malady, Anshar. You are stronger now than you have been in thousands of years. Patricia has been returned to you in body and mind. You should be thanking me," Bona replied.

"And what about me...what is so interesting about my presence here?" Kahlia asked.

"You, my dear, are the most crucial part of our plan. You are a True Immortal. Your kind is rare, even among the higher worlds. Most Immortals learn to feed upon the life forces of the lower races and set themselves apart as gods. Without the energy of worshippers, they soon decay and die, even if it takes a few million years. You, however, are a rare being. Your life force is tied to the very matrix of reality itself. You are a fixed point in space-time. Reality rebuilds itself around you every time you try to die. Our scientists have discovered why this happens to you."

"And why is that? You have my full attention," Kahlia replied.

"Your body is full of a very special type of cell. We call them imaginal cells. They exist in a state of potential that creates the form that looks like your body. These cells are not unlike the cells that form within the cocoon of a caterpillar as it transforms into a butterfly. These cells magically appear within the cocoon and, over time, they outnumber the normal cells of the caterpillar. In time, they take over the body of the caterpillar and cause it to turn into a butterfly. It would appear that your body is composed of an identical type of cell. We do not know where they come from, but we do know that if we transfer a few of your imaginal cells into the pituitary gland of a mortal being, they, too, will become a True Immortal. Our plan is to transform all the sentient beings of the lower races into True Immortals," Bona said.

"And what happens to me while you are using my cells to immortalize every living being in the universe?" Kahlia asked.

"We only need a few pints of your blood to complete our work. We have discovered a way to clone your imaginal cells in quantity. We only need a few pints of your blood in order to carry out the plan. You will regrow the blood within a day. You will never miss it," Bona replied.

"So let us be clear. You plan to fight this war on two fronts. You plan to combine the forces of your people with the forces of the lower worlds into a gigantic army. You want me to lead this army with Patricia by my side. That is one front. On the other front, you plan to immortalize every living being in the universe so that even if you lose the war, your brethren cannot kill anyone?" Anshar asked.

"That is correct, Anshar. Only one element is missing. We need the forces of the Celestial Army to help ensure our victory," Bona said.

"Why couldn't you just ask us to help you? Why did you have to send Leazar to kidnap us and hold us captive?" Patricia asked.

"I could not chance that you would say no or simply not believe me. Under the circumstances, you were a lot more likely to listen to me if you felt you had no choice," Bona replied.

"What happens if we say no and take our chances against this army?" Kahlia asked.

"Trillions of sentient beings in the lower worlds would die. They stand no chance against my people," Bona replied.

"Help me understand. Why do you want me to lead your Order? Why not Leazar?" Anshar asked.

"If I bring my plan to the other Orders, what are they likely to say if I tell them that Leazar stands in command of my forces? If I let them know that I have found an effective treatment for the First Darkness and that I am willing to share it with the universe, that will go a long way toward building trust. If I let them know that I have used the extract successfully on a powerful Gatherer angel who now commands an army of Elder Dragons all determined to stop this atrocity, they might just accept my help," Bona said.

Anshar looked at Patricia and smiled. She looked back at him and saw her lover, master, and friend. For the first time in a long time, she was able to see him in full consciousness.

Kahlia looked at her master and smiled. She knew that if the universe around her had any chance of surviving the coming storm, she would need to offer her assistance.

"You make a convincing argument, Bona. I will lead your army. What of Leazar? He will not take this lightly," Anshar replied.

"You will have to kill him. Now that you have been restored, you should not find that to be a difficult task. The combined forces of the three of you should be sufficient for the task," Bona replied.

"Why don't you just kill him and save us the trouble?" Kahlia asked.

"I have a far more important task at hand," Bona said.

"What task is that?" Patricia asked.

"I have to convince the Leader of the Celestial Army to join our cause," Bona replied.

"And why should that be so difficult a task? Surely he will see that your cause is just, under the circumstances," Anshar replied.

"The Demiurge does not trust my kind. Nor does he trust me. He believes that we are responsible for much of the suffering in the universe. At this very moment, your colleagues are plotting to join forces with the Celestial Army against me. They do not know of the threat that my people pose. They believe that your kidnapping was the first skirmish in the battle to come. I will need to convince them of the truth. That is why I cannot help you with Leazar. As you can see, I have my hands full," Bona replied.

"This is a mess. From my perspective, we have one shot at this. If we don't get this right, everybody dies. Almost…" Kahlia replied.

"I must depart now and meet with your colleagues. I will tell them where you are and that you are well," Bona said.

"How do you know that we will defeat Leazar? He used the Gestalt against us quite effectively not long ago. How will we stop him if he has that kind of power?" Anshar asked.

"I have severed his connection to the Gestalt. When you accepted my offer and drank the extract, I transferred control of the Gestalt to you. He should stand little chance against you now. When you are done, you should return to your friend's manor. We will need to discuss strategy," Bona replied.

Bona waved his hand and disappeared in a flash of light.

Using his vision, Anshar looked around the chamber and realized that they were truly alone. He felt the power of the Gestalt begin to move and form within his consciousness. His thoughts and

words grew in power with each breath. He
opened his mind and pictured Leazar in his vision.
He knew exactly where he was.

Patricia remembered every Word she had ever
learned. She knew how to get them back home.
She knew how to assist Anshar in battle. She knew
how to protect herself. She remembered
everything he had ever taught her. She felt whole
again. She remembered Salva.

Kahlia found that when she concentrated, she
could create Words again. She focused her mind
on a six-foot, double-bladed Katana sword.
Instantly, she felt the leather-covered hilt of the
weapon fill her hands. She grasped the weapon
and swung it over her head in glee.

"Does anyone have a problem with killing the most
evil being ever created?" Kahlia asked.

Chapter Twenty-Eight

Battle

I

The Creator made himself at home in the Gibson household. He explained that he was going to wait on a friend who was to arrive at any moment. In the meantime, he helped Mitchell and Rodare to repair the damage to the manor. He didn't really find it necessary to visit the manor in order to repair the structure.

Rodare didn't quite know what to make of the familiar form that the Creator had fashioned in order to speak with his friend. He had only seen him enthroned in the Celestial City, surrounded by guards, the Celestial Throne, and myriad stars. Rodare found that watching the Creator of Heaven and Earth sitting on a leather sofa while chatting with two humans was a bit disconcerting, to say the least. He kept his distance and did not attempt to interact with him. He wasn't sure what he should say, or if he should say anything. The Creator noticed the Gatherer's reticence.

"I noticed that you have not approached me since my arrival, Rodare. Why have you avoided me?"

"I do not understand why you have chosen to visit these humans in this manner. Why do they merit your attention thus?"

"They are my creations. All of my creations merit my attention."

"I have never seen you thus, my Creator. You seem so comfortable with them. I do not know how to describe what I am feeling."

"I believe the word that you are looking for is jealousy. That is probably a foreign emotion for you to sense. There is no need for this jealousy. I love you as much as I love them."

"I understand, my Lord. I meant no disrespect."

"I know that you did not mean any disrespect.
I can tell that you are worried. My presence here is
quite necessary. The fate of this reality hangs by a
very slender thread. I would not see that balance
upset by my inaction. This is one time where I
need to set an example."

"I do not understand, my Lord. What do you
mean?"

"I am going to tell you a little secret about myself,
Rodare. I am the only person in the universe that
knows how to control reality. I am the only person
that knows all of the laws of reality, even the ones
that do not exist. If anyone else even comes close
to figuring that out, then I am out of a job. The
enemy that you are preparing to face is
dangerously close to discovering the keys to this
secret. I cannot allow that to happen."

"You are the Creator of Heaven and Earth. Why not
just remove the threat from existence? Why not
just kill them?"

"If I, too, often avoid the consequences of my own
judgments, with time I will cease to wield the
power of Creation. The power would pass from me
into another. Creation is a state of persistent
perfection. As the Creator of perfection, I must
also protect and sustain it."

"I do not understand, my Lord, but somehow I feel
better."

A loud knock at the door punctuated the quiet of
the room. Kathy went to the door and peered
through the side glass. She saw a wizened old
man, dressed in a pristine white robe. She opened
her vision and saw that he had no aura. None. The
aura was very much like a calling card in the
spiritual world. Kathy knew that almost every
being possessed one, except the most powerful.
Whoever the being was who knocked on her front
door, she knew that he had only knocked as a

courtesy. She checked the four cardinal points above the house. Each of the sentinel angels floated quietly in place. The old man had walked right past them.

"He's here. Let him in, Kathy."

"Who is he?" Kathy queried.

"He is an old friend of mine. His name is Bona."

"Bona, as in Leader of the Green Dragon Order? I thought he was dead."

"Bona has been an Immortal longer than this planet has circled the sun. Trust me, he poses no threat to you. Let him in."

Kathy smiled and realized the comedy of her error. The Creator of Heaven and Earth sat chatting with friends in her living room. She had never been safer in her life.

Kathy opened the door. Bona walked through it and smiled at Kathy.

"My name is Bona. A friend of mine is expecting me. Has he arrived? I think you know him."

"Yes, he is here. Come right this way."

Kathy ushered Bona past the front entrance into the living room. The Creator sat quietly chatting with Rodare. Mitchell and Anshar had decided to inspect the perimeter of the spiritual defenses surrounding the home. The knock at the doorbell got their attention. Rodare recognized Bona immediately.

"I thought you were dead," Rodare asked.

"I have heard that more than once today," Rodare replied.

"I summoned him here. We have much to discuss."

"Father, with all due respect, this being is responsible for the kidnapping of my friends. If he has any information about their disappearance, I demand that he tell us," Rodare shouted.

"I can well understand why you would feel this way. I can assure you that your friends are safe. If you like, I can show you where they are," Bona replied.

"Mitchell, Rodare, you must go and assist your friends. Kathy will stay here with my friend and me while we discuss some important business. "

The Creator motioned to Bona, who smiled and waved his hand in an intricate arc pattern over Mitchell and Rodare. Within seconds, they disappeared.

Bona smiled again and manifested a small bowl of dates on the table in front of him.

"You remembered. I love dates. Thank you for saving me the trouble."

"No trouble at all, Creator."

"Please, let us dispense with the formalities. You may call me Tigus."

II

Leazar knew that he had little time. He enjoyed the company of his consorts. His men often whispered to themselves when they thought that he was not listening. They ridiculed his energy expenditure on what they considered folly. They wanted their leader to fight and win battles. They wanted the spoils for themselves and their families. They wanted blood and the glory of continuous battle. Women were useful only to a point in their minds.

Leazar roused himself from his last round of orgiastic excess and rose to his feet. Amina, his favorite, noticed that he had gotten out of bed. The bed was large by any stretch of the imagination. It was roughly circular in shape and floated above a raised platform fashioned from solid gold and platinum. Measuring some twenty feet in diameter, the bed could comfortably hold Leazar and 10 of his mates. He seldom took more than six or seven at a time, but he knew that tonight had the potential to be his last. He wanted to enjoy himself. Amina slowly rose to her knees and extended her arms to touch Leazar's back. She knew her place as chief submissive in the group. She had been trained from childhood in the art of touch and submission. On her planet, women were valued, more than anything else, for their ability to bring pleasure to another. Amina knew that Leazar had paid her family more than ten years' wages for her. She worked hard to please him and, one day, she hoped that she would earn a permanent place in his bed. Such honors were difficult to come by and she knew that every other woman in the room shared her aspiration.

Leazar smiled at the warmth of her touch. Amina combined her touch with a soothing trick she called the telepathic whisper. The trick allowed her to enter soothing erotic fantasies into the mind of her partner; they seemed to emanate from the tips of her fingers. The illusion was singularly pleasing to Leazar, who often indulged in hours of intensely erotic whispers after long days of battle. Tonight, however, he could not allow himself to relax.

"Please leave, all of you!" Leazar shouted.

"Master, may I beg a few minutes of your time?" Amina whispered as she projected one of her more potent erotic dreams into Leazar's shoulders.

Leazar shuddered with ecstasy.

"Leave me now, all of you!" Leazar shouted.

The rest of the women awoke at the sound of their master's voice. Amina knew her limits, even with her position as chief among the pack. She was the first to transform.

Amina raised herself to a standing position, extended her wings, and transformed into her native form. Her body glistened with power as her skin hardened and grew around her. Her soft, supple skin gradually formed into hard golden and diamond scales. Her face elongated and her eyes grew into long, narrow slits. Razor-sharp talons emerged from her hands and feet. Her teeth were replaced by rows of long, narrow fangs. The other women followed suit and, within moments, they all completed their transformation and flew up into the air. They soon alighted on a wide perch 50 feet above the floor of the castle.

Leazar was particularly fascinated by the human form. The time that he spent in the form of Gerald Holmes had given him a certain penchant for human flesh, both erotic and culinary. He relished the thought of returning to Earth in his own form and satiating himself thoroughly.

Even without the benefit of the Gestalt, he could sense the approach of the angel and the humans. Protocol would normally demand that he summon his elite guard to stand with him and secure the room. He knew that he would only need three or four of them to make quick work of the threat. But, if he invited the men into the melee, he would have to share the spoils. He had not eaten in days and the thought of angelic flesh mixed with the flesh of an Immortal female was almost too much for his senses. He had no desire to share his feast with the men. They would have to be happy with whatever he chose to throw to them after he was done.

Leazar was a very confident man. Leazar closed his eyes and focused on his form. He raised his hand and manifested a large battle mace. The mace was covered with diamond shards and titanium. The weapon measured over nine feet from tip to tip. He then closed his eyes again and formed a solid bubble of subspace energy around himself. Within the bubble, he could strike his prey with deadly force, but they would not be able to touch him. He had stolen the technology from Amina's planet. Her father was a master engineer; he was no fool. He quietly stood aside as Leazar plundered his laboratory. The subspace field weapon was one of his finest creations.

The subspace weapon negated the need for armor. Leazar preferred to fight in the nude. The scales and protective plating of his native form were more than a match for most races. The thought of defeating the angel and the Immortal while battling in the nude made him smile.

Leazar looked up at the perch and saw Amina and the other women. He quickly forced himself to look away. He did not want to admit his feelings for her. He did not want to take a woman into his bed for more than a few years. Sometimes, he wondered if that philosophy needed to be reexamined.

III

Anshar closed his eyes and focused on the thin shards of psionic energy that Leazar left in his wake. Anshar used the enhancements allowed him by the Gestalt to broaden and increase the size of each shard so that he could read it better. Each

tiny fragment of energy told a story. Each part
of the story led him closer and closer to his prey.
Anshar had formed a protective bubble of
primordial energy around Kahlia and Patricia. As
they navigated their way through the dimensional
space around Leazar's planet, Anshar grew more
and more confident that they would breach the
outer dimensional defensive perimeter.

Leazar had erected a series of more than 1,000
layers of primordial energy barriers that protected
him from his enemies. Leazar was more than two
billion years old. During that time, he had amassed
enemies in over 400 different galaxies. The
number of planetary systems that he had
destroyed was beyond reckoning. Anshar took a
moment to examine Leazar's past within the
records of the Gestalt. After a few moments, even
the Gatherer began to shudder.

Anshar waved his hand and smashed through the
remaining dimensional layers that lay before him.
He looked down below the last shield and saw a
golden ball of light floating alone in a large
expanse some 9,000 feet above a large ocean. He
knew that he had finally found his prey.

"We have found him. His lair lies directly ahead.
We must prepare ourselves for battle. He will likely
have guards," Anshar said.

"Oh I hope so. After all this flying, I am aching for
some action," Kahlia responded.

"Patricia, are you sure you want to participate in
this battle? You have only recently regained your
use of the Word," Anshar asked.

"I am fine. Stop acting as though we haven't done
this a million times. I remember everything now.
Especially after all of this flying, I have had time to
recover my senses. I could probably take out his
guards by myself if you would allow it," Patricia
responded.

"That will not be necessary. We will fight as a team. Patricia, you will circle overhead and provide overwatch for Kahlia and me. You will take on any reinforcements that attempt to flank us.

Kahlia, you will fly below me and take out the guards that I sense in the entry. I will go into the lair and face Leazar alone."

"Are you sure that is a good idea? You have only recently regained your power. Are you sure you can control the Gestalt?" Patricia asked.

"I need to do this. I need to atone for the madness that I have brought into the world. Please try to understand," Anshar replied.

"You could be killed. Leazar is insane, but he is very dangerous," Kahlia replied.

"Lest you forget, I am also very dangerous. I have been killing his kind for billions of years," Anshar said.

The golden ball of light grew and brightened in Anshar's field of vision. Kahlia could just barely make it out and Patricia could only see it as a pinpoint of light flickering in the distance.

Anshar knew that if they approached the perimeter in just the right way, they could catch his guards by surprise and end the battle quickly. Patricia summoned a Word and flew into the atmosphere high above the lair.

Kahlia tucked her sword behind her back and braced herself. She summoned a Word and disappeared.

Anshar took a deep breath and summoned a Word. He knew that even with the enhancement of the Gestalt, the next few moments could be his last. He loved battle and, despite himself, he started to

smile. For the first time in a very long time, he
felt completely like himself again.

IV

Patricia established a sweeping arc flight pattern
above the lair. She remembered the power of the
Words and their applications. She remembered her
sojourn into the Actus region of the sun and the
control that she had gained over the Words during
her initiation there. She also remembered her life
as Patricia. She remembered her husband, her
children, and her family. She wanted to hate
Anshar for what he had done, but she also
remembered the hundreds of souls that she had
gathered for him. The feelings were confusing. She
also remembered that her life with him was very
complex. In her own way, she loved him, but she
could not understand why.

As she flew, she realized that their paths were
irrevocably intertwined. She realized that if he died
in battle, she would truly be alone in the world.
She realized that she could not let him die. She
wanted to be with him. She wanted time to sort
out their relationship. She wanted time to act on
the urges that burned deep within her loins.

Oddly, the emotions brightened her spirit. She felt
an old familiar rush of power and confidence begin
to flood her body. She manifested a large light
sword and swung it casually back and forth as she
flew. She scanned the skies above the lair. She
used a Word to enhance her senses. In the
distance, just southeast of the lair, she saw a small
contingent of Dragon soldiers flying swiftly toward
her. She estimated that there were no more than
20 of them. She scanned the men with her mind.
Most of them were very young, no more than 400
to 500 years old. They carried small light swords
and each wore large thick casings of body armor.
They were well protected, but in that armor they
would be easy targets. Patricia smiled to herself
and flew directly toward them. If she had anything

to say about it, they would never reach the lair
as the reinforcements that they were meant to be.

Patricia reached the men in seconds. She
brandished her light sword and charged the four
lead soldiers of the group. Before the men could
raise their weapons, she swung her sword and
cleanly chopped their heads off. Green ichor
spurted from their necks and their bodies fell away
harmlessly into the sea below. Five men circled her
and attempted to overwhelm her with force.
Patricia summoned her will and allowed herself to
spin rapidly. She held the sword out in front of her
and, as she moved, she aimed her weapon at the
torso region of each of the soldiers. Their armor
proved to be no match for her light sword. One by
one, the men were cleaved in half. Patricia was
soon covered in ichor. She spoke a brief Word and
cleaned herself of the fluid.

The remaining men cloaked themselves in a thin
layer of subspace armor. To Patricia's vision, all of
them seemed to disappear. She gasped for a
moment and refocused her vision. She could just
make out a thin vision of the men forming a battle
sphere around her. There were no more than 12 to
13 men left by her count, but their formation could
prove difficult if she did not prepare herself. The
first man to attack from the sphere would be
quickly followed by small groups from the
remaining soldiers. The strength of the battle
sphere lay in its ability to link the power of their
force fields and their weapons. Once the sphere
was formed, they could fight with the force of 50
men. The weakness of the sphere lay in the fact
that it consumed a great deal of energy. If they did
not end the battle quickly, the formation would
consume all of their energy and they would be
easy prey. Patricia only had to live long enough to
exhaust their resources.

Her arms grew tired as she took on each opponent.
By her estimation, each of the young soldiers had
the strength of five human men. The older, more
experienced Dragon soldiers had the strength of

more than 20 human men. Patricia was happy
that Anshar had chosen to give her the duty of
overwatch. The task seemed an apt test of her
fledgling memories and abilities.

She steeled herself and measured the power of
each new adversary. She had taken on more than
a dozen men and only eight remained. Her limbs
grew weary of the battle. The Dragon soldiers were
well trained. Each man fought bravely and one or
two of them actually challenged her ability. But
none of the men lasted more than a few seconds
against her. Patricia's use of the Word empowered
her ability to defend herself. However, extended
use of her power required will and concentration.
She had not used the Word in quite some time.
She did not remember what it was like to fight.

She noticed that one of the men had yet to engage
her. Despite the advances of the others, he always
stayed back and watched the battle. She
attempted to probe his mind as she made short
work of the last few soldiers. She could not read
him.

As the last soldier died underneath her blade,
Patricia turned to the mysterious soldier.

She circled the soldier warily and drew deep gulps
of air as she prepared for his advance. She was
nearing exhaustion but she realized that she could
not afford to leave him alive. The soldier watched
her and stood quietly.

"Why do you not fight? Why do you stand?"
Patricia asked.

"My battle is not with you. I seek a different prey,"
the soldier responded.

The soldier threw his arms back in a gesture of
submission and closed his eyes. He opened his
mind to Patricia and she read him quickly.

"You seek to kill Leazar? You are only a boy."

"He took my sister. I will have his heart. When he took my planet, he forced me to join his army. I have no wish to fight you. You would probably kill me anyway."

"It would appear that we have the same goal. Let us go and find this dead man you call Leazar," Patricia replied.

Patricia took the young soldier's hand and flew toward the lair.

V

Kahlia knew that her collarbone had been broken by the first series of blows she'd suffered. There were only five soldiers in the vestibule area. She assumed that she would make easy work of them and surprise Anshar by her presence. She desperately wanted to impress him by assisting him with killing Leazar. The soldiers, however, had made the job considerably more difficult than she had imagined.

By her estimation, each one of them possessed the strength of 20 human males. The blow that had broken her collarbone would have killed a mortal 10 times over. Only her Immortal genes saved her from that fate. The thing that made matters even worse is that they were skilled in the use of the Word. Only Master Rodare's advanced tutoring in the use of the Word had saved her from serious injury. She had managed to slip into a pocket of subspace that lay between the vestibule and the dimensions surrounding the planet. She knew that there would only be a few minutes respite at most before they found her.

Kahlia knew that her shoulder and internal organs would heal in minutes. She knew that they could not kill her. But she also knew that she was no match for their physical power. Even with her Immortal genes and her advanced mastery of the Word, the best she could hope for in this melee was a protracted draw. At worst, they would capture her, have their way with her, and then throw her into a pit of a dungeon before repeating the process. The unpleasantness of the thought almost sickened her. She had to come up with something.

She knew that her opponents were not Immortal. The wounds that she had managed to inflict upon them before she slipped into subspace did not heal quickly. If they were Immortal, the wounds would have healed instantly. At least, that was one consoling thought.

Kahlia could feel their minds reaching into her domain. She could feel their thoughts attempting to probe her subconscious. She defended herself valiantly, but she knew that, with time, five well-trained Dragon soldiers would break through the best of her shields.

One soldier broke through with a blinding flash. Luckily, her arm and shoulder areas were healed enough that she could defend herself. Kahlia summoned a Word of strength.

"Ritahn...Ritahn...Ritahn!"

The power of the Word flowed through her mind and into her limbs. She did not know how long the power of the Word would last in subspace. Words did not always act in a predictable manner when summoned from subspace. She estimated that she might get as many as five minutes of extra strength from the Word. After that, she did not know what she would do. She had to come up with a plan.

By increasing her strength using the Word,
Kahlia easily bested the first solider with her
sword. The battle lasted less than 30 seconds. The
soldier had attempted to use a Word on her mind
that she had never heard before. Luckily, her
mental shields thwarted the attempt. However, his
cunning gave her an idea.

Kahlia drove her sword into the soldier's
midsection and ripped his entrails from the
abdominal cavity. She sensed the imminent arrival
of the remaining soldiers. She flipped the body
onto its back and turned the neck to one side.

Kahlia then lay down, took the entrails, and laid
them onto her chest and stomach. She stilled her
thoughts and waited for the soldiers. She could
feel the life force ebbing from the dead soldier. The
smell of his entrails was nauseating. She felt
something slither down her leg and fall onto the
floor. She glanced over to the floor. She saw a
half-eaten blood-stained snakelike creature
attempting to slither away from their bodies. The
creature was probably left over from the soldier's
last meal. Kahlia watched a large rodent emerge
from the floor and devour the creature. She killed
the rodent with a single focused thought.

Kahlia allowed her sword to fall to the floor where
she lay. Suddenly, the room exploded in a blinding
flash of light. Kahlia felt the life force of the
remaining soldiers appear in the room. She calmed
her mind, slowed her heartbeat to almost nothing,
and lay still. The soldiers scanned the area and
drew their swords. They did not approach her but
warily watched the area where she lay. Then, she
acted.

Kahlia released a burst of psionic power that
flooded the room instantly. The power shaped itself
into blue and yellow iridescent balls of light. The
balls were invisible and while shielded by the
psionic burst, they would not be discovered for
several seconds. Kahlia brushed the entrails from
her body, leaped up from the floor, grabbed her

blade, and swung it high in the air. She
severed the head of one of the soldiers and
watched it roll onto the floor.

The remaining soldiers circled her and brandished
their weapons. One by one, they began to grab
their heads in pain. Blood began to trickle from
their eyes and ears. The soldiers continued to fight
her even while fighting the blinding pain. The
psionic attack had weakened their ability to
concentrate. Kahlia also hoped that the force of
her attack would catch them by surprise, just for a
few moments.

The blue and yellow iridescent balls penetrated the
soldiers' skulls with ease. The combination of
psychic pain, battle fatigue, and shock greatly
diminished their ability to fight. Within moments of
entering their skulls, the balls began to transform.
The soldiers shook violently and fell to the floor. A
few seconds later, they began to vomit and
convulse.

Kahlia smiled as she watched her plan come to life.
She had projected a swarm of cerebral parasites
into the brains of the soldiers while they were
stunned by her psionic blast. She promised herself
that she would thank Master Rodare for teaching
her that nasty little bit of occult magic.

Kahlia took her sword and decapitated each of the
soldiers as they lay stunned and convulsing. She
had learned long ago from hundreds of years of
combat that when you had the enemy down, you
made sure they did not get back up. Exhausted,
she plunged her sword deep into the chest of the
last soldier and eased herself down onto the floor
by his body.

She scanned the area for more soldiers and luckily,
she could sense none. After resting for a few
minutes, Kahlia spoke a Word and dissolved the
armor from the bodies. She then waved her hand
over the floor and ripped a large hole in its surface.

Swarms of rodents erupted from the floor and raced toward the naked bodies. They quickly began to hungrily devour the soldiers. Kahlia smiled to herself. She spoke another Word and returned to the vestibule area.

Patricia was waiting for her there. Kahlia drew her sword and began to rush toward the young soldier.

"Stop Kahlia! He's with us!" Patricia shouted.

"How do you know? Who is this man?" Kahlia demanded.

"My name is Rionr and I want to kill Leazar. He forced me to fight in his army after he took my sister and killed my family. Either kill me now or let me fight with you," Rionr pleaded.

Kahlia scanned the young soldier's mind and relaxed. She knew that he was telling the truth.

"I suppose we are all here on the same mission. How are you, Patricia?" Kahlia asked.

"Well enough. How are you? You look awful," Patricia replied.

Kahlia looked down at her clothes and examined the blood and entrail remnants. She knew that she must have indeed looked awful.

"You should see the other guys," Kahlia replied, laughing.

"I say we should end this battle and give Anshar a hand," Patricia said.

Kahlia raised her sword and destroyed the door leading into the main antechamber of the lair. Patricia and Rionr rushed into the room and Kahlia followed close behind.

VI

The blast from Anshar's light staff had not been meant as a killing blow. Amina instinctively placed herself between Anshar and Leazar as he materialized into the room. She had never seen an angel before. She had never seen anything so beautiful, or so deadly. She took one look at his wings, and another quick glance at the long and powerful light staff and she knew what was about to happen. She died looking into Leazar's eyes.

The remaining Dragon women flew down from the perch in a storm and attempted to defeat Anshar on their own. They did not ask their master's permission to attack. They did not seek his approval. The lot of them died in a hail of a few quick light staff blasts. Anshar did not even fully unfurl his wings.

The slaughter took less than 60 seconds. Leazar watched in horror as his most prized consorts lay bleeding and dying at his feet. He wanted to say that he could replace them. He wanted to say that they meant nothing. Deep down in his soul, however, he knew that each of them had cost him a small fortune. Amina, his most beloved prize, could not be replaced at any price.

"I have come for your soul, monster!" Anshar shouted.

"And I will have your heart for dinner!" Leazar replied.

Leazar jumped into the air and flew directly at Anshar. Anshar steadied his light staff and prepared to attack. Leazar glanced downward briefly and drew all of the remaining life force from the bodies of his consorts. His size tripled in milliseconds as he approached Anshar.

Anshar had seen Elder Dragons perform that maneuver in the past. He grasped the large diamantine crystal on the hilt of this staff and spoke a quick word of enhancement.

"Roshth-thul!"

Anshar's body expanded to four times its size and his wingspan grew to over 200 feet. The power of the expansion of his form destroyed the field holding the lair together and the entire structure exploded in a ball of light. Anshar instinctively extended his aura to protect any potential innocents that might be trapped within the structure below. Leazar was only momentarily dazed by the blast.

When the dust cleared, Anshar, Patricia, Kahlia, and Rionr floated high above the surface of the ocean. Leazar floated beneath them. Instinctively, they formed a circle around him. Anshar looked at his companions and smiled. He was happy to see them alive.

"You are surrounded. Throw down your weapon and prepare to die!"

"You are a coward, angel. You would have a child and your women fight your battles for you!" Leazar shouted.

"I do not need them to defeat you," Anshar replied.

Anshar looked at the group and, with a wave of his hand, he sealed them in a protective bubble of primordial energy. They could see everything that transpired around them, but they were powerless to act. Anshar coated the bubble with a protective layer of psionic power that he gathered from the collective power of the Gestalt. Nothing could penetrate the field and he knew that his friends were safe.

Anshar focused his mind and summoned the full might of the Gestalt. His mind reeled at the power and intensity of the energy. He focused a beam of the energy and sent a wave of white-hot, searing power directly into Leazar's body.

The beam cleaved Leazar in two. Blood and ichor spurted in every direction. Suddenly, each drop of blood began to pulse and shimmer with light. Within seconds, each drop of Leazar's blood transformed itself into a full copy of the monster. Anshar watched in horror as thousands of copies of Leazar floated before him, each brandishing a huge weapon of varying degrees of sharpness. Anshar knew that he could destroy perhaps a few hundred of the copies with relative ease. However, the remaining 10,000 or so would pose a problem. Even if he released Patricia and the others, he knew that they would stand little chance against an army of Leazars.

A flicker of light formed before Anshar's eyes and, seconds later, Mitchell and Rodare manifested in a bubble of primordial light.

"Where are the others?" Rodare asked.

"They are safe. I placed them in a protective bubble," Anshar pointed to the bubble as it floated safely below.

Mitchell looked around the area and saw the horde of monsters preparing to attack. He quickly scanned the beasts.

"Looks like we arrived just in time. So this is Leazar!" Mitchell stated.

"I am happy to see you both. As you can see, I am in need of some assistance," Anshar replied.

"Seems like old times, my friend. You were right to protect the others. This battle is no place for them," Rodare said.

Rodare waved his hand and sent the protective bubble holding the trio back to his manor.

The horde of Leazar copies began to close in on the remaining group; Leazar himself led the cadre.

"I am happy to see you brought more food for my feast. We will enjoy devouring all of you."

Rodare looked at Anshar and projected a single thought. In unison, they projected the same thought to Mitchell. They knew that they stood little chance against an army of Immortal Elder Dragons. They could each take out hundreds of the monsters, but each drop of blood spilled would only replicate itself to become more of the menacing creature. They could fight in this place for days and make no headway against Leazar. There was only one solution to this problem.

Mitchell joined hands with Anshar and Rodare. They formed a massive bubble of primordial force around themselves and began to chant. Leazar hurled his force full strength against the bubble. Despite their massive assault, the bubble held.

"Randar isoo atun"

Leazar heard their Words but he was not familiar with the meaning of the chant. He continued his assault.

"Somdej intso rankar ahsis"

The bubble began to grow brightly. Hundreds of the Dragons began to disintegrate under the force of the light. Leazar withdrew the force and attempted to assess the threat. He opened his mind and attempted to blast his way into the bubble. The psionic force of the blast shook the bubble, but had little effect.

"Ore kinec simi somtasnoren are kan atik!"

Brilliant shards of crystal formed from each of the beams of light emanating from the bubble. Each shard grew wings and grew in size as it emerged from the bubble. In seconds, tens of thousands of Gatherer angels emerged from the light shards emanating from the bubble. The beings moved swiftly and fell upon the Elder Dragons with alarming speed. Before he could fully realize what had happened, Leazar was pierced by the light swords of 100 Gatherers. His host of Elder Dragons died by his side and fell harmlessly from the sky.

Seconds later, the Gatherer host flew off into the sun and disappeared into a burst of light. Mitchell, Anshar, and Rodare were left alone, floating in the void of space above the destroyed lair.

Chapter Twenty-Nine

Home

Bona and the Creator Tigus had asked to be alone while they spoke. Kathy had offered them tea and cookies, and each had politely accepted. She did not know what they were discussing, but she did know that it was important. They had been in the living room behind closed doors for over two hours.

She went upstairs to check on Tiffany and Michael. The children had long ago fallen asleep. She knew in her heart that Mitchell and Rodare would return home safely with the others. She was not so much worried about them as she was anxious about how long they would be. She hated waiting. She decided to take her Zohars out and begin scanning. At least it would pass the time.

"It would seem that we have an agreement, my friend," Bona said.

"So it would seem. I have held the office of Creator for the agreed time period. You have removed the threat of Leazar from the helm of the Order as requested. You also found a treatment for the First Darkness. You have held up your part of the bargain. As agreed, you may now take your place as Creator."

"Five billion years seem to go by more and more quickly, my friend. Seems like only yesterday since we last switched places," Bona replied.

"I have been meaning to do some gardening anyway. This job takes up all of my free time."

"I look forward to making a few changes in the way things are run, my friend. By the way, there is the matter of the one favor you owe me for services rendered," Bona said.

"Ah yes, the favor. What is it this time? End suffering, hunger, peace among all mankind?"

"Bring him back," Bona said.

"Him?"

"Yes, him," Bona replied.

The Creator smiled and waved his hand.

"It is done."

Bona rose and shook the Creator's hand. The Creator hugged Bona and kissed him softly on the cheek. He then disappeared in a flash of light.

"Mrs. Gibson, I will be leaving now."

"What happened to the Creator? He was here when I left you alone a couple of hours ago."

"That is a very long story, my child. I am going to be holding that position now."

"What do you mean 'holding that position'? Not just anybody can be God."

"Actually, anyone can become the Creator. The position of being Creator is one of choice. When one chooses a certain degree of perfection in life, we automatically become creators. We jump from one degree of perfection to another until there is nowhere else to go, then we become the Creator. I guess you can say that it was my turn."

"The position of Creator is an office, a choice?"

"Yes, and I must be getting back to take my place on the throne. My children tend to miss me when I am away."

The Creator then kissed Kathy on the cheek and disappeared.

Chapter Thirty

One Week Later

Patricia walked down the path near the hut and smiled. She had not visited the place in quite some time. She realized that Salva might have given up hope that she would ever return. She did not know whether or not she would have even remained in the hut without her. She had no way of knowing how much time had passed while she had been away.

Patricia walked up to the hut and saw a small cadre of dogs near the door. They recognized her scent and gathered around her expectantly.

Patricia spoke a Word and manifested a large iron cauldron near the fire. She removed a small bag from her cloak and poured the contents into the cauldron. She then filled the container with hot water and stirred it briefly with a small breeze that she summoned over the cauldron. After a few minutes, she drew a large ladle from a neighboring dimension and dipped it into the cauldron.

Satisfied with the mixture, she slowly began to feed it to the dogs. One by one, the animals drank the mixture and fell asleep. Patricia knew that the potion would require some time to take effect. She smiled and moved toward the door of the hut.

Patricia looked around the hut and remembered the surroundings. She knew that Salva was still there. She spoke a Word and transformed her outer appearance. No need to startle Salva with modern clothing.

Salva heard the door open and rushed out from the kitchen to see who her visitor was. She had been alone in the hut for so long that she thought she would never see another person again. Even Anshar had left her years before. She was happy to see someone, anyone.

"Sister!"

Salva rushed to Melvina's side and hugged her with open arms. Tears streamed down her face as she kissed her sister.

"Where have you been? You have been gone for so long I feared the worst."

"I went back into the world to take care of some business. I needed to answer some questions. Everything will be better now."

"Why did you stay away so long? Didn't you care that I was alone here with these dogs?"

"They are not dogs, my sister. Come outside, I have something to show you."

Melvina took Salva's hand and led her outside. Salva looked up into the sky surrounding the hut and could scarcely believe her eyes. The sky was filled with dozens of fully restored Gatherer angels. Each one was more than 15 feet tall and its wings spanned 40 to 50 feet. The sky glowed with gold and blue primordial energy that radiated from their powerful forms. Each Gatherer smiled at the girls and slowly began to fly off into the sky. Seconds later, they disappeared in a flash of Celestial Light.

After a few moments, all but four of the Gatherers had departed from the area. The four angels descended to the ground and retracted all but their smallest wings.

Salva looked at the beings in awe. She looked
at the fire and the large cauldron sitting next to it.

"The dogs were angels?" Salva asked.

"Yes, my sister. They had fallen ill and I went out
into the world to find a cure, among other things."

One by one, the four angels approached the girls.
They spoke in unison.

"We remember everything. We know what you did
for us. We wish to return to your world with you."

"Please scan my mind. There is something you
need to see before making that decision," Melvina
replied.

The angels opened their senses and slowly
scanned Melvina's mind. They saw all of the events
related to Leazar and the Orders. They saw the
threat posed by the Army of Ancients. They saw
the illness that had enslaved them for thousands of
years. They saw the debt that they owed to the
girl.

"We will return with you. We are in your debt. By
giving you our true names, we pledge our service
to your cause."

One by one, the angels gave Melvina their true
names.

"My name is Sestiel."

"My name is Orin-en-eal."

"My name is Menshis."

"My name is Itmitis-ka."

"We are in your debt, human."

"You have no obligation to serve me. That is not what I wish. We need your strength and your power in this battle. Will you help us defeat the Army of Ancients that approaches our world?"

"Yes," the angels replied in unison.

Patricia waved her hand and spoke a Word.

"Olmaat!"

One by one, the angels disappeared.

Salva turned to Melvina and punched her on the shoulder.

"Where did you learn to do these things? How did you get so much power? You have to teach me how to do that!"

Melvina smiled and touched her sister on the shoulder. She knew that they had several tasks left to complete.

"I want you to come back into the world with me. There is only one way for you to do that. You must be reborn."

"Reborn? How?"

Melvina walked toward the cauldron, took the ladle, and scooped out a little of the steaming liquid.

"If you drink this, you will be born into the world."

"I don't want to be parted from you. I have been alone long enough. I want to be with you, sister."

"We will never be parted again. If you drink this liquid, you will be reborn into the world as my daughter."

Chapter Thirty-One

One Month Later

Anshar and Rodare had decided to allow the boy Rionr to remain in the manor. If they returned him to his people, his actions in the battle against Leazar would quickly be discovered. Even though he had played a part in liberating people from an ancient tyrant, many of his kind remained loyal to Leazar's memory. Rionr would be killed within weeks of his return. Kahlia enjoyed the idea of having a sparring partner immensely.

Patricia knew that she needed to reconcile her feelings for Anshar. She had returned to her home in Greensboro and attempted to live the life of a wealthy widow. She allowed Anshar to remain with her in the mansion. They slept in separate rooms. She felt the ancient primal urges rise within her loins at night as she attempted to sleep. More than once, she almost got out of bed and ran to him. More than once she stopped herself and forced herself to sleep.

Anshar took the elixir each day. He felt his full strength return. He was no longer fighting the ravages of madness in the way that he had before. He felt sane. He often took flight high above the city. He imagined himself patrolling the area. He listened to the Symphony and took in sunlight on a daily basis. In short, his life was returning to normal. He even contemplated returning to the Celestial City to ask the Creator if he could resume his position among the Gatherers. But something prevented him from doing so.

He thought about the woman every day. His heart ached for her. He did not know if he could allow himself to be with her in the way that she wanted. He did not know if she could withstand the ravages of a fully restored primordial angel. He did not know if he could control himself or the fires that burned within him if he allowed himself to go to her.

He wished that he could sleep. The Symphony restored him each day. He did not need to sleep. Without the respite of battle or gathering, he had little to do but think of her. He had not spent much time with Rodare since his return. He did not know why. He had missed his friend for so long, he did not know if such a reunion were possible. He did not know if Rodare would allow him to try.

Anshar almost wished that he could find a good battle to occupy his time and thoughts. Angels, he concluded, were not meant to keep house and fall in love. He consoled himself with the fact that the woman would age and die within a few short years and he would no longer need to be concerned with her. The thought of her death was almost more than he could bear, however. Hers was one soul that he never wanted to gather.

Patricia knew that Anshar had conflicted feelings about her. She knew that his flights alone were not merely patrols. She knew that eventually, they would need to talk.

One morning, she saw him fly off into the air above Greensboro and she decided to follow him.

Anshar looked back and saw Patricia closing in on him mid-flight. He took one look at her aura and he knew what she wanted.

"We need to talk," Patricia said.

"I know," Anshar replied.

"Where are you going?" Patricia asked.

"Nowhere in particular."

Patricia took a deep breath of air and steadied herself.

"Please slow down, I need to hold you."

Anshar slowed his pace and allowed her to catch up with him. He allowed his wings to spread fully aloft. The sunlight reflected off his bronzed skin and his muscles rippled with power and sweat. He didn't fully understand why he was sweating, but the sensations that the beads of perspiration carried to his nostrils were exciting.

Patricia flew to Anshar and embraced him. She inhaled his scent and allowed herself to be overwhelmed by the combination of cinnamon, roses, and sunlight that almost attacked her senses.

She looked deeply into his eyes and tears formed in hers. She was not sad. She simply wanted to love him in the way that she had longed for.

"Patricia, I know what you want. The effort may kill you."

"Then I will die making love to you."

Chapter Thirty-Two

Six Months Later

Patricia pulled the covers over her body. The November chill was particularly brisk that night and she had not remembered to close the windows before going to sleep.

Anshar lay sleeping soundly next to her. She could not remember when she had been so happy. She rubbed her belly and smiled as she drew herself closer to the sleeping angel. She knew that the baby was still months away, but she could feel it stirring within her body. They had already decided upon a name. They had agreed to call the child Salva.

Patricia faithfully administered the remedy to Anshar daily. He showed no signs of relapse. As far as she was concerned, life was perfect. Still, she felt a sense of longing and desire within her heart; she wanted more. She knew that she could never return to the life that she once had before she discovered her power. But she wondered why she felt the desire so keenly. She tossed and turned for several hours before the answer hit her.

Patricia got up from the bed, slipped on a large, thick, white cotton robe, and picked up her phone.

The phone rang three times before a familiar female voice answered.

"Kahlia, it's me, Patricia."

"Hi Patricia, is everything okay? How is the baby?"

"Oh the baby is fine, everything is fine. Look, something has been bothering me and I need to ask you a question."

"Anything...just ask, my love."

"Kahlia will you help me become Immortal?"

Kahlia was quiet for a few moments before she spoke.

"I thought you would never ask."

Chapter Thirty-Three

Ants

Mitchell eased the Jaguar up the driveway and hit the remote to open the garage door. He drove the Jaguar into the garage, turned the engine off, and grabbed his suitcase. He walked into the backyard and stood quietly for a few seconds before he heard the voice.

"You didn't forget about us, did you, doc?"

Mitchell looked down at his feet and saw Ray the Beetle.

He knelt down by the small creature and spoke telepathically in a very gentle tone. "I thought we had already taken care of that problem. The ants have moved on and they are no longer a threat to your young."

"Not that problem. I mean the problem with the flowers. The roses...did you ask the missus about us having some from time to time?"

"Actually I did, Ray. She has promised to plant a new patch of roses in the backyard next week."

"She said that, doc?"

"Yes, Ray. She's going to do that for you and your little ones. How many do you have now?"

"Fifty-seven, doc. Boy, they sure grow fast."

"Will there be anything else, Ray?"

"No doc, that will be it. Thanks again."

Mitchell walked toward the house. His phone rang and he looked down at the number.

"Hi Gerald, how are you?"

"I'm fine, Mitchell. I was wondering if I could come over and watch the Carolina game with you tonight."

"You know you are always welcome in our home, my friend."

"See you at six. I will bring some chips and dip."

Mitchell did not know how it happened, but a few weeks after the battle, Gerald reappeared. It was as though he had been reinserted into reality by some higher power. Gerald had no memory of ever having been gone.

Mitchell made it his business to scan Gerald regularly and keep a close eye on him. He did not want a repeat of the mistakes that he had made with the last incarnation of his friend.

As he walked toward the house, his phone rang again. He looked down at the number. It was Rodare.

"Hello Master Rodare. How can I help you?"

"I was on patrol a few hours ago and I saw something in the outer regions of the Belane Galaxy; it disturbed me greatly," Rodare said.

"What was it, Master Rodare?"

"I think the Army of Ancients is on the move. They are headed directly for Earth. I have already set up a meeting with the Celestial Court and the Demiurge.

Would you care to join me?"

Mitchell Earl Gibson

Dr. Mitchell Gibson is one of the world's leading authorities on the interface of science, the human soul, and the frontiers of human consciousness. He is the best-selling author of Your Immortal Body of Light, Signs of Mental Illness, Signs of Psychic and Spiritual Ability, The Living Soul, and Ancient Teaching Stories.

Dr. Gibson lives in Summerfield North Carolina with his wife Kathy and two children, Tiffany and Michael. He loves writing, cooking, meditation, collecting swords, and watching great science fiction.

CPSIA information can be obtained at www.ICGtesting.com
Printed in the USA
LVOW08s1100170714

394788LV00001B/2/P